THE GUNNER

JASON RYAN

ISBN: 978-1-950109-31-9

Cover design and interior design:
Deborah Perdue: www.illuminationgraphics.com

This book is a work of fiction. Any resemblance to actual persons, living or dead, or real-life medical institutions and events is purely coincidental. The story, characters, and incidents portrayed in this book are products of the author's imagination and are not intended to represent the typical experiences of medical students.

Throughout the pages of this story, the author takes creative liberties to explore the comical aspects of medical education in the modern era. The situations, mishaps, and humorous anecdotes are crafted for entertainment purposes and should not be mistaken for accurate depictions of the medical education system.

Medical education is a serious and vital pursuit, and this book does not seek to diminish the dedication and hard work of medical students, educators, or healthcare professionals. Instead, it aims to entertain and engage readers with the fictional journey of its protagonist.

Remember, laughter is the best medicine.

Enjoy the story with an open mind and a sense of humor.

Jason Ryan
August 2023

For my students

1.

"You know that clock ain't right," Momma calls to me from the living room.

I'm in the kitchen, pushing scrambled eggs in a pan, the butter sizzling, heat rising to my face. I should be getting dressed. I'm still in pajamas, and I need to leave soon. But Momma insisted I make her some food.

"What'd you say?" I call out to her, turning down the heat. The eggs are nearly done.

She calls back, "I said, you know that clock ain't right, don't you?"

I glance at the stove. It's 12:01 p.m. I have plenty of time before I have to leave.

You know that clock ain't right, don't you?

Suddenly, a jolt of fear shoots down my spine. Did the power go out again last night? Nothing works right in this rundown apartment. I grab my phone from the kitchen counter to check the time.

It's 1:01 p.m.

My heart plummets. *Shit, shit, shit.* How could I have let this happen on today of all days?

I turn off the stove and race from the kitchen.

"Where you running off to?" Momma asks as I enter the living room. She's planted in her wheelchair before the TV in a robe and pajamas. She rarely gets dressed or leaves the apartment these days.

Before I can reply, I stumble over my brother's boots and nearly fall to the floor.

Damn, Jerome! This apartment is too small for you to leave your crap everywhere.

I kick the boots aside, then snake around the small coffee table and sofa.

"I gotta get dressed," I say to Momma before I scurry down the hallway to my tiny bedroom. I scan the space, trying to think of what to do next. Where are my clothes? My shoes? I spy my outfit on the floor by the window, a plain blue skirt and white blouse I picked out last night for today's event. I quickly pull off my pajamas, pajamas I should have shed hours ago instead of lounging all morning like a sloth. So stupid! I yank on my outfit like a fireman pulling on gear then hurry toward the mirror that hangs crookedly on the far wall. I give my hair two quick brushes, tugging the tangles left from last night's sleep. That's all I have time for. Makeup and jewelry I'll have to skip, a casualty of my lateness.

As I toss the hairbrush on my desk, I see the two letters that have set me toward the destiny I'm late for today. I've read them both so many times, the words are forever fixed in my memory. The first letter reads:

Dear Ms. Sophia Abney:

Midtown Community College is pleased to inform you that you are the winner of the Albert Mitchell Scholarship in Medicine. The scholarship committee was thoroughly impressed with your academic record at Midtown, as well as your strong personal statement and letters of recommendation. This scholarship covers tuition at any U.S. medical school and provides a small monthly stipend for living expenses. More details will be forthcoming. Congratulations!

The second letter states:

Dear Sophia:

Congratulations on your acceptance into the State Medical School class of 2026. We are very excited to welcome your class into our community. Your school activities will begin at 1 p.m. on Monday, August 22nd, with our annual White Coat Ceremony, which will be held in the Academic Rotunda. At this event, you will receive your white coat to use for the remainder of your medical school training. This is a very exciting time. We look forward to seeing you soon.

That's today: August 22nd. And it's now 1:05 p.m.

I've been given the chance of a lifetime for a poor city kid like me, and I'm missing it. So stupid!

"Where you going?" Momma asks when I rush back into the living room. She's still in her wheelchair before the television. Two years ago, she had breast cancer that spread to her spine. She's in remission, but the loss of function in her legs has practically turned her into a piece of furniture.

"Medical school, Momma," I state tersely as I scan the room for my car keys. "Don't you remember your daughter is going to be a doctor?"

"Ah, right," she says, staring at the TV. "Can you get me my eggs before you go?"

I'm told there are families that leap for joy when a son or daughter gains admission to medical school. I'm told they call relatives to announce the good news and throw lavish parties to celebrate the occasion. My family is not one of those. Momma hardly blinked when I was accepted. Today she's more concerned with her scrambled eggs than wishing me good luck on becoming a doctor.

She's like this because she hates doctors. She met hundreds of them when she had cancer. She says they didn't listen to her and treated her rudely. She told me I should get a normal job like my brother who works at Burger King. She told me not to spend four years becoming a sadist. But she'll see. When I finish school, I'm going to make enough money to finally get my family out of this shitty section of this shitty city. I'm going to get us a new life.

I hurry to the kitchen to get Momma her eggs. She'll hound me until I do, so I might as well do it. I grab a plate and scrape the eggs from the pan. I start to bring them to her but then remember she needs a fork, which I get from the top drawer. Seconds later, I hand Momma her food.

"You pay the electric?" Momma asks as she mashes her eggs with her fork.

Scanning the room for my car keys, I reply, "Yes, Momma, I paid it. What do you think—"

"Well, last month—"

"Last month I forgot. It was just one time. You don't need to hound me."

I crouch to look under the recliner for my keys. It's crazy that I'm twenty-one years old and I manage the bills for this apartment. But Jerome's not organized enough to keep finances, and Momma . . . well, between the wheelchair and her moods, the bill paying just falls to me.

Glancing at my watch, I see it's 1:12. If I don't hurry, I'll miss the entire White Coat Ceremony.

I spy my keys on the table beside the old sofa and quickly grab them.

"Love you, Momma," I say, to which she simply nods in reply—her typical response. She lost Daddy three years ago, then got cancer and lost her legs. There's little she loves anymore. A week ago, I asked her to come with me today to the White Coat Ceremony, but she said it was "too damn far to go in a wheelchair."

As I head toward the door, my phone rings in my purse.

"Where's Jerome?" an irate voice says in my ear when I answer the call. It's Randy, Jerome's supervisor at Burger King. I went on a date with him last year. It was just a coffee, and I ghosted him after that. But he still tries to flirt with me whenever I see Jerome at work.

"Nice to talk to you, too, Randy."

"Jerome was supposed to be here a half hour ago."

"So call him."

"He's not answering. He don't show up soon, his ass is fired."

This is bad. Jerome needs his job. Or really, *we* need his job. To pay the rent for this apartment, plus food and bills, we need his income, plus Momma's Social Security and my stipend.

"Hold on," I say to Randy. I mute the call and ask Momma, "Where's Jerome?"

"He's working."

"Randy says he ain't there."

Momma shrugs. "Well, I'm not his biographer."

I stomp to Jerome's room and bang on the door. No response. I swing the door open to find Jerome hunched before his computer with headphones on, a screen full of zombies, soldiers, and guns before him. The smell of dirty clothes and beer hits me like a punch to the face. I march over to him and yank the headphones onto the floor.

"Hey!" he yells at me. "I was in the middle of a game."

I unmute my phone and say to Randy, "He'll be there in ten minutes." Then I end the call.

"You know what time it is?" I say to Jerome.

A pause. "Aw, I forgot."

"You didn't forget shit. You're gaming with Fernando, and you didn't pick up when Randy called you." Jerome lives online with a gaggle of other twenty-five-year-old screen addicts who smoke weed and stay up past midnight, then sleep all day. His real address is somewhere in cyberspace, not here with his mother and baby sister.

"I was gonna go," Jerome says. "I was just gonna be late. That's all." I smell weed coming from his baggy jeans and New England Patriots T-shirt, the same clothes I saw him wear to bed last night. The pot smell could get him fired if someone notices at work.

"You can't lose this job, Jerome. This isn't a game. Momma needs you. I need you."

"I know that," Jerome fires back angrily. He hates when I scold him, but someone has to. "Damn, girl, I can look after myself. Besides, you're the one who just quit your job. If you'd just go back to work, we'd have plenty."

He's referring to the fact that until a week ago, I worked the front desk at the emergency room across town. I had to quit because school is starting.

"This has nothing to do with that. You get your ass to work now, damn it."

"Your old job paid good."

"I'm getting a stipend."

"Five hundred bucks a month? That ain't close to what you had before."

He's trying to change the subject, but I won't have this argument again. "Go to work. Now. Or I swear I'll throw your computer out the window."

I turn from Jerome and dash out of the apartment, mad at my brother for making me even more late.

Outside, it's a sticky August afternoon on Riggs Avenue. Townhouses go as far as the eye can see, all with cracked sidewalks out front and chain-link fences. A dog barks woefully in the distance. Although this dreary street is mostly white families like mine, a block in either direction and you'll find Jamaicans, Asians, and Mexicans. But Momma says there's really only one type of people in Capitol City: broke. And God, ain't that the truth.

I open the door to my car parked along the curb. It's a rusty, white 2002 Ford Festiva, a twenty-year-old shitbox that isn't even made anymore, probably because it's so embarrassing to drive. I slide into the driver's seat and look at my watch: 1:19. I am so late.

I slam my keys into the ignition and turn. Just a click.

Odd.

I try again. Another click. It won't start.

No, no, no.

Two more clicks, then nothing.

This cannot be!

I try again about ten times and get nothing but clicks.

"Damn it!" I howl, punching the steering wheel so hard the horn sounds. My car did this last month, but Mr. McKernon, our upstairs neighbor, got it started for me and it seemed to be fine after that. Of course, on today of all days, it dies again.

I wonder if God is trying to keep me from medical school? I half expect the sky to turn gray and hail to fall from the heavens any second. I consider skipping the entire event. It's just a White Coat Ceremony. Sure, I want a white coat with my name on it, but it's not like I can't get one later. I'll simply explain that my car died, and surely they'll excuse my absence.

But then I think of how hard I worked to get to this day.

I got straight As in college, which some might say wasn't hard being as I went to a community college, but they're wrong. I put in long hours at the library while also working part-time at the emergency room. Then came the MCAT. That was the hardest test I've ever taken in my life. Questions about biology, organic chemistry, and physics, plus tons of reading comprehension. And the whole time I was studying for it, Momma and Jerome kept asking me why I wanted to do more school instead of keeping my job.

But besides all that, this day carries enormous meaning for me for another reason. I'm tired of living in a rundown city. I've seen it a hundred times in my mind: one day a moving truck will arrive in front of this crappy apartment, ready to move my family away to a better place. When I was accepted to medical school, I saw an escape for me and Momma and Jerome. Doctors make a lot of money, more money than I could earn in a lifetime doing menial jobs with my community college degree. Medical school is so much more than a place to learn for me; it's my chance to break out. It's freedom.

No, I think. *I'm not skipping today's ceremony. I am going to get my white coat, damn it. And then, after that, I'm going to become a doctor.*

I pull out my phone and call Jerome again.

"I'm gonna go to work!" he says when he picks up. "Just changing my clothes."

"Hurry up," I say. "You gotta drop me off at the med school on your way."

2.

JEROME DRIVES ME ACROSS THE CITY in his rusty pickup at what feels like a turtle's pace. When he drops me on the sidewalk beside the medical center parking lot, it's 1:35 p.m. I am so damn late.

I look up at State Medical Center, three towering glass buildings reaching toward the blue sky. One houses the medical school, one a hospital, and the other a research center. The beautiful glass towers, twinkling under the sunlight, are nothing like the surrounding urban decay of the city where I live. Momma says they're like a reverse cancer—the one healthy thing growing in a body of sickness.

Seeing these buildings always brings a surge of memories. Daddy was brought here after his heart attack. There's a green, squishy couch in the waiting room outside the ER where I learned he was dead. And Momma gets all her cancer treatments here because it's the only place that takes Medicaid. She calls it the "hospital for the hopeless." Up until now, these buildings meant only sickness and death for my family. I guess it's not surprising that Momma and Jerome don't want me to study here for the next four years.

I scamper through the parking lot as the August heat hugs me like a blanket. I hope I don't look like a sweaty monster when I reach the ceremony. Inside the building ahead of me, the others in my class await. I wonder what they look like? I wonder if I'll make any friends?

I pass Hondas and Acuras and Nissans, plus a few Audis and even a beamer. They're newer models without the dings and scrapes and rust of my car or Jerome's truck. Most of these probably belong to my fellow classmates or their parents, a reminder of how different I am from my class. People on Riggs Avenue do not have cars like these.

Then I notice that many of the vehicles have college stickers on the back windshield. The first one I see is Boston College. Our neighbor Little Jeff applied for a scholarship there but didn't get it. He told me the tuition was sixty grand per year. I could never afford that. Then I see Holy Cross, Lehigh, Amherst. And then I spot some Ivy Leagues: Brown, Columbia, Cornell, Harvard, Yale. There's no one from Midtown Community College like me. I'm a rusty penny entering a school full of shiny silver dollars.

I try to shove these thoughts away as I hurry up the stone steps of the medical school. When I enter the building, the elegant marble lobby is empty of people but holds tables of crackers and cheese, plus bottles of wine. This is for the reception with faculty, students, and parents after the ceremony, a reception I will sadly attend by myself. I spy a sign that says "White Coat Ceremony" with an arrow. I follow a hallway until I reach a massive set of double doors, where I can hear murmuring from just beyond. I put on my mask, which I always wear in crowds. The last thing I want is to bring some virus home that strikes Momma in her debilitated state. Then I take a slow, deep breath and open the doors.

I enter the Academic Rotunda for the first time in my life. It's a massive space with a domed ceiling a hundred feet overhead. The room is packed with people, the warmth of their body heat hitting me as I enter. Rows of people are seated in chairs before a small stage on the far side. They must be the other students in my class. I can tell by their young faces and nervous twitching as they gawk at the stage.

Dozens of others line the circular wall around the room, standing with their gazes fixed on the stage, a few in masks, but most without. These are clearly the parents. The men have stately gray hair and dark suits. The women wear dresses and skirts with earrings and makeup. They have the look of money. It's hard to describe, but when you grow up poor, you know money when you see it. They may not be billionaires, but they're rich by my standards. They're doctors or lawyers or PhDs. They own homes in the suburbs and drive nice cars with college stickers on the rear window. They don't live on Riggs Avenue.

On the stage are several serious-looking men and women sitting on chairs, all wearing white coats. I see a table with folded white garments, clearly the coats intended for the students. This is good news, because it means I haven't missed the important part of the ceremony when I'll receive my coat. A portly woman with short dark hair is speaking from a podium. She looks about fifty years old and wears a white coat over a stylish navy dress. I recognize her from a photo online. She's Dr. Sylvia Weaver, Dean of Students for the medical school.

"You are an elite group," she states with pride, her words booming from speakers along the walls. "State Medical School received over five thousand applications this year. The eighty-nine students in this room outworked and outcompeted thousands of others to become the SMS class of 2026."

I notice the parents along the wall beaming over these words. I can see their lips turn up into slight smiles, their spines straightening so they stand a little taller. They love hearing that their children are the chosen ones. They're ready to provide anything required to succeed: words of encouragement, family connections, money. There's none of that for me.

"Be very proud of yourselves," the dean says. "You are the best of the best."

These words should fill me with pride, but they only make my heart pound. The other students in my class may be elite, but I'm a lowly city girl. I got lucky. The admissions committee liked my personal statement about how Daddy died of a heart attack, which inspired my interest in medicine. They were wowed by my full scholarship, plus my grades in college. But it is precisely these things that make me different. I don't come from a family with the money to pay for medical school. I didn't attend an elite college. It's a matter of time before the others in my class figure that out. Then I'll endure four years of snickers, smirks, and whispers—if I don't fail out first because of my pathetic community college education.

As the dean continues her speech, I slide into an empty seat in the back row of the students. I'm glad to sit, because the heat and stress have made me feel faint. Beside me sits an elegant blonde woman in a stylish yellow dress. She doesn't wear a mask, probably because her family is in perfect health, unlike mine. Her white skin is bronzed, clearly from sunbathing at a pool or beach somewhere. About my age, she appears to have spent more money on her hair than the monthly rent for my apartment.

"Hi," she says in a perky voice.

I'm so nervous and flustered from arriving late, I'm in no mood to talk. I just want to focus on the ceremony.

"Hi," I say back in a low whisper, then turn my gaze toward the stage.

"We're going to be classmates," she says.

I nod.

"I'm Jennifer Mercer," she says. "I went to Harvard. My father is the chief of neurosurgery."

Her words hit me like a sledgehammer. I abruptly sit back in my chair.

I went to Harvard. My father is the chief of neurosurgery.

What kind of person opens with a statement like that? Is this the norm at medical school? To announce your Ivy League pedigree and occupation of your parents? If so, I'm doomed to be a laughingstock. I think of the cars, the windshield stickers, the parents, and now Jennifer Mercer, Harvard graduate and daughter of the chief of neurosurgery. It feels too much to bear. I am so goddamned different from everyone here.

"Are you alright?" Jennifer asks when I don't respond.

I shake my head and wave a hand at her. "I'm . . . I'm fine."

From the podium, the dean announces, "We will now call the students up one at a time to receive their coats. Sophia Abney."

I silently curse Daddy for having a name so close to the start of the alphabet. A sudden urge comes over me to abandon my quest. Maybe people like me don't become doctors? I feel so painfully out of place. I can't imagine ever feeling at ease in a group like this. Did I make a mistake? I could go home now. Get my old job back working the desk at the emergency room. Jerome would love that.

But I can't turn away. The terms of my scholarship require me to pay back the money if I quit or fail out. I've never told this to Momma or Jerome—they'd freak if they knew. I signed my name on the scholarship documents last week in ink, but it might as well have been in blood. The first tuition payment was made five days ago. It's more money than I could earn in a year. Once you take money like that for med school, there's no turning back. I'm becoming a doctor, or else my family will be bankrupt and on the streets. There is no other option.

Mustering all the courage I can, I rise on shaky legs and walk toward the podium. I feel the heavy weight of the eyes in the room upon me. All my fellow students are staring. And I don't know how, but somehow, they *know*. They know I'm not like them.

I went to Harvard. My father is the chief of neurosurgery.

I climb the steps to the stage. The dean and other faculty smile at me, but I'm certain these are smiles of pity. *Oh, you poor child. Didn't someone tell you how different you are from the others?*

The dean holds out a white coat, and I see my name on the lapel: Sophia Abney. My heart swells with pride because I worked so hard to get here. But in all my visions of this day, I never thought of how foreign I'd feel among my class.

I turn to face the audience as the dean slides the coat over my shoulders. For the first time, I look upon my class as a whole, all eighty-eight others. The windshield stickers flicker through my mind: Boston College, Holy Cross, Lehigh, Amherst, Brown, Columbia, Cornell. My classmates study me on stage as if studying some disfigured lab specimen. *Look at this one. A fascinating case. She came to medical school not realizing she didn't belong.*

I step down from the stage and back toward my seat. Medical school is going to be even harder than I imagined. Everyone else *belongs* here. They were destined for this place their whole lives. Not me. I was destined for clerical work in the ER, or a job at Burger King like Jerome. I'm a pawn who's snuck into a world of kings and queens.

That's when I decide not to return to my seat. Instead, I weave through the people along the wall, then exit the back door of the rotunda, leaving the faculty, students, and parents behind. I won't stay for the reception, which is "optional and not mandatory" according to the email I received yesterday. These people are aliens to me, and I don't want to make small talk with them. I have my white coat. I got what I came for. Now, I'm going home to Momma and Jerome. I need to rest tonight and prepare for what's coming.

Classes start tomorrow.

3.

THREE WEEKS LATER, I'M ONCE AGAIN in the Academic Rotunda, this time for class.

From the speakers I hear, "When the glomerulus senses a high sodium load, the distal tubule will . . ."

In the middle of the rotunda is a podium where Dr. Robert Murrow is speaking, a feeble seventy-year-old man with thick glasses and a balding head. He's a professor of medicine who holds a PhD in cell biology. He's also an awful teacher. His head is so filled with medical science and terminology, I can't possibly understand him.

"The nephron filters electrolytes . . ."

He might as well be speaking another language. I'm lost.

I scan the rotunda, studying the other students, looking for confusion in their faces, but I see none. The room has been completely rearranged since the White Coat Ceremony. The stage is gone and so are the rows of chairs. Now, dozens of circular tables are spread about the cacophonous space, each surrounded by medical students with laptop computers. My entire class, all eighty-nine of us, is here under the domed ceiling, listening to Murrow.

I wonder if I'm the only one bewildered by his teaching? I could ask some of the others if they understand what he's saying, but I won't. In fact, I'm quite proud of the fact that, since starting school three weeks ago, I haven't spoken to a single soul in this room. I attend labs and lectures alone, then leave quickly when class concludes. I don't go to clubs or interest groups or happy hour. This has kept me from conversations about my background, which is so different from everyone else's. It's kept my anxiety at a level I can bear.

Murrow's computer projects from the podium onto a massive screen on the rotunda wall. I stare at his PowerPoint slide, white with large black letters saying: "Sodium = Volume." I tap on my laptop keyboard to record this in my notes, hoping I can decode what it means later.

"So, now that we've reviewed yesterday's material," Murrow continues, "let's move on to the case for today's TBL."

TBL. Just hearing this makes me quietly groan to myself. It's short for Team Based Learning, the dreaded exercise we're assembled for today. The idea behind TBL is for groups of five students to answer questions about clinical cases together as a team. It's supposed to help us learn to work with others. But Murrow calls on random students to stand and present their team's diagnosis in front of the class, and he isn't kind to those who give wrong answers. It's basically a sinister lottery where the prize is potential shame and embarrassment with everyone watching. I didn't get called to speak last time, but today I may not be so lucky.

The four others seated at my table, all of us assigned together as a TBL group, listen to Murrow's instructions, just as I do. One of them, sitting directly across from me, is Jennifer Mercer, the same Jennifer Mercer I met at the White Coat Ceremony, the one from Harvard with the neurosurgeon father. I notice her rolling her eyes.

"God, I fucking hate TBL," whispers Mercer to Randall Collins, the student beside her at the table. She wears a Harvard sweatshirt, even though it's early September and seventy degrees outside. She's worn some item of clothing with Harvard on it every day for the past three weeks. I wonder if she has a Harvard tattoo across her chest, so if she dies stark naked, the world will know where she went to college.

"I hate TBL, too," Collins whispers back to Mercer. He folds his beefy arms across his chest, his biceps easy to appreciate because he wears blue scrubs with short sleeves. He's worn scrubs every day since school started because, as he will tell you any chance he gets, he plans to become an orthopedic surgeon. I think he dreams of being ready for an emergency surgery. *Attention medical students! There is a trauma in the ER, and we need someone to hold pressure on a bleeding tear in the aorta. Is there anyone in scrubs who can assist?*

It's widely known that Collins and Mercer are fucking. I know this because even though I haven't spoken to anyone in my class, I've listened to whispers in the lecture hall and labs. Medical students love to talk, and they love to talk about each other. Just from the hushed conversations, I've learned many things, like an anthropologist silently observing a primitive culture. For example, two girls in my class have eating disorders, and one of the boys has a restraining order against him from his ex-girlfriend. There's also one student, a spindly man with Coke bottle glasses named Barnaby, who supposedly masturbates in the library study rooms. I have no idea how this became known. I only wish I knew which room, so I could avoid it.

I'm pulled from my thoughts when Mercer decides to share more of her opinions on TBL with Collins. "If they gave me a choice between a rectal exam and TBL," she says, "I'd take the gloved finger." She thinks for a second. "I might even take two."

"Same," Collins replies. "One hundred percent agree."

I've heard sentiments like this before. My class would rather have their bodily cavities invaded than attend Team Based Learning. I'm not sure why they hate it so much. They're all geniuses from fancy colleges, unlike me. I guess no one likes to be called upon to stand and speak before the class.

"You may all now read the first case," Murrow announces from the podium, his words echoing in the vaulted chamber. He then projects a slide onto the screen describing a patient with a kidney problem.

I read the words of the case carefully, knowing I may soon be called upon to stand and state a diagnosis.

It begins: *A thirty-year-old woman presents with a chief complaint of fatigue.*

The case descriptions always start like this. *A {insert patient age} man/woman presents with a chief complaint of...* It makes the patient sound like a whiner who complains all the time. I wonder if this is how doctors see their patients? I wonder if Momma's doctors think she's a complainer, too? Maybe that's why she hates them so much.

The case continues: *She is a runner and thinks she may have "overdone it" last week with a long run . . .*

The patients in these cases are always mistaken when they tell the doctor what they think is wrong. They have headaches they think are brain tumors but are caused by simple stress. Or they have belly pain they think is indigestion, but it's actually cancer. Seems to me they should show us cases where the patient is right. When Momma first got breast cancer in her spine, she knew something was seriously wrong, but her regular doctor said she had strained a muscle. It took another month and three more doctors until the correct diagnosis was made.

"They don't listen," she said to me at the time. "They never listen."

The rotunda falls briefly silent as my class reads the rest of the case, but soon murmurs rise from the tables. We have ten minutes for group discussion before Murrow selects a victim at random to present his or her group's conclusions. During the last TBL, I stayed quiet, while my team debated the case. No one seemed to care that I wasn't part of the discussion. Honestly, I'm not 100% sure they even know my name.

Collins is the first one at my table to speak. "She has a kidney stone," he says confidently.

Mercer taps at her laptop screen. "I'm not sure that's right," she says. "The patient has muscle pain. Doesn't that go with rhabdomyolysis?"

She says the word "rhabdomyolysis" with obvious pride. She'd probably shout it to the room if this was allowed: *Attention Little People: I know what the word rhabdomyolysis means!* Mercer and Collins love to say fancy medical words as if they speak them every day. Last week, Collins casually said the word "pancereaticoduodenectomy" and I thought he was going to get an erection.

"There's no imaging in this case. How are we supposed to make a diagnosis without an X-ray or CT or something? The future radiologist in me is offended." These words spill from the mouth of Avtandil, the fourth student assigned to our group. He's going into radiology, in case you missed it. He says it over and over and over, a hundred times a day.

Everyone calls him Avi because his name has too many consonants and too few vowels. All the kids with foreign names get a nickname. Kirollos is Kirk, Anidita is Annie, and Chandrashekhar everyone just calls Bob.

Celia, the fifth member of our team, is holding her phone above her head tilted down. She flashes a broad smile and takes a selfie. Then she pecks at her screen to upload the photo to the web. Celia calls herself a "medical influencer." She started an Insta page (@futuredoccelia) her freshman year at Brown, where she documented everything she did to get into medical school, everything except the part where her father, a prominent oncologist, called the dean of admissions on her behalf. She has 1,218 followers, a piddly number by most standards, the bulk of them probably bots or family. Nevertheless, she claims this makes her a celebrity.

"One of my followers told me to watch the Boards and Beyond video on glomerular disease for this TBL," Celia says. "It totally slayed."

"I didn't know Boards had a glomerular disease video," Mercer says to Celia, her eyes narrowed in concern. Nothing strikes fear in my classmates like hearing about some video, app, book, or study sheet they didn't know existed.

Collins and Avi peck at their computers, no doubt searching for the video Celia watched. No one ever consults the textbook from the syllabus. In fact, no one even reads the assigned textbook chapters, as far as I know. Instead, they use videos to study, all of them available online with a subscription: Pathoma, Boards and Beyond, Sketchy Medicine. They cost hundreds of dollars each, money I cannot spare. I stick to the syllabus and assigned readings from textbooks. These are the materials we're supposed to use. They're all available for free at the library.

Suddenly, Mercer turns to me and says, "Well, what do you think, Sophia? You didn't speak a word in our last TBL. Don't you have anything to add about this case?"

I freeze. Believe it or not, this is the first time since I started school that someone has spoken to me directly. I'm so quiet, the other students act as though I'm invisible.

I should respond, but I'm so confused by what we're learning; I'd probably blurt out something ridiculous. Mercer went to Harvard, Collins to Yale, Avi to Boston College, and Celia to Brown. They know so much more than me. So I simply look down, hoping if I remain quiet the group will move on.

But they don't move on.

"I saw you in the library last night," Collins says to me. "You were reading the textbook, right?"

Celia's eyes widen. "You actually read the textbook? Are you, like, a low-key genius or something?"

"She got in here from community college," Avi says. "She must be super smart."

I suddenly feel exposed. The med students talk about each other so much, I should have realized they'd talk about me, too. *She got in here from community college. She must be super smart.* Is he serious? This logic astounds me. It's as if they're worried I know something they don't.

I again say nothing and keep my gaze down. I don't want to talk about how I study or where I went to college, not with this group of Ivy Leaguers.

The others exchange puzzled looks when I don't respond.

"Maybe she's, like, mute or something," Celia says.

"I heard she doesn't speak to her anatomy group," Mercer says. "They were dissecting the left shoulder and she worked on the right by herself. Bizarre."

She's calling me bizarre? I'd like to respond with, "Bizarre is saying you're from Harvard and your father is a neurosurgeon to everyone you meet," but I don't want to start an argument. I just want to think about this case by myself. Why don't they just ignore me like they did last time?

"There's a fourth year who never talks to anyone in his class," Avi says. "Miles Sebastian. You guys know him? Supposedly, he used some secret underground resource to study. It was next level, had all sorts of mnemonics and memory tricks. Guy crushed his exams but hardly speaks to anyone in his class. They all fucking hate him."

"Sophia," Mercer says, "if you have some resource we don't know about, you better damn well share it."

I try to wrap my brain around the absurdity of this statement. Jennifer Mercer, the Barbie girl from Harvard, is demanding study tips from me, the poor kid from community college. *You better damn well share it.* I'd like to punch her in the face for speaking to me in such an obnoxious tone, but once again, I don't want to argue or make enemies. So I remain quiet, just looking at my laptop, waiting for time to pass.

"There was a thread about med school loners on Reddit the other day," Celia says. "Pretty much every class has one. Personally, I think it's pretty sus. I mean, like, what do they have to hide?"

It's widely known that Celia posts in Reddit forums almost every day. She's so dense, she chose the handle "CeCeIGinfluence," which the whole class knows is her. She posts questions in the med school threads like "What's the best way to learn the brachial plexus for an exam in two weeks?" on the exact day our class begins studying the brachial plexus for an exam in two weeks. She basically self-doxes.

"Look, Sophia, it's not cool to keep your study habits to yourself," Avi says. "Look at me. I'm going into radiology. Super competitive field. I need every advantage I can get. But still, I share what I know with my classmates, because I'm a decent guy."

Why are they assuming I have some secret study strategy? Just because I'm quiet? I use the assigned textbook, that's it.

"You know, it's not professional to keep your study tools to yourself," Collins says. "Someone's going to file a PURF on you if you don't share."

A hush suddenly falls over the others at my table. They gawk at Collins as if he's mouthed the unholy words of Satan himself. He's brought up the Voldemort topic of medical school: professionalism. And the reason it's so dreaded is because of the sinister PURF.

From the medical school student manual:

The professionalism underperformance report form (PURF) exists to ensure professional behavior among students. All incidents of professional misconduct witnessed by students must be reported via PURF. This may include lying, stealing, cheating, drug or alcohol abuse, rude behavior, stigmatizing language, or demeaning comments to marginalized persons. The PURF is available electronically and can be submitted online by any student.

It's basically a formal way of snitching. You can report your fellow students anonymously for anything you consider bad behavior. The idea is to promote "professionalism"—whatever that means; no one ever really defines the term—among students by having us spy on each other.

"Don't say that word, PURF," Mercer scolds Collins. "Don't even think it."

"You guys hear about Jasper, the fourth year?" Avi asks. "He snuck out early from a surgery lecture to play Grand Theft Auto. Someone filed a PURF, and he had to write an apology to his entire class. Then Jasper filed a payback PURF against another M4, Franklin, the one he assumed was the snitch. He said Franklin took food from a demented patient's breakfast tray in the hospital—a brilliant charge, since it's impossible to disprove. Franklin swore it wasn't true and begged the dean for mercy. He was let off with a warning. Now, rumor is that Franklin keyed Jasper's car. It's all-out fucking war."

"Who the hell came up with the idea for the PURF?" Celia says. "It's savage. Anyone can stab you in the back anytime. Why'd you bring this up anyway, Collins?"

"He brought it up because Sophia is being unprofessional," Mercer replies.

I give Mercer a look. She seems to have it in for me.

"I'm just trying to help Sophia out," Collins says. "You don't contribute, it's gonna be PURF city for you."

I try to comprehend the madness that's occurred over the last few minutes among my TBL group.

Don't you have anything to add?

Maybe she's, like, mute or something.

Someone's going to file a PURF on you.

Sophia is being unprofessional.

I seem to have triggered my TBL team with my lack of engagement. It occurs to me that the others—in an amazing display of paranoia—see my silence as a threat. Because I don't engage, they think I must know some secret to getting ahead. They want me to speak my thoughts aloud so they can assess what I know, and how much they should fear me. The whole thing pisses me off. To hear these children of privilege—all of them graduates of expensive, elite colleges, all of them with parents who shower them in money and support—call me selfish. Unreal.

That's when I know I'll have to speak. I can't keep up

my silence any longer.

Drawing in a deep breath, I scan the others at the table with eyes of steel. "Listen, I have no secret resource. I go to the library each night and check out the assigned textbook that's on reserve. I could buy my own copy, but I need to save money, so I use the school's book. I take notes, then return the text. That's the sum total of my study method. It's what the syllabus tells us to do. There's nothing complicated about it."

I turn from the group and look at my laptop screen.

"Now if you all will just move on, I want to think about this patient's problem in case Murrow calls on me."

4.

The four others in my TBL group stare back at me in silence. The only sound is the dull background noise of the surrounding tables discussing the case. My group appears shocked that I can speak. I wonder if they really thought I was mute?

Mercer breaks the quiet by laughing. "You only read the textbook? Are you serious?"

Her tone is snide and insulting, and the fighter in me begins to boil. "What's wrong with that? Don't they have textbooks at Harvard?"

Mercer glowers at me.

"You don't use any TPRs?" Celia says.

I give Celia a puzzled look.

"TPRs," Celia repeats. "Third Party Resources. You know, the stuff online we all use to pass medical school. It's totally basic."

This group clearly has no idea what it means to lack money. And they're all looking at me like I'm from another planet because of how I study. It's infuriating.

"I can't even afford the textbook. How would I afford online resources?"

"You don't buy them," Collins says. "Get them off the Google Drive."

Again, I show a puzzled look.

"You don't know about the drive?" Avi exclaims. "Oh my God. I can't believe it. How are you surviving without the drive?"

I look at Avi for a second. "What's the Google Drive?"

"Pirated videos from all the online teaching sites," he replies. "Also pirated practice questions from UWorld, Amboss. There's even a pirated PDF of the textbook. You don't need to go to the library. You can have your own copy. None of us pays for these things."

I stare back at Avi with my mouth hung open in surprise. These guys are pirates? They're so rich, at least compared to me. Mercer's father is a neurosurgeon. Surely she can afford any study tool she wants. Don't they worry about having a PURF filed on them?

"I didn't think it was possible to survive med school without the drive," Avi says.

"Maybe it's not," Mercer replies. "We haven't had our first exam yet. Who knows, Sophia may fail."

I give her a look, thinking of the jabs she's sent my way this morning.

Don't you have anything to add?

You only read the textbook?

Sophia may fail.

I've had enough of her spoiled ass picking on me.

"What's your problem with me?" I say to Mercer. "What have I ever done to you?"

Mercer thinks for a few seconds, the others glancing from her to me like they're sitting ringside at a prize fight.

"You're not a team player, Sophia," Mercer replies. "What can I say? It pisses me off."

Before I can respond, Murrow speaks, his voice booming through the speakers. "Alright, alright. Quiet down, everyone. We'll now go through this case together."

My anger at Mercer suddenly switches to fear of being called to speak by Murrow. We spent all our group time talking about PURFs and TPRs. I never came up with a diagnosis for the case.

Slowly, a hush falls over the rotunda. Murrow pecks at his computer on the podium. We know what he's doing. The random name generator will select a student from the class who'll be called on to state a diagnosis for the case. Time ticks by as we wait for the executioner to identify his next victim.

"Let's hear from someone in team four," Murrow says.

I let out the breath I was holding. My group is team seven. I've been spared the gallows, at least for now.

The five students in team four stiffen with fear. Now Murrow will choose one of them to stand and speak. He takes a long pause, probably to make everyone in team four sweat.

"Let's hear from Kaamya Chigurapti," Murrow finally says. He butchers the pronunciation of her name: Kim-ee Chig-rit-ee. The Diversity, Equity, and Inclusion Committee will massacre him for this—mispronouncing a name is considered a microaggression—but for now no one complains.

Across the room from me, Kaamya slowly rises to her feet. She's a tiny stump of a woman, her skittish gaze fixed on Murrow. A lamb brought to the slaughter.

"Uh, er, yes," she begins. "For this patient . . . my team wasn't sure exactly what was causing her symptoms—"

"Oh, wasn't sure, eh," Murrow says from the podium. "Your future patients will love to hear you say that. 'Yes,

Mrs. Jones, we're not exactly sure why you're dying.'"

Kaamya darts her gaze to the others in her group, clearly searching for a hint of something to say. Then she looks back at Murrow. "Well, we knew she had muscle pain and red urine—"

"Yes, well, it told you that in the case description, so you certainly should *know* it. But can you put it together? Come up with a diagnosis?"

I swallow hard, knowing I could do no better than Kaamya is doing right now. It's a matter of time until Murrow calls on me. I just pray it isn't today. I feel so lost. If he calls on me next week, by then I'm sure I'll have a better handle on the class material.

"Dr. Murrow, my group thought this might be a case of rhabdomyolysis," someone shouts out. The words come from Thomas McKinney, a stout, round-faced guy with a goatee. McKinney raises his hand and speaks every chance he gets in TBL or lectures. Honestly, he's got guts. I'd rather hide under the table than give an answer in front of everyone.

"Excellent," Murrow exclaims, turning toward McKinney. "Now, how did you come up with that diagnosis?"

McKinney launches into a monologue on the diagnostic criteria for rhabdomyolysis. I wish I could say what he's saying now, but I'm so confused by the material, I couldn't possibly. But I'm thrilled he's speaking. Each minute he talks, I get another minute closer to the end of TBL.

I notice the others at my table whispering to each other. As they talk, they occasionally glance at me, then look away. Mercer appears to be the ringleader, looking from one to the other.

"Now, the next question we must answer is, why did this otherwise healthy woman of thirty years of age develop rhabdomyolysis?" Murrow says. "Let's hear from another group."

Murrow taps at his computer, no doubt using the random name generator to identify another medical student to torture. I feel the blood drain from my face.

"Uh, Dr. Murrow, may I ask a question?" someone says. The voice comes from Martin Chad, a tall, rail-thin classmate of mine dressed in a periodic table of elements T-shirt. He's an MD-PhD student. Yes, you read that correctly. He's earning a degree both as a doctor of medicine *and* doctor of philosophy. Insanity, if you ask me. Med school alone is hard enough. Apparently, he wants to cure cancer in a research lab or something.

Murrow nods at Chad, who continues. "Do you know if rhabdomyolysis has an association with protein marker six-five-seven? I'm writing my thesis on six-five-seven, and I wondered if someone has studied it in rhabdo patients?"

Protein marker 657. Chad lives and breathes for this microscopic particle, whatever it may be—I have no clue. At some point, during every lecture, lab, or TBL, Chad name-drops this thing as if he's casually mentioning he knows Kayne West. A lot of my class finds him irritating, but I don't mind him. His questions kill time in TBL.

Murrow clears his throat. "Well, er, I'm not aware of any recent papers on rhabdomyolysis and six-five-seven." He then rambles on for a minute about cell surface molecules and immunoglobulins. None of it makes any sense to me.

After a short back and forth with Chad that no one listens to, Murrow returns to his laptop. He's about to choose a student to speak. Once again, my heart plummets.

"Let's hear from team seven," Murrow says.

My heart slams against my chest. He's called on my team! There's a one in five chance he'll say my name with his next breath. I close my eyes. The seconds tick by like hours. I can feel the weight of the class as it stares at my table.

"Sophia Abney," Murrow says. "Let's hear from you."

The room spins, and I feel like I could pass out. The day of my execution has arrived. Why does it have to be today? Any other day but today.

I slowly rise to my feet, a slight tremble to my hand.

"Why would this otherwise healthy woman of thirty years of age develop rhabdomyolysis?" Murrow asks. "What conclusion did your group come to?"

I dart my eyes to the others at my table. They have smug looks, no doubt thrilled I was called and not them. Mercer gives a sinister, satisfied nod as she smirks at me.

I'm doomed. Murrow's lectures on the kidney are incomprehensible to me. I read the assigned textbook chapter, but there was nothing about causes of rhabdomyolysis. My mind is completely and utterly blank. The room is deathly silent. Everyone is staring at me.

"Well?" Murrow says.

Suddenly, Mercer leans toward me and whispers, "Hartnup disease."

She appears to be giving me a hint. Maybe, I think, she's extending an olive branch, trying to help me out as a friend? The name Hartnup disease sounds familiar, but I can't recall the symptoms of the disorder. Where have I heard it before? Could I have read it in the textbook chapter last night? I can't be certain, but maybe I did.

Knowing I must say something, I blurt out, "She could have Hartnup disease?"

The room is silent for a moment, then I hear snickers arise from the tables. When I look again at Mercer, she's laughing together with Collins, Avi, and Celia.

"Hartnup disease?" Murrow exclaims. "That's a metabolic disorder that affects babies. It has absolutely nothing to do with rhabdomyolysis." He rubs his forehead with the palms of his hands. "Good God, what are you thinking? Let's move on to someone who has some clue about what's going on . . . uh, let's hear from team twelve."

The others in the room turn their attention from me, but the damage is done. I saw how everyone looked at me. The quiet girl, the one who speaks to nobody, is an imbecile. I could have just answered that I didn't know, like Kaamya. Instead, I spouted the name of an idiotic disease with no bearing on this case.

Mercer is still chuckling with Collins, the two of them looking at me with wide grins. She insulted me in front of my group during the discussion period. And now she's embarrassed me before the entire class.

I slump into my seat and quickly wipe a tear from my eye. I don't want to give Mercer the satisfaction of seeing me cry. I think of Momma. What would she say if I told her what just happened? I already know the answer. She'd tell me to fight back. Momma didn't raise me to be a doormat.

That's when I decide: Mercer will regret what she did today.

This is going to be all-out fucking war.

5.

A WEEK LATER, I'M STUDYING in the library, tucked away in a cubicle deep behind stacks of books. I like it here where it's quiet and secluded, far out of sight of the others in my class, like Jennifer Mercer, and away from the Rotunda, where Murrow makes us stand and opine on topics we barely understand. Here, I feel safe so I can learn in peace.

I gaze at my laptop, studying the various emails I've received today. My inbox is brimming with notifications of student interest groups. For God-knows-what reason, medical students are obsessed with interest groups. They segregate into these things with feverish intensity like wild animals forming packs to fend off predators. There's one for every specialty from abdominal imaging to geriatric psychiatry to undersea medicine. Every ethnicity has a group from the Russians to the Chinese to even a tiny group of coastal Alaskan natives called the Alutiit. There's also an interest group called Social Media in Medicine which, of course, Celia joined. She vowed to become the president by third year. Two days ago, she proudly modified her Instagram profile to read, "Member, Social Media in Medicine Interest Group" as if she was bragging about her induction into Mensa.

Suddenly my phone vibrates from the desk beside my laptop computer. I glance at the screen and see it's Jerome.

"What? I'm studying," I say into the phone.

"Uh, Soph, you . . . you gotta go to the ER at the hospital."

His tone is grave. My body clenches. "Why? What's wrong?"

"I'm . . . I'm at work. But Momma fell or something. She didn't want to call you when you're studying. She called Mr. McKernon, and he called 911. She's at the ER."

My shoulders tense. "Well, is she okay? Dying? What?"

"I . . . I think she's okay. Hit her head. Has some bruises. But you gotta go down there and check on her. You know how she is around doctors."

I most certainly do. "I'll check on her right now."

I end the call, realizing my studying will be cut short—again. Last week Momma called, asking me to pick up Tylenol on my way home. Before that she called because we were out of Pepsi. Apparently she'll interrupt me for those things, but not when she falls. I'll never understand her brain.

As I'm about to pack up, an email comes in on my laptop. *Ding.* It's from a student in my class.

From: Hannah Foley <hfoley@sms.edu>
Sent: Monday, September 12, 2022 12:47 PM
To: Sophia Abney <sabney@sms.edu>
Subject: <blank>

How could you do this, Sophia?

Hannah Foley
MS Biological Science, Brown University 2022
M.D. Candidate, Class of 2026
Flu Shot Coordinator, Camp Driftwood
Burn Victim Sympathizer, Eternal Rest Hospital

I have never spoken to Hannah Foley and have no idea what her email means. As I try to make sense of this, another email dings, this one also from a student in my class I've never spoken to.

From: Yvette Nunes <ynunes@sms.edu>
Sent: Monday, September 12, 2022 12:49 PM
To: Sophia Abney <sabney@sms.edu>
Subject: Rat

You have sold our entire class out.

Yvette Nunes
MA Gender Studies, Vanderbilt University 2022
Pronouns: she/her/hers
M.D. Candidate, Class of 2026
Food Services Volunteer, Woeful Saints Homeless Shelter
Hall Monitor, Sunken Stone Day School

My mind races to understand these two emails. What could I have done? I can only think of one thing, but it should have no bearing on Hannah or Yvette.

Yesterday, I filed a PURF against the other members of my TBL team.

After they embarrassed me in front of the class, I couldn't take their prank idly. My mind spun and spun with anger and rage. I tried to let it go, tried to tell myself to focus on school and forget about what happened, but the image of Mercer smirking at me burned like a hot poker in my chest. At twenty-one-years of age I know my brain pretty well. I realized I'd never be able to move on until I did something to get back at them.

But I bided my time before taking revenge, letting a week pass so I could study for our first major exam. This pause, this brief armistice, lulled them into a false sense of safety. They saw me in lecture and lab, and in the hallways and cafeteria, but I said nothing. I didn't even look at them. I wanted them to think I was beaten and cowed.

Then yesterday after I finished the exam, I submitted the following message to the dean through the online PURF portal:

I have been made aware that four students are using a secret Google Drive to study. The drive contains pirated videos and test questions used in violation of copyright. As future doctors, we should not use pirated materials. The four students are Jennifer Mercer, Randall Collins, Celia Chalas, and Avtandil Khurtsidze.

That was it. Just fifty-one-words meant to destroy the lives of my TBL group for humiliating me. Maybe it was a bit harsh. After all, they simply pulled a prank on me and I retaliated by threatening their careers. But as Momma likes to say, "If you mess with the bull, you get the horns."

Since submitting the PURF, I've been quietly waiting for my TBL team to learn their fate. Any time now, I expect one of them to confront me in fury. They'll suspect I sold them out since the PURF was filed just a week after they told me about the Google Drive. But I'll deny submitting it. They can never prove what I did—submissions are anonymous to all but the dean. Hopefully, the dean makes them write a thousand-page essay on the importance of US copyright laws. Or maybe something worse. I don't care, so long as they suffer.

But why the emails from my other classmates, like Hannah and Yvette?

I'm pulled from my thoughts when someone yells, "Sophia!" The sound reaches over the tops of the book stacks around me.

Mercer stomps around the corner and marches to my cubicle. She's wearing her Harvard sweatshirt and shorts, just like always. She glares at me with eyes of rage.

"You crazy bitch!" she exclaims.

"What are you talking about?"

"Did you tell the dean about the Google Drive?"

I respond by pleading innocence, just as I'd planned. "I have no idea what you mean."

Mercer puts her hands on her hips. "The dean called our whole TBL group down to her office. Everyone except you. She brought us in one at a time. Said she knew about the Google Drive. There's only one person in the entire class who doesn't use that drive: you. So you better fucking explain yourself."

Suddenly my heart races.

Only one person in the entire class who doesn't use that drive.

I knew students outside my TBL group probably used the drive, but I had no idea the *whole class* used it. Could this explain the emails? How many people did I get in trouble? My stomach twists into a knot.

I decide to continue pleading innocence. "Well, I don't know anything about that."

"Bullshit," Mercer says. "We know it was you. *Everyone* knows it was you. Celia and Avi broke down and confessed to the dean. They showed her the drive. She took it down this morning. Now none of us can use it ever again. And she's calling an emergency assembly to confront everyone over this."

My hands go cold, and the hairs on my neck stand up. Mercer will tell everyone it was me. I'll never be able to lie my way out of this. This is my worst nightmare. I've gone from the silent and withdrawn girl in class to the most hated person. But goddamn it, my hand was forced. Mercer pushed me to this.

My laptop pings over and over with incoming emails. I glance at the Inbox on my screen:

Inbox ☆	
From	**Subject**
Rivers, Emily Rose	We want YOU in the Cleft Palate Interest Group!
Lopez, Isabella Sofia	Hard Flow, the Urology Interest Group meets tomorrow
Patel, Nathan Alexander	Can't Move, the Constipation Interest Group meets tonight
Carter, Olivia Grace	Serbian Medical Student Weightlifting Interest Group
Sillivan, Ethan Michael	Hirsutism and Baldness Interest Group next Tues 8pm!!
Foley, Hanah Hazel	<blank>
Nunes, Yvette Marie	RAT!
Mitchell, Grace Elizabeth	SELL OUT!
Foster, Alexander Willian	YOU SCREWED US!
Turner, Daniel Charles	SNITCH!!!
Bennett, Jacob Thomas	SNITCH
Hughes, Robert Mason	RAT!
Adams, Sophia Evelyn	SQUEALER
Campbell, Liam Patrick	U R SO CRINGE!
Jenkins, Zoe Alexander	SNITCH!
Walker, Noah Benjamin	SNITCH!!!!!!!!!!

The emails are pouring in. *Oh, my God!* Everyone hates me.

I study Mercer closely, her golden, tanned legs, her bleach-blonde hair. She has everything and decided to pick on me, the poor kid from community college.

"You humiliated me in front of the class," I say to her. "You can't attack someone like me and expect nothing in return."

Mercer's eyes widen. "We were just kidding around. It was a harmless prank. But you . . . you've ruined the whole class. Are you insane? I could've been formally disciplined if my father didn't help me out with the dean!"

My phone buzzes with a message from Jerome: *text me soon as u get to Momma so I know shes ok*

I shove my laptop into my backpack. Mercer watches me do this, her hands still on her hips.

"I have to go," I say, sliding my phone into my purse and standing.

"Of course you do," Mercer says. "Don't want to answer for what you did."

I glower at her. "My mother's in the ER. I got no time for your bullshit now."

"You'll never hear the end of this," she says. "You'll regret this for the rest of your life."

I try to ignore her, even though the words sting.

I march out of the library, eyes down as I pass other students.

The words of Hannah's email reverberate through my mind: *You have sold our entire class out.*

6.

"I'm going home," Momma says to the ER doctor. "I'm fine."

Momma doesn't look fine. She's sprawled on a gurney in her red bathrobe and nightgown, the outfit she always wears at home. There's a large purple bruise on her forehead as I sit beside her in ER room twelve, the smell of antiseptic in the air. Outside the room, voices buzz in the busy emergency department.

Since her cancer entered remission three years ago, Momma's health has been stable. The hemiplegia of her legs is permanent, but according to her doctor's she's otherwise without life-threatening illness. Despite this I've feared some evil lurking within her body would announce itself like thunder someday. Recurrent cancer? Heart disease? Diabetes? There are so many ways her body could turn against her. I hope today isn't the day that happens, but my stomach is aflutter over the notion that it could be.

"Mrs. Abney, we need to scan your head," says the ER attending physician. She stands at the foot of Momma's gurney, her face covered by a mask. Everyone in the ER wears a mask these days. It feels like Momma's being tended to by space travelers.

"No, no, no," Momma says. "I'm going home." She turns to look at me. "Soph, go get your car. Let's go."

Momma hates the medical system after all she endured with her cancer treatment. She hates the waiting on doctors. She hates the thousands of questions: *How did you fall? Are you having trouble breathing? Do you have any allergies?* She says doctors don't treat patients; they interrogate them.

"Mrs. Abney," the attending doctor says, her tone growing irritated, "we're trying to make sure you're okay. We need to do a CT scan of your head. If you don't want to do that, you can sign out against medical advice."

The attending's name is Dr. Miller, who I know from my old job at the front desk. A short woman in scrubs, her hair is pulled back in a bun, a weary look in her eyes. I admired her when I worked the desk, just like I admired all the doctors here. They're kings of the ER, so powerful and knowledgeable. One of the reasons I went to medical school was to become like them.

Momma shakes her head. "I just fell trying to get off the toilet. I didn't want to come here. I told McKernon not to call an ambulance. That old fool. I just wanted him to help me off the floor. Can't you see I'm fine?"

I try to focus on the conversation, but my mind swirls with guilt over the PURF. On the way here, my inbox blew up with messages of scorn from my class. They all hate me.

"Look, it's your life," Dr. Miller says to Momma. "You want to leave, you could die. But if you sign the AMA form, you can go."

Dr. Miller is surprisingly short and sharp. She almost seems to *want* Momma to sign out AMA.

Momma swings her gimpy legs over the side of the

gurney. If I don't do something, she'll leave the ER.

"Just wait a minute," I say to Momma. "Give me a second to talk to her."

"I'll give you a second, but I'm not staying," she replies, sitting on the edge of the gurney.

I step out of the room and motion to Dr. Miller, who follows me. We stop in the busy hallway outside as ER staff hurry past.

"Is she safe to go home?" I ask Dr. Miller. "I don't think I can get her to stay."

"I don't know, Sandy. She won't let us complete her evaluation."

I'm such a little person to her she doesn't remember my name. "Sandy is the other girl who works the desk," I say to correct her. "I'm Sophia."

"Oh, well, fine. Look, your mom's anemic. I haven't told her yet, but her red count dropped from where it was a month ago. It needs to get worked up."

My stomach twists into a knot. "Is that serious?"

"Can't say without more tests. Now, is your mom staying or not?"

"She's just scared, is all," I explain. "She almost died of cancer. She's afraid if you do more tests, you'll find something else. Maybe if you can reassure her she'll be okay?"

"I don't have time for scared," Miller says in a sharp tone, almost as if I've offended her. "Look, I'm working a sixteen with a three-quarters nursing staff. I can help your mom if she wants my help. But if she doesn't, she can leave and take her chances."

Miller turns and walks away, leaving me floored. *I don't have time for scared.* Some bedside manner. And I used to work here. I thought she'd give extra attention to Momma because of me. But then again, she doesn't even remember my name. I'm not even sure she cares much about what happens to Momma. I begin to think Momma is right to leave this place.

I slip back into Momma's room, where she's somehow managed to climb from the gurney into her wheelchair. She sits in her robe with bare feet, hands on the wheels, like a race car driver anticipating the starting horn.

"Let's go," she says.

"You don't even have shoes!"

"I'm fine."

I don't want to mention the anemia, because it'll scare Momma, but she needs to stay. "You have to let them run more tests."

"I'm fine. I just slipped. I have a bruise, but I'll heal. Let's go."

I can tell there's no stopping her. "Well, you have to sign the paper," I say. I pick up the AMA form, which the nurse left by the sink.

Mama gives an irritated sigh, then takes it from my hand. "I need a pen," she demands.

I fish inside my purse, then hand Mamma a PaperMate I use to take notes in class. She scribbles her name using her thigh as a desktop, then thrusts the AMA form onto the bed.

"Let's go," she says.

She pushes herself from the room, with me following behind. Her wheelchair moves as fast as a scooter. The ER is so noisy and busy, no one notices us leave. We move through the ambulance bay doors and into the parking lot. It's a warm September afternoon, with a cool breeze.

"Where's your car?" Momma asks. She's quite a sight sitting in the parking lot in bare feet, a bathrobe, and night-gown, with a huge bruise on her forehead. In the sunlight, I see how bony her face looks. She's lost so much weight in the past year. The cancer is supposedly in remission, but she looks like she's dying.

I point to my car and wheel her toward it. When we reach my Festiva, I freeze.

Spray-painted on the back window is the word "SNITCH" in white letters.

Bile rises to my throat and I think I might vomit. I stare at the vehicle, sunlight reflecting off the roof. Falling to one knee, I cover my face and weep. It's too much. They're never going to stop coming after me, not after what I did. They'll dog me until I quit. And Momma is in a wheelchair. How can I go to school when she could need me anytime?

Momma places a hand on my shoulder. "Who did this?" she asks, looking at the rear windshield.

I sniffle, then tell her the whole story. About how I kept quiet to avoid embarrassment over my background. About how they picked on me for not speaking. And about the PURF I filed yesterday.

Just as I finish, a pickup truck rumbles to a stop beside me and Momma. It's Jerome. He cuts the engine and hops from the driver's seat, the warm September sun on his scraggly face. He has on his Burger King uniform, his sleeves stained with grease.

"Oh, shit," he says, looking at my car.

"You're supposed to be at work," I say.

"Randy let me go. I told him Momma fell." He motions toward the word on my car. "Who did this?"

"Kids in her class," Momma replies. She taps my shoulder. "Come on, now. Stand up, Soph."

I do as she instructs, her voice like the command of a drill sergeant. I'm hoping she has some words of wisdom to help me navigate my disastrous circumstances.

"I'm sorry they did this to you," she says. "Do you wanna call the police?"

I'm already the most hated person in my class. If I send the police after everyone, it'll only get worse.

"No," I say. "I want to forget all about this."

"Then let's go home," she says. "Jerome and Randy will get the paint off. You rest and do your work. You gotta get back to school tomorrow."

Her words catch me by surprise. This is the first time she's ever encouraged me over medical school. I wonder if the bump on her head has affected her personality.

"Why'd they do this to your car?" Jerome asks.

"They hate me," I reply.

"Because you're city, right?" he says. "Because you got no money like them, huh? You gotta do something, Soph. Fight back."

Suddenly, I fill with rage. My hands tremble, and I feel blood rush to my face.

"Fight back?" I say. "How am I supposed to do that with you hounding me to get my old job?" I turn to Momma. "And you . . . you care more about making sure we have Pepsi in the fridge than me getting my studying done. I'm all alone. Everyone else has their family behind them, but not me."

I bury my face in my hands and weep. There's too much resistance. I can't go through four years of med school if I have to push against Mercer, Collins, and the rest of my class, plus Momma and Jerome.

"Stop those tears," Momma says. "I didn't raise my girl to cry. You get yourself together."

Slowly, I collect myself. "I'm just being real, Momma."

She thinks for a second. Her face softens while she looks at me. Every once in a while, sometimes just for a moment, she rises from the gloom of her cancer and Daddy's death. Then I get the old Momma back, the one who nurtured me as a child, the one who taught me to be a fighter.

"Why are you altercating with these kids by tattling on them?" she says. "Baby, you're brilliant. You've always been my brilliant girl. Just do what you do. Exams. Awards. Do it all. You leave the other kids in the dust."

Jerome nods his head. "Yeah, Soph. Show these kids up. Don't let them win. You're the smartest person I've ever seen."

I let out a small laugh as I wipe the tears from my face. Only now, with my class united against me in hatred, do I finally get the support of Momma and Jerome. I shouldn't be surprised. We may be poor, we may live in an apartment that's a dump, but we're tough. And if there's one thing we can't stand, it's seeing one of our own picked on.

"So now you want me to go to school?" I say to Momma.

"I want you to follow your heart. If you believe this is the right path, I'm with you."

"But I thought you hated doctors?"

"I know this is what you want. And I also know you'll be different."

Just do what you do. Exams. Awards. Do it all.

It occurs to me that I've handled my situation poorly. I never should have allowed myself to become so lost in TBL that Mercer could pull that prank on me. I have to refocus on school. Every time I've set a learning goal for myself, I've achieved it. Mercer and the others may come from fancy schools, but that doesn't mean I can't outwork them. I've started slowly, but I can catch up. What did Avi say about that one fourth-year student?

Guy crushed his exams but hardly speaks to anyone in his class.

That's exactly what I'm going to do. Let them hate me if they want. I don't need them at all.

Sometimes just one sentence from Momma is all the advice I need.

You leave the other kids in the dust.

Damn straight, I think. *That's exactly what I'm going to do.*

7.

THE NEXT MORNING AT 8:09 I sit nervously in a chair before the imposing desk of Dean Sylvia Weaver. The good news is that Momma slept okay and seemed fine this morning, despite abandoning the ER yesterday. After Jerome and I hounded her, she promised to see her regular doctor for more tests of the anemia this week—a huge relief.

The bad news is that I received this disturbing email last night:

From: Lois Armstrong < larmstrong@sms.edu >
Sent: Monday, September 12, 2022 7:49 PM
To: Sophia Abney <sabney@sms.edu>
Subject: Meeting with Dean Weaver

Dean Weaver would like to meet with you tomorrow at 8 a.m. Her office is located on the second floor of the academic tower. You will be excused from TBL for this meeting.

Lois Armstrong, MA
Administrative Assistant, Dean Weaver
Office of Medical School Administration

Winner, Best Office Assistant, 2018 and 2021
Runner-up, Ladies Sewing Circle Mitten Competition 2019

Normally, anything that gets me out of TBL would be a godsend, but this is different. I have no idea what the dean wants to discuss with me. Does she want to talk about the PURF? Did someone file a revenge PURF against me? Or is there some innocent reason for this meeting I don't know about?

Needless to say, I barely slept last night.

I shift in my seat as Dean Weaver sits regally behind her desk, her hands clasped before her. She's a large woman but carries herself well, spine straight, chin up. She always wears makeup and tasteful earrings. She's always clothed in refined dresses under her white coat. Surrounding her are cramped bookshelves and diplomas. I notice a large text, *Diseases of the Thyroid Gland*, which she authored. There's also a diploma from Yale University, B.S. in Biology, that looms high on the wall. Reminders of my inferior community college are everywhere.

"Thank you for coming," she says. I notice a large box of tissues on her desk. I presume these are for tearful students when she delivers bad news. I wonder if I'll need them today?

"Uh, of course. Sure," I reply nervously.

"The first thing I'd like to say is: thank you. Thank you for submitting that PURF. We have a major problem with professionalism in this school. I need students like you who are willing to speak up. There is a code of silence I am trying to break."

I consider telling her my class hates me because of the PURF. I consider telling her about "SNITCH" on my car. But getting the dean involved with those things won't help.

"Well . . . I, uh, just didn't think it was right what they were doing."

Weaver picks up a pen from her desk and twiddles it in her large hand. "It wasn't right. This school is teeming with unprofessional behavior like that. You'd be amazed at what goes on."

"So, is that why you asked me here? To talk about the PURF?"

"Unfortunately, no. Sophia, I'll get right to the point: you failed the first exam."

My heart plummets. "Wait? What? Are . . . are you sure?"

"We finalized the grades yesterday. They'll be released this afternoon. But I wanted to tell you about yours personally. I know this can be devastating news."

The room seems to spin around me. Failed? That can't be. I've never failed an exam in my life. The questions on the test were hard. I did a lot of guessing. But I never imagined a failing grade. That's not something that happens to me. Jerome, sure. But not me.

"That . . . that's . . . I can't believe this."

"Lots of students struggle on the first exam. It's part of the adjustment to medical school. Don't worry. I'm here to support you. You're part of our family now. Would you like some candy?" She gestures toward a bowl on her desk. "We have tissues, too, if you need them."

Her tone is as sugary as the candy on her desk. I've overheard other students say how nice the dean is. The school prides itself on being "supportive." I overheard an upperclassman say, "The exams and pressure may crush your soul, but when you crumble, the dean's ready with a smile and a Starburst."

"Can I see my exam? I want to know which questions I got wrong. There has to be a mistake."

"You can see your exam later today, during the review period—"

The phone rings on Weaver's desk. She looks at the Caller ID, then says to me, "One second." She picks up the receiver, and I hear murmurs spilling into her ear. "When?" she says, her voice suddenly grave. "Do you have it? I'll be right there." She hangs up the phone. "Come with me," she says. "There's something I have to do, but we can chat while we walk."

Weaver lifts her large frame from the chair behind her desk and ambles out of the office with me following behind. I should ask where we're going, but I can't stop thinking about my exam.

You failed the first exam.

How could this have happened? Horrible thoughts flicker through my mind: *Maybe I don't belong here. Maybe it was crazy to think a poor city girl like me could become a physician.*

We walk from her office down the hallway outside as other students pass by, some studying me closely, no doubt wondering why I'm walking with the dean. Weaver leads me toward the elevator bay.

"Let's talk about study habits," she says. "Medical school is different from college. You may need to change the way you study. Sometimes that's all it takes for a student to improve."

It's hard to focus, my mind so frazzled by the news of my exam. "I . . . I studied by reading the assigned textbook chapters. And by going to lecture. I . . . I wrote down everything Murrow said."

Weaver waves at a colleague who passes by, then says, "Well, there must be something we can work on. You're the only one in your class who failed. So there must be something you're missing."

My jaw falls open. *The only one!* I feel nauseous, like I just ate rotten meat.

"I can't be the only one. That's impossible. My class doesn't even read the textbook. Most of them don't go to the lectures."

We reach the elevators and Weaver presses the call button. "Well, maybe you just have a unique learning style? Would you like to meet with our learning specialist? Maybe you're a visual learner? Or an auditory learner?"

The walls feel like they're shrinking around me. Suddenly, it's hard to breathe. This is unbelievable. Any plan to outperform my class feels ridiculous. Now I'm wondering if I can even make it to graduation.

"Don't get worked up, darling," Weaver says as she waits for the elevator to arrive. "Dr. Murrow will meet with you for one-on-one teaching. We'll help you get on top of this material."

One-on-one with Murrow sounds like medieval torture. The reason I'm in this mess is that he's a terrible teacher. How will more time with him help?

"Besides," she says, "your grades in the first two years are pass-fail. After you meet with Dr. Murrow, you can enhance, and no one will ever know you failed."

"Enhance?"

"We give you a similar exam to the one you failed so you can demonstrate your enhanced understanding of the material. Pass that and your failed exam will never appear in your permanent record."

"So, you mean I'll get a retake exam?"

The dean's face turns dour. "We don't use terms like retake or remediate. Those can be stigmatizing to learners like yourself. At SMS, we allow students to *enhance* their understanding of medical science."

I'm going to be pretty fucking stigmatized among my classmates because I didn't get a passing grade on the test—it doesn't really matter what they call it. I can already hear the gossip. *Did you know that Sophia failed the first exam? She's that bitch who filed the PURF. Maybe she'll drop out.*

And another exam is hardly a relief. My class has already moved on to new material. How will I keep up and also find time to study for a retake or enhancement or whatever they call it?

Suddenly, the image I had of medical school changes. During the first two years of lectures, labs, and group sessions like TBL, there will be another dozen exams. Am I doomed to struggle each time I'm tested? Then after second year comes the Step 1 licensing exam, an eight-hour behemoth of a test. How will I pass that if I can't pass the school exams? So many tests. If I can't pass the first one, how will I pass all the others?

The elevator doors swing open, and I step into the car with Weaver, my feet shaky. She hits the button for the first floor. All I can think about is her words: *You're the only one in your class who failed.*

As the car rumbles downward, Weaver sees the concerned look on my face. "Is the stress getting to you?" she asks. "First year can be overwhelming. We can set you up with one of our counselors. We also have a wellness curriculum. There's yoga, tai chi, meditation."

"I don't need any of those things," I reply.

"Well, we have to do something. If you fail the enhancement exam, you'll have to go before the academic advancement committee. I don't want to see that happen."

My skin turns cold at the mere mention of the academic advancement committee. Its name is Orwellian genius. It is widely known that the AAC suspends or expels students for poor performance.

The elevator doors open, and I step out into a long corridor. I try to shake off the haze from my failed exam so I can see where I'm going. This hallway leads to the library, rotunda, and anatomy lab. Several men in white coats are huddled in the corner near the soda machine, apparently waiting for Weaver. I recognize their faces. They're the anatomy faculty who supervise us as we cut into the flesh of our cadavers.

Weaver walks toward the men, telling me to wait by the elevator. "Let me see it," she says.

The group turns toward the dean. One of the men holds a slim stack of papers in his hand which he gives to Weaver.

"Found it on the floor of the anatomy lab this morning," someone says to Weaver.

She thumbs through the papers with a grim expression. "Is there anything on the cameras?" she asks.

The men shake their heads, and one of them murmurs something I can't hear. Weaver mutters back to them, then returns to me.

We go back to the elevator where she hits the call button and the doors swing open. "Come," she says. "Let's go back to my office."

After the doors shut; I say, "What were those papers they showed you?" Maybe I shouldn't pry, but I can't help myself. The dean and the faculty seemed so grave over the documents they found.

Weaver's eyes narrow in anger. "Answers to the RAT questions. Someone from the upperclasses typed them up to share. Pigs. Unprofessional pigs."

Once a week during TBL, my class takes a Readiness Assurance Test, otherwise known as a RAT. It's basically a quiz which counts as a small portion of our final grade. Everyone hates these weekly mini exams. The name is fitting since we feel the same way about these quizzes as about disease-infested vermin. I've heard that some upperclassmen secretly record the questions and pass them down to students in my class. Someone is in big fucking trouble if the dean nails them for this. Maybe Mercer got the answers to the RAT questions. Maybe she'll get kicked out of school for this. God, that would be glorious.

Weaver turns to me and says, "We need more students like you, Sophia. Students who send us PURFs. This school is overrun with professionalism violations. I am determined to do something about it. Just wait. You'll see."

It's nice that she appreciates my PURF, but the truth is: I'm done reporting my classmates to the dean. I can't even pass my exams. Reporting professionalism violations is the last thing I want to do now.

As the elevator car whirs, Weaver says, "Now, let's get back to your studies. I want to help you. And we have to do something to get you back on track. I want to be sure you pass the enhancement exam. What are you going to do to improve?"

I stand frozen next to Weaver, thinking over what's happened. I'm the only one who failed the exam. I'm also the only one from Midtown, a small community college. Why did I ever think I could handle medical school? I knew it at the White Coat Ceremony: I don't belong.

But then my mind races through the questions from the test. They were nothing like the material covered in the textbook or in lecture. How did my class do so much better than me? Is this the result of my inferior college education? Or maybe this happened because my class used those stupid TPRs? That's probably why they passed and I didn't.

It occurs to me that the study habits that served me in college don't work here. I need new skills. But I don't want to meet with Murrow. And I don't need a learning specialist or yoga or meditation. What I need is someone who can tell me how to prepare for med school exams. They're nothing like college. In college, they test you on the things they teach in class. In med school, the teaching is gibberish, and the exam questions aren't even similar to the gibberish. My class apparently knows how to navigate this gauntlet. I need someone who can show me how they do it.

Suddenly, I remember what Avi said last week in TBL: *There's a fourth-year who never talks to anyone in his class, Miles Sebastian. Guy crushed his exams.*

"Do you know Miles Sebastian?" I ask.

The elevator car halts, and the doors open. The dean's smile suddenly fades. "Yes. Why? Has he been giving you advice?"

We step out of the elevator into the hallway. "No, but I wonder if you could introduce me to him. I hear he does very well on exams."

The dean shakes her head. "That is not a good idea. Mr. Sebastian is . . . well, let's just say I don't recommend you get help from him."

What? Avi said the guy crushed his exams.

"I'd like to meet him. Just for a quick conversation."

The dean scrunches her face in concern. "Mr. Sebastian has had professionalism issues. He is not a person you should try to emulate. I think you'd do much better to meet with Dr. Murrow to review your exam."

That Weaver doesn't want me to get advice from Miles Sebastian only makes me want to meet him more. Why would a student who excels in school be disliked by the dean? Besides, I failed my exam after doing exactly what the school told me to do, things like reading the textbooks and attending lectures. Maybe if I do something the school *doesn't* want me to do, I'll actually get ahead.

Weaver starts marching back toward her office, with me following beside her. "So, when are you free to meet with Dr. Murrow?" she asks. "I'll set it up today. I'm also going to have you see our learning specialist."

"Oh, anytime is fine," I say.

But this is just something to satisfy her. I'll go to the meetings, but Dr. Murrow and the school's learning specialist aren't the people I want to see.

The truth is as soon as I get out of here, I'm going to find Miles Sebastian.

8.

"You can sit down," Miles Sebastian says to me after I introduce myself.

He peers at a computer screen showing the medical record of one of his patients. It's late morning, and the hospital work station is crowded with nurses and other staff, all pecking at computers nearby.

Tick-tack. Tick-tack.

I'm on the second floor of the building, the general medical ward. One of the patients must have a bowel disaster, because the faint smell of feces lingers in the air. It's gross, but what can I do? I need Sebastian's help.

I study his features closely. A lanky, beanpole of a man in scrubs and a short white coat, he's definitely over six feet but can't weigh more than a hundred and fifty pounds. His mask sits atop a goatee that appears neatly-trimmed from the edges I can see. He has thick, dark hair and brown eyes—handsome in an average sort of way, not bad looking at all, but also not the kind of guy to make women swoon with his looks. There's nothing about him that says super genius, but that's his reputation.

I slide into a chair next to Sebastian. "I'm sorry to bother you when you're working, but the online schedule said you'd be here. We don't know each other, but I heard you did really well on your exams. I was wondering if I could ask you—"

"You have to wear a mask," he says.

"Oh, uh, right." I fumble in my purse and withdraw my mask, sliding it over my mouth.

"Don't mean to be difficult," he says, "but the nurse manager will get pissed. And she fills out an evaluation on all us students."

"No, uh, it's fine. I'm just a first-year, so I'm not in the hospital much."

Sebastian returns his gaze to the screen, studying a CT report. "Did you fail the first exam?" he says.

My spine stiffens. "How did you know that?"

Sebastian turns to look at me. Above his mask, I see his brown eyes study me up and down. "I just figured. I went to Midtown, like you. And I also failed the first test. It's hard to adapt to this place from community college."

I didn't think anyone at SMS other than me went to Midtown. And Sebastian is a fourth-year. He's somehow navigated this school with just a meager community college education behind him. I must know more.

"I . . . I didn't know there were other Midtown students here," I say.

Sebastian eases back in his chair. "Just you and me. Everyone else is from bougie schools. They all have sticks up their asses. Maybe you've noticed."

A petite nurse beside Sebastian glances at him when he says this, then turns back to her computer. It feels eerie to have this conversation in such a public place, but I'll talk anywhere if Sebastian will help me.

"Who told you I went to Midtown?" I ask.

"I saw it on the incoming class list. And besides, ever since you ratted out your class with that PURF, everyone in this school knows about you."

I feel my skin go cold. I knew my class hated me, but until now I didn't realize I was despised by the upper classes, too.

Sebastian swipes his badge to log off the computer in front of him. Then he rises and says, "Come with me. We can talk while I work." As I follow him down the hallway, he says, "I've actually been wanting to meet you. Look, you're in a big hole. Your class wants to throw you off a cliff, and you failed the first exam. It sucks. But I may be able to help."

I thought I'd have to plead with him to help me, but he seems eager to give advice. I scurry to keep up with him as he walks. "So, how did you pass your first-year exams? I need some pointers."

"Look, there's a lot I can tell you. But it's not worth my time unless you're a certain type of person. What specialty are you going into?"

An odd question. I'm only a first-year. I don't need to pick my specialty until year four. "Uh . . . I'm not sure. Maybe oncology. My mother . . . she had cancer."

"Oh, God. If you're going into oncology, I can't help you at all."

"What's wrong with oncology?"

We reach the stairwell doorway and hurry through. Sebastian walks quickly downward. "Let me ask you a question: What's the purpose of modern medicine?"

Now this is really getting weird. "I thought you were going to give me study tips?"

"I will," Sebastian replies, turning as we reach a landing. "Well, maybe. But first let's get some things out of the way.

What is the purpose of modern medical care?"

"What . . . I don't know. What kind of question is that?"

"Come on. Humor me. It'll all make sense in a second."

This is fucking bizarre, but I decide to play along. "Fine. Okay, um . . . what's the question again?"

"The purpose of modern medical care?"

"It's . . . to cure disease. To heal. You know, to help people."

"Wrong. The purpose of modern medical care is to produce documentation."

We reach the bottom floor and leave the stairwell into a long, brightly lit corridor. A sign on the wall says "Pathology." Sebastian walks quickly down the hallway, headed for God-knows-where.

"Listen," I say, "I just came here because I thought you could help with my classes."

"I can," he says as he walks.

"Well, I don't see how a discussion of the purpose of medicine will help."

"You'll never succeed in medical school, or medicine as a profession, unless you truly understand the field. That's what I'm trying to tell you. The purpose of modern medicine is to produce documentation."

"What are you talking about? The purpose is to help the sick. Same as it's ever been."

He stops, then turns to look at me. "Sometimes the sick are helped, sometimes they aren't. But the production of documentation never stops. The hospital? The clinic? Just big factories churning out documents like an assembly line."

A man walks past us, wheeling a gurney. It carries a large figure covered in a white sheet. It occurs to me he's transporting a dead body. I've seen the dead before in anatomy lab, of course. Plus, I saw a few people who died in the ER when I worked the desk. But it still creeps me out.

The gurney passes us slowly, the wheels squeaking as it moves away down the hall. I wait to speak until the corpse is out of view.

Then I think back to Sebastian's comment about how the purpose of medicine is to produce documents. "So, you're one of those cynical types, then? Medicine is all about documents, insurance companies, blah, blah, blah."

"Not at all. In fact, I love medicine and I love that I'll get to practice it for as long as I like. But I see it for what it really is. You'll be happier if you do, too."

"And I presume this is something you'd like to explain to me now."

"Look, all the important things that doctors do generate documents. Examine a patient? You put your findings in the chart. Cut out a gallbladder? You write an op report. Interpret a chest X-ray? You generate an imaging report. Nothing important happens in medicine without a document being generated. And those documents are *extremely valuable.* Once you create one, insurance companies will send you cash. And without that cash, the entire system would grind to a halt."

"Yes, but you can't create documents without helping people. All those things—examining a patient, doing surgery, reading an X-ray—they all help patients. That's the goal."

He glances at his watch, then starts moving again, taking long strides down the hallway. I follow along beside him.

"Go to your phone. Search up 'obituaries.' You'll find thousands of people who died. Most of them got a lot of medical care in their lives, especially at the end, but they still died. But that doesn't mean we couldn't document things. All of them, every single person in the obit section, sourced a hundred, maybe a thousand documents before they went to the wrong side of the grass."

I see where he's going with this. "Fine, people die. But we *try* to help them. That's our goal."

"Yes, but help or not, we generate reports. And those reports are turned into cash by the hospitals and clinics. You're right that patients get helped by us, at least some of the time, but that's *incidental.* You could help a thousand people, but if you don't produce documents, you won't get paid, and you won't have a job. What maintains the system—the very system you're going to depend on for your career, by the way—is the generation of documents. And the most powerful doctors are the ones who can generate the most valuable documents."

"And what makes a document valuable?"

Sebastian walks through a doorway with a sign overhead labeled, "Autopsy Room." We enter a large space reeking of formaldehyde, the heavy smell making my stomach turn. Six naked bodies lie on gurneys, one with the chest cracked open, another with the head removed. It reminds me of the anatomy room where we dissect cadavers, only these bodies are freshly deceased from the hospital. It occurs to me that I'm going to continue my conversation with Sebastian among the dead. Medicine is a strange field.

Sebastian hurries toward the nearest of the deceased, an older man with purple lips and the blank look of death in his eyes. A small stack of papers rests on the man's thigh. The dead are apparently used as tabletops around here.

Sebastian picks up the papers and scans them. "Ah, perfect! Cause of death, retroperitoneal bleed."

"Was he your patient?" I ask.

"Yes. He arrested suddenly yesterday."

"And you wanted to know how he died? That's why you came down here?"

"Doesn't really matter to me why he died, but my attending will want to know. So, I came down here to get the early results. Then I report it to the attending, and bingo: superstar evaluation. I've mastered the art of obtaining glowing reports on the wards. One of many things I can help you with."

He's cocky, which I normally don't like. But it also seems like he can teach me a lot about performing well in medical school.

"So, anyway, what were you saying? Something about the most powerful doctors are the ones who can generate the most valuable documents?"

"Ever seen an op report for open heart surgery? Pure fucking gold. Worth thousands of dollars. It's like holding a diamond in your hand. And you can't get a report like that without a heart surgeon. So, heart surgeons make bank."

"So, you want to be a heart surgeon?"

"Hell, no! Too much call." Sebastian takes the autopsy report and walks to a copier in the corner, with me following behind. "Don't go into any specialty where you have to get up in the middle of the night. You'll never be happy. Sure, it might be okay for a while. But do you really want to be fifty years old and driving into the hospital at three a.m.?"

"So, what, then? Primary care? Emergency medicine?"

"Ah, no! Never, never, never." Sebastian slides the papers in his hand into the feeder tray for the copier which sucks them in with a whir. "Don't go into any specialty on the front lines. Any patient can stroll right up to you with their bleeding this or their aching that. You'll get the unwashed hordes complaining of everything. You *have* to be a specialist. You have to go into some field where patients only get to you after they've seen another doctor first. Use the other doctors as a shield that blocks the craziness."

"So, what's your perfect field, then? I presume one that isn't on the front lines, has no call, and produces super valuable documents?"

Sebastian turns toward me. He bows his head slightly and clasps his hands. He appears almost prayerful, and I briefly wonder if he'll genuflect or make the sign of the cross.

Then, in a low voice he replies, "Dermatology."

I think for a second. "Isn't that, like, the most competitive specialty? Super hard to get into?"

The papers slide out of the copier one at a time. "Last year, hundreds of med students applied in dermatology and didn't get a spot. The competition for residency is brutal. And for good reason. Dermatology has a good lifestyle. Great salary. Easy to make over four hundred thousand a year. You know why?"

"The documents?"

"Exactly. A clinic visit takes five minutes. Look at rash, prescribe cream, next. And you know what lots of rashes require? A skin biopsy. Takes under a minute, snip-snip, but it generates a document as good as a surgical procedure. Then you look at that biopsy under the microscope. Boom. Another document for the path report. The specialty is a gold mine for documentation. And you'll never get woken up in the middle of the night. There is no such thing as a derm emergency. The rashes, the zits, the warts, they can all wait until Monday morning."

He clearly has strong feelings about this topic. I suspect he could talk about it forever if I let him, but I need to get help with my studies.

"So, what's this got to do with my exam grade?"

Sebastian returns the report to the dead man's thigh, and we walk from the autopsy room. As we dash down the hallway again, he says, "This journey you're on—medical school—is brutal. You have piles of material to learn for your exams, which are ridiculously hard, but the teachers are terrible. You think Dr. Murrow sucks? Wait until you meet some of the others in third year. So you spend four years trying to learn on your own, while the school throws bad teachers in your way. Then when it's all over, you go into residency, where you can easily work eighty-plus hours a week for years. The only specialty that's worth all that trouble is dermatology."

"So, you'll only help me if I'm going into derm?"

"I'm in the top ten percent of my class. I aced every exam except the first one in the past three years. I have a dozen research publications, plus community service. I am the *ultimate* applicant to dermatology. To get here wasn't easy, but I've devised my own system that really works. I've got study guides, insider tips, and a hundred other things to help you succeed. I've been looking for someone to pass all this on to since I'm graduating in May. You're perfect. Another lost kid from Midtown, like I was. But I'm not giving you my opus if you're going to waste it by going into pediatrics or cardiology or allergy or some other shit field where you'll be miserable. I'll only help you if you want to become a gunner."

I think for a second. "What's a gunner?"

"You've never heard that term? Seriously? Not in college or high school?"

"I went to high school in the city. At PS Fifteen, when they say someone's a gunner, you better run."

"Well, in med school it's different. A gunner is . . . I don't know how to say it exactly. It's a person who wants to be the best. Isn't that what you want? To be the best in your class?"

"I'll settle for just passing my exams."

"Did you really come to medical school just to pass? Don't you want to be at the top? If you do, then you're a gunner. That's what I am. I wear it as a badge of pride. It just means I know what I want and I go after it."

The elevator doors open, and I step inside the empty car with Sebastian. Soon, the car begins to rumble upward as I consider what Sebastian has said. I'd love to become a top student in my class. I'd revel in watching Mercer look upon me with jealousy. But Sebastian is all about dermatology. The truth is: I have no idea what specialty to choose. There are so many. And it's not like I come from a family of doctors who can tell me about each one.

Sebastian makes some good points. I don't want to go through years of medical training, then end up burned out. Driving into the hospital at 3 a.m. scares the hell out of me. Could I do it? Sure. But would I be happy doing it for the rest of my life? I have no idea.

The elevator doors open, and I step out onto the second floor of the hospital with Sebastian. "I . . . I just don't know. I want your help, but I'm not sure I can choose my specialty now. I mean, I've only been in school a month. And I just failed the first exam."

Suddenly, my phone vibrates from my purse. The Caller ID says, "POLICE."

A nurse walks up to Sebastian and they begin talking. As this happens, I answer the call.

"Uh, Soph, it's me," Jerome replies.

His tone sounds grave. "What's going on? Why does your Caller ID say police?"

A pause. The sound muffles for a second. "I got arrested.

Can you come get me out?"

"What! What happened?"

"I'll explain when you get here. Can you just come? Come now. I don't want to talk about it on the phone."

I agree, then end the call.

The nurse walks away from Sebastian, and he turns his attention back to me.

"Look, I have to go," I say to him. "I'll have to think about what you said."

Sebastian reaches into the pocket of his white coat and slides out a slip of paper. "Take this," he says. "Dermatology interest group meeting is tomorrow night. You should come. I'll write my number on the back."

Sebastian places the paper against the wall and scribbles on it with his pen. Then he hands it to me.

"I'm offering you the chance of a lifetime," Sebastian says. "I can basically guarantee you'll match into derm if you follow my instructions. Think of the money you'll make. Think of the lifestyle you'll have. A lot of people in your class would jump at this opportunity."

I listen, but my mind is occupied with Jerome. What could he have done? Could he go to jail? What if he can't work anymore? How will we afford to pay the bills?

"I've got to go," I say. "I'll think about it."

Then I hurry for my car to drive to the police station.

9.

"I HAD TO PAY FIVE HUNDRED BUCKS to get you out," I say to Jerome as we depart the police station downtown.

It's evening, the sky dark, lamplights buzzing. My car is parked a few blocks away, the only spot I could find. As I walk with my brother along the sidewalk, I'd like to strangle him for getting mixed up with the police, but his brain needs all the oxygen it can get.

"You know we don't have that kind of extra money," I say. "I had to put it on the credit card."

"I'll get it back."

"How are you going to get it back?"

We pause at an intersection, waiting for the walk signal. "I'm gonna get off," Jerome says. "I get a public defender. They'll tell the judge I didn't do anything. Charges get dropped. Then I get the bail money back."

I don't share Jerome's confidence over this, but I decide to let it go. What I want to know is how he got arrested. "Care to explain why you were charged with possession of narcotics?"

"It wasn't me. It was Fernando."

Fernando, if you can believe it, is half as smart as Jerome. I find it hard to conceive of him dragging my brother into mischief. "You let that fool lead you around?"

The walk signal comes on, and we resume our march toward my car. "Fernando told me to wait in my truck for him. Then he goes into Big Freddie's house. He comes out, says, 'Let's go.' Five minutes later, the cops pull me over. Fernando had fentanyl in his backpack. Got it from Freddie. But I didn't know he had that. And Fernando will back me up. So, they're gonna let me off."

I consider the story my brother just told me. I know him too well. He's not this stupid.

"Where's Fernando now?"

"His grandmother paid his bail."

"You mean to tell me you didn't know what he went to Freddie's house for?"

Jerome shrugs. "He said he had to get something. What, I'm supposed to interrogate him when he asks a favor?"

From the look on his face, I'm certain my brother is lying. I stop walking and pull my phone from my purse. Jerome stares at me with a puzzled look as we stand in front of a bodega. I find Fernando in my contacts and call him. A second later, he answers.

"Yeah?" he says in his low, stoner voice. This man probably puts weed in his Cheerios.

"You realize what a mess you've made for my brother? Huh? Do you?"

"Soph, don't do that," Jerome says, but I ignore him.

"What I'm supposed to do?" Fernando says over the phone. "Apologize?"

Jerome reaches for my phone, but I swat away his hand. To Fernando I say, "You mean to tell me Jerome had no idea you were carrying drugs in your backpack? *Absolutely* no idea? And so help me, Fernando, if you lie to me. You know my Momma and your grandmother are close. You lie to me, and I'll see your grandmother learns every damn thing you do online at night with my brother. And don't think I don't know what sites you two land on. My room's next to his. I can hear through the walls."

Jerome's eyes narrow like hot pokers. He's not just mad because I called Fernando. He's mad because he knows Fernando will tell me the truth.

Fernando says nothing for a beat. Then he lets out a laugh. "The truth?" he says. "Truth is, the whole thing was Jerome's idea."

I end the call and glower at my brother. "You mind telling me what *really* happened?"

Jerome presses his palms to his forehead. "God, you're frustrating." Then he lets out a sigh. "There's a dude comes into work every day about noon. He's this tall, scraggly dude always gets a Whopper and a Coke. Anyway, I come to find out he sells fentanyl at the gym. You know, that workout place over on New Park? Anyway, he says he's being watched. He can't pick up his supply himself. He says he'll give me five hundred dollars a week if I do it. It's easy money, Soph. I get the stuff from Freddie, then put it in his Burger King bag."

I start hitting Jerome with my purse.

"Ow!" he shouts.

"Damn you, Jerome! This is the last kind of trouble our family needs. Why can't you just go to your job like a regular person? Don't you have any kind of brain in that head?"

"I was thinking of you and Momma," he pleads. "You can't tell me that five hundred dollars a week wouldn't help."

"This is not the way to earn extra cash."

"Well, what am I supposed to do, huh? What? For just

once, I wanted to bring home a fat payday. And don't try to tell me you don't understand. You just quit your job. You said it's so you can go to med school, but I know the truth. You got dreams of dollars, same as me, and you jumped at the opportunity when it came. I know it. Well, what school am I gonna go to? None. I took the best option I got. For people like us, when you're presented with an opportunity, you gotta take it."

Something about Jerome's comments sting. I find myself feeling defensive.

"I went to med school to help people."

"Oh, please, girl. There's a thousand ways to help people. You coulda been a cop, a teacher, a firefighter, whatever. But you picked the job that pays. Don't think I can't see that. I may not be smart as you, but I'm not blind."

My brother, for all his weed smoking and online gaming, has a sharp eye. The reality is, I didn't go to medical school just to help people. That was part of it, sure, but if I'm honest with myself, I went for the money.

I stare at my brother, his face in a shadow beneath the streetlamp. "Going to med school isn't against the law."

"Yeah, well, if I had options that were legal, I'd take 'em, but I don't."

Somehow, this conversation has drifted far off topic. "You gotta find a way out of this. You can't go to jail. Me and Momma need you working."

"I know," he shoots back. "What, you think I haven't thought of that already?"

He appears on the verge of tears. I can tell I've pressed too hard. He feels bad. I don't need to rub it in.

"Alright, then," I say. "Let's get home."

As we resume our march down the sidewalk, my mind drifts to Jerome's words.

You coulda been a cop, a teacher, a firefighter, whatever. But you picked the job that pays.

He's right, of course. For some reason, it feels dirty to say you're going into medicine to make money, but I am. Maybe it's because medicine involves caring for the sick. It seems wrong to profit off the suffering of others. But the reality is that I'm in medical school to get rich. So is everyone else probably. Mercer knows what her father earns as a neurosurgeon. No doubt she had dollar signs in her eyes when she applied to medical school. Collins, Avi, Celia: I'm sure they've all thought of the money they'll make down the road. No one talks about it. We put on this charade that we're in school, working our asses off, solely to help others. But the truth is we all want to get paid.

For people like us, when you're presented with an opportunity, you gotta take it.

When we arrive at my car, I reach into my purse and retrieve the folded slip of paper with Sebastian's phone number. I can just read it under the dim streetlights. To pass on Sebastian's guidance would be insanity. He could help me get to the top of my class. He could guide me to a life of wealth beyond anything I've ever imagined. If I'm going to work my ass off in medical school, it's only logical to aim for the highest-paying specialty with the best lifestyle.

My mind is made up: Tonight I'll call Sebastian and take him up on his offer of help.

And tomorrow when I wake up I'm going to become a gunner.

10.

The next day I meet Sebastian at Starbucks. We sit at a counter, the two of us on stools, a lame cup of water in front of me. It's pathetic but I always ask for water at Starbucks, which they usually give me for free. I never order the drinks—they're too expensive. The café bustles with the noise of customers, but I tune it out, my mind focused on learning what I must do to become a wealthy dermatologist.

Last night after bringing Jerome home, I kissed Momma goodnight then rushed to my room. I turned on my laptop and searched "physician salaries by specialty." I quickly found this list:

Top Ten Average Annual Physician Salaries

1. Plastic Surgery: $576,000
2. Orthopedics: $557,000
3. Cardiology: $490,000
4. Otolaryngology: $469,000
5. Urology: $461,000
6. Gastroenterology: $453,000

7. Dermatology: $437,000
8. Radiology: $437,000
9. Ophthalmology: $417,000
10. Oncology: $411,000

My heart soared. $437,000 a year for derm! And that's the *average* salary. I could earn more, because when in life has this girl ever been average? Sebastian was one hundred percent right: dermatology is super lucrative. And of the top ten highest paid specialties, it's the only one where you're never up in the middle of the night. How could I *not* go into this amazing field when I have a mentor in Sebastian to guide me along the way? After seeing the salaries, I almost woke Momma up to tell her to start searching for big houses in the suburbs.

"Let's start by talking about Anki," Sebastian says, drawing me from my thoughts.

I think for a second. "What's Anki?"

"What's Anki?!" Sebastian exclaims, grabbing his chest, making a faux swoon. "You can't be serious. That's like asking, 'What's oxygen?' or 'What's water?' Anki is the life-sustaining force of a medical student. Without it, you will die."

"Well, somehow I got into medical school without hearing of it."

"That's a minor miracle," he says. "You should let the Vatican know. Seriously. It's on par with turning water into wine, healing leprosy, all that shit. The Pope may want to talk to you himself."

I roll my eyes at Sebastian's joke and sip my water. He proceeds to explain the glory that is Anki, a glory somehow I'd never heard of until now. At a basic level, Anki is a memory program. You can get it on your PC or laptop, or as an app on your phone. It flashes "cards" at you with text like, "Streptococcus is a ______ bacteria." I'm supposed to read this, think of the answer in my head, then signal the program to show me the answer. If I'm right, great. If I'm wrong, I commit the answer to memory and mark the card. Then I move on to the next card. Anki shows me cards I got wrong more frequently than those I got right. That's essentially it. Very, very simple.

"The true power of Anki," Sebastian explains, "is in the decks. You have to find the perfect deck."

"What's a deck?"

Sebastian slurps his beverage, a grande cappuccino with caramel drizzle, which he claims "all the dermatology residents" drink. I saw him order it—it costs $5.34. Unreal.

"A deck is a collection of cards on a particular topic, like cardiology, neurology, whatever. There are thousands of these decks out there. But because you're lucky enough to know me, I'll give you the best deck in the world. Go through the cards over and over, and you're practically guaranteed to ace your exams."

"What's so special about your deck?"

"Three years ago, just around the time I was starting medical school, I met a Russian girl online. We briefly dated, but she turned psycho because I'm part-Polish and . . . well, that's a long story. But anyway, her father was a Soviet spy during the Cold War. Around that time, he infiltrated the U.S. medical system. They wanted to get Russian doctors into medical research facilities to see what the Americans were up to. So the KGB acquired U.S. board exams, carefully examined the questions, and turned them into study guides so their spies could climb the ladder at U.S. medical schools and residencies. Well, this girl took her father's old study guides and turned them into Anki decks. They're pure fucking gold! And because you've decided to become my protégé, I'm going to pass them on to you."

"You like that expression, 'pure fucking gold,' don't you?"

"It's fitting. The goal of a gunner is to dig for med school gold: anything that gets you ahead of the pack. These things aren't always obvious. You need a sharp eye. Consider my Anki deck your first discovery."

"So, you're going to give me the study tools of Russian spies?"

"Look, if you want to become a dermatologist, you're going to have to use a lot of tricks to get ahead. Profiting from foreign intelligence is the least of your worries."

I take another sip of my water. I suppose benefiting from Russian spies is a minor crime if it gets me into dermatology. I can't imagine this is explicitly outlawed in the academic policies manual anyway.

"So I should start going through the cards tonight?"

Sebastian shakes his head. "No, no, no. You have to start right now. As soon as we're done here. If you want to go into derm, you have to get through a minimum of two thousand cards a day."

I almost spit out the water in my mouth. "Two thousand!"

"If you want to match into dermatology after graduation, you have to follow the Gunner Rules. And Gunner Rule Number 1 is: ANY MINUTE NOT DOING ANKI IS A WASTED MINUTE."

I roll my eyes. "Gunner Rules? Are you serious?"

"Don't make fun. These rules are guaranteed to lead you to the promised land of dermatology. Ignore them at your own peril. Here's what I did first year: Get up at five a.m. Knock off five hundred cards before school starts at eight. Do another two hundred at lunch. Another five hundred in the afternoon. Then do eight hundred at night before bed. The average medical student does five hundred Anki cards a day. If you want to go into derm, you have to quadruple that."

It seems my quest for dermatology will be harder than I thought. But I worked my ass off to get into medical school. I can do it again to become a dermatologist. Especially if it pays $437,000 a year.

Sebastian slides his phone from his pocket and taps at the screen. He shows me a small grid of boxes, each box filled with a shade of green, some light, most dark.

"What's that?" I ask.

Sebastian shudders as if I've just said something shocking. "Oh, my. I have so much to teach you. This is my Anki heat map from first year."

"A heat map?"

Sebastian points at his phone screen. "It's part of the Anki app. Each box represents one day. The darker the shade of green in each box, the more Anki cards I did. You don't know it yet, but what you're looking at is a fucking masterpiece. I may print this out and frame it. It could actually end up in the Louvre next to the Mona Lisa. Da Vinci himself would tip his hat if he saw this. My heat map is epic. Most kids in my class had maps with a bunch of yellow, some light green here and there. What you're looking at, all this dark green, is a legendary achievement. This right here: this is how you get into derm."

I study the screen which looks like a mishmash of green colors that make odd shapes, almost like a Rorschach test. It seems unremarkable to me. Funny that this is the key to getting into derm rather than reading textbooks about skin disease. Medical school is bizarre.

"Ok, I get it," I say. "I'll start doing Anki right away and work on that, uh, heat map thing."

"That's only the beginning," Sebastian says. "Gunner Rule Number 2 is: NEVER LEARN FROM SCHOOL INSTRUCTORS."

"What's that supposed to mean?"

"Forget going to class or lab or anything else unless it's mandatory. The way to really learn is to watch videos and do practice questions on your own every day." He pulls out a flash drive from his pocket, a small, black rectangular device. "I made this for you. It has every video from Pathoma, Boards and Beyond, Sketchy Medicine, Dirty Medicine, Osmosis, and Lecturio. You need to watch at least two hours of videos per day. Watch them at 2x speed or faster, so you can do more. There are also practice questions on here from the best Qbanks. I've given you bootlegs from UWorld and Amboss and Kaplan. You need to do at least one hundred questions per day."

Watch them at 2x speed or faster. Is he serious? And how am I going to do videos plus practice questions plus Anki every day?

I study the jet-black flash drive he holds in his palm like some wizard's gem with magical powers.

"Where'd you get all the videos and questions?"

"Telegram. It's an online file sharing site."

File "sharing." Sounds so benign. But I know what he means: the videos and questions are pirated. Sebastian is offering me the study tools my classmates use. He's telling me to do the exact thing I just reported to the dean in my PURF.

"It makes me nervous to use those things without paying for them."

"What are you, some kind of Girl Scout or something? You can buy all these things if you want. It'll cost you about two thousand bucks. But I'm guessing you don't have that.

One of many ways kids without rich parents get screwed by the system. You either pirate this stuff, or you fail."

I twiddle my hair, a nervous habit I've had for years. "But I just turned in my class for using pirated videos from a Google Drive."

"And you know what? Your class already made another Google Drive. There's a reason you were the only one who failed the first exam. It's because you went to class and paid attention. It's because you didn't watch these videos and use these practice questions. Goody Two-Shoes don't become doctors."

There's a reason you were the only one who failed the first exam.

God, I was so naïve. All I did was read the textbook and take notes in lecture. That's like riding a bicycle in a NASCAR race.

A flutter of doubt suddenly courses through me. I never realized I'd need all these pirated resources. I never knew dermatology required hours and hours of work I'll have to do while juggling Momma's health and Jerome's stupidity. Maybe I'm aiming too high?

Just then, the door to the café swings open and Jennifer Mercer walks in. I silently curse myself for picking a public place to meet. Sebastian sees my gaze drawn toward the door and looks over his shoulder. Mercer catches us eyeing her and freezes. For once she's not wearing a Harvard sweatshirt, but she still looks like a spoiled brat in her Vineyard Vines fleece, with diamond earrings dangling from her lobes like chandeliers.

She approaches the counter where I sit with Sebastian.

"Hello, Miles," she says, purposefully ignoring me.

Bitch.

"Oh, hi, Jennifer," Sebastian says. He turns toward me. "This is Sophia. Do you two know each other?"

Mercer rolls her eyes. "We've met," she says.

I don't reply, hoping she'll leave so I can resume my conversation with Sebastian.

"You know," Mercer says to Sebastian, "Sophia sent a PURF about our class Google Drive. Maybe you heard? Not sure why you're hanging around with the class snitch?"

My shoulders tighten in anger. I'm reminded of the word "SNITCH" painted on my car. I know Mercer was the one who did it. I'd like to punch her, but I stay quiet, waiting for her to walk away. This is no place for an argument.

"Sophia and I went to the same school," Sebastian says. "We're swapping old stories of community college."

"*You* went to Midtown?" Mercer says. "I had no idea."

She uses a tone like Midtown is a school for defectives.

"It's no Harvard, but it got me here," Sebastian replies. "So anyway, maybe I'll see you later at the clinic?"

"For sure," Mercer says. Then she walks toward the counter to place an order, swinging her hips like a runway model. God, I hate her.

When she's out of earshot I say, "How do you know Mercer?"

"She's always floating around the derm clinic," Sebastian says. "She's kissed every attending's ass so much, they have lipstick on their internal sphincters."

Realizing what this means, I swallow hard. "Mercer is going into derm?"

"Yep. She's been gunning for it since day one. Her father introduced her to the chair. She shadows in clinic all the time."

The notion that Mercer and I will be competing for the same specialty makes me sick. I want to see less of her, not more.

"She hates me," I reply. "Even before the PURF. She

just doesn't like me."

"That's because she's an inbred and she knows it."

"What's that mean?"

"Her father got her into medical school. People like us, people who got in on our own merit, strike the fear of God in her. She thinks we're smarter than her since we made it here with no help. She worries we'll expose her for the nepotistic trust fund baby she is."

"I can't believe she feels threatened by someone like me."

"Last year, five students at SMS applied for dermatology, but only one got in. The competition is brutal. Mercer knows this. She'll shit her fancy jeans when she hears about you."

I like the idea of Mercer shitting her pants over me, but hearing that four people didn't get into derm makes me tense.

"What happened to the people who didn't match?"

"A couple went into pediatrics instead. One did emergency medicine, I think."

"Those are the fields you told me to avoid!"

"Don't panic. You have something Mercer doesn't: me. Remember, if I can do it, you can, too."

His confidence slightly calms my nerves. Slightly. I watch Mercer place her order at the counter. She asks for a grande cappuccino with caramel drizzle, just like Sebastian did. Then she slaps down a credit card. Surely it's her father's. The cost of coffee or clothes or jewelry is nothing to Mercer. Meanwhile, I'm drinking a cup of water. I'm reminded of last night when I put down my own credit card to get Jerome out of jail. I bet Mercer doesn't have a deadbeat brother like me. Or a handicapped mother for that matter. Her life is so fucking easy. And yet she chooses to pick on me.

I find myself clenching my fists, tired of being the poor girl from the poor family who lives in a poor apartment. I want to get paid. *Really* paid. I don't want to earn a hundred and twenty grand a year as a family medicine doctor or internist or pediatrician. That seems hardly better than Jerome's job at Burger King. I want $437,000 with eight hours of sleep every night. I want to be the envy of the doctor world. For once, I want to have something other people want but can't get.

I reach for the flash drive and take it from Sebastian's hand. Suddenly I'm not afraid of the long hours and hard work ahead. I'm actually *excited* to grind.

I ask Sebastian to excuse me for a moment. Then I rise from my stool and walk toward the counter where Mercer waits for her grande cappuccino with caramel drizzle. I tap her on the shoulder and she turns toward me.

"I'm not actually meeting with Sebastian to swap old college stories," I say.

Mercer twiddles a strand of her long blonde hair. "Er, okay. Whatever. Good for you."

"I'm really meeting with him for advice on matching in dermatology."

Mercer stops twiddling her hair, her face suddenly scrunched with worry. This news will drive her bonkers. The more students who apply for residency in dermatology from our school, the harder it is for each one. She and I will compete for recommendations from the same dermatology faculty, and we'll compete for the same precious interview slots at residency programs.

After a few seconds of thought, she says, "You won't match. It's *super* competitive."

This is exactly what I thought she'd say. "Well, we'll see about that. Anyway, I wanted you to know what I was doing. I wanted to make *absolutely* sure you know I'll be competing with you for derm. See you around."

Her face turns to a most satisfying frown as I spin and stroll back to Sebastian.

I don't care how hard I have to work. I'm going to become a goddamn dermatologist. And I'm going to steamroll over Jennifer Mercer as I do it.

11.

One week later, I sit in the library in my usual spot: a small wooden desk tucked deep in the stacks, my laptop glowing before me. It's perfectly quiet at 7:40 p.m., just twenty minutes before closing. I suspect I'm the only student here since it's Friday night. My classmates are probably out on dates, or at movies, or at bars or parties, but I'm not jealous. Those things hold little excitement for me now. I want only to learn.

The reason I'm so excited to study is that I passed my enhancement exam. And I didn't just pass, I crushed it. I owe all my success to Sebastian. His KGB Anki deck is exactly what he said: pure fucking gold. During my week preparing for the exam, I drowned myself in Anki cards. I did the two thousand a day he recommended, even hitting 2,134 on a freakish Thursday when I woke up early and stayed up late because I couldn't sleep. My mobile phone is no longer a phone; it's a portable Anki machine. I pull it out wherever I go to squeeze in a few Anki cards. I can do ten cards while peeing, twenty-five during my morning poop. When I buy Momma's Pepsi or Tylenol, the checkout line is usually good for a dozen cards. I'm barely human any longer. I'm a machine built for the consumption of Anki cards. My heat map, although still in its infancy, is turning green as a forest—a beautiful sight.

ANY MINUTE NOT DOING ANKI IS A WASTED MINUTE.

Over the past week, I've also watched tons of the teaching videos on Sebastian's flash drive in dumbstruck awe. The explanations of medical science in these videos are *so good.* Topics that left me baffled in textbooks or Murrow's lectures melted before my eyes, transforming into such simplicity that even a kindergartener could understand. Why doesn't Dr. Murrow teach like this? In fact, the videos make me wonder why the school is receiving tuition money on my behalf. I could learn everything I need to know on my own. Imagine all the time and money medical students could save if we simply learned from online videos.

Because the dean insisted, I went to my required enhancement session with Dr. Murrow, where he creepily studied my breasts as I sat in his office. My sessions with him and the school learning specialist only slowed me down. They taught me nothing and cut into my Anki and video time. Giant potholes in the road on my journey toward $437,000 a year.

NEVER LEARN FROM SCHOOL INSTRUCTORS.

I also did the practice questions on Sebastian's flash drive. They devastated my confidence because I answered so many incorrectly. But during the exam I saw dozens of nearly identical questions. My heart leapt with glee during the test because of this. For once, I *understood* what the exam questions were asking. It was as if the test was in a foreign language and the practice questions made me fluent. I'm convinced every teacher in every school in the world should give students hundreds of practice questions prior to exams. Failing grades for motivated students would become a thing of the past, like pay phones or landlines. Children would chuckle as they asked their parents, *Daddy, is it true people used to fail exams?*

The loudspeaker comes on: "The library will be closing in fifteen minutes."

This pulls me from my thoughts and I refocus on my laptop screen. Just for fun, I open Outlook to reread the email I received from Dean Weaver notifying me that I passed my exam. I've already read it a dozen times, the words practically memorized. But I want to see it again because it's so awesome.

From: Sylvia Weaver <sweaver@sms.edu>
Sent: Monday, September 26, 2022 12:49 PM
To: Sophia Abney <sabney@sms.edu>p
Subject: Enhancement exam

Dear Sophia:
I am pleased to inform you that you have passed the enhancement exam with a nearly perfect score of 96%. Clearly, your meetings with Dr. Murrow and our learning specialist were beneficial. Dr. Murrow has a knack for helping students in one-on-one sessions. You should meet with him anytime you feel confused.

Best of luck going forward and congratulations!

Sylvia Weaver, MD, MPH, JD, MS
Professor of Medicine
Dean of Students, State Medical School
Winner, Cornelius Snicklefritz Achievement Award
Chief, National Society of Defective Thyroid Glands

It dawns on me that the school has no clue how students learn. They take credit for our accomplishments even though we achieve despite the school, not because of it. I wish I'd known this when I started in August. They ought to tell everyone on the first day: *Make sure you ignore the instructions of our faculty. They will only confuse you and lead to failure on exams.*

NEVER LEARN FROM SCHOOL INSTRUCTORS.

Thank God I found Sebastian.

I push through another dozen Anki cards. I'm preparing for the exam next week, one that will cover cardiology, pulmonary, and renal. I haven't looked at the textbook even a single time for the upcoming test. I've also skipped Murrow's lectures—they're not mandatory—since they would just confuse me. I learn only from TPRs. They're my lifeblood now.

Soon the lights flicker, telling me I have five minutes to leave the library. I pack up my laptop, slide my purse over my shoulder, and head for the exit. As I turn the corner around one of the bookshelves, a man barges into me, spilling a pile of books and papers to the floor.

"Oh, uh, sorry," he says, quickly squatting to pick up his things.

I kneel down to help, studying him closely. He's a classmate of mine, but I can't remember his name. I've seen him in TBL and lectures. A squat little man, round as a keg of beer, he wears glasses and has a thick crop of hair.

We both stand once he's collected his books and papers. "You're Sophia, right?" he asks.

Oh, God. Here it comes. Another classmate who's going to call me a snitch. I just want to get home, so I can do a couple hundred more Anki cards before bed. "Yes," I reply, bracing myself.

"I'm Charlie," he says. "I've actually been hoping to run into you."

Why would he want to run into me? Probably so he can call me names to my face.

"Hi," I say. "I have to get going."

I start to walk away. He holds up a finger, and I stop. He pauses for a second, almost appearing nervous.

"I . . . I just wanted you to know not everyone in our class is mad at you about your PURF."

My eyes widen. This isn't what I expected to hear. But it doesn't matter. I need to go.

"That's fine. Whatever. I don't care. That's behind me now."

"Look, I don't pirate anything. I pay for all my stuff. I don't use any Google Drives or anything like that. I've always wanted to say something about the others, but I never had the guts. You're very brave."

I let out a laugh. "You can't be serious."

"I am," he protests, pushing his glasses up from the tip of his nose. "Not everyone in medical school is a gunner."

"And yet, you're in the library on a Friday night."

"What's wrong with that? I wanted to get ahead in the reading. The things we're learning in class, someday I may need to know them to save someone's life."

I briefly consider examining Charlie's clothes for a Boy Scout badge. He can't really be this much of a goody-goody.

"What specialty are you going into?" I ask. "If you're here on a Friday night, you must be gunning for orthopedics or radiology or something."

"Oh, no, not me. There are too many specialists in the world. I'm going into primary care. Care for the elderly in this country is terrible. They have so much trouble finding good doctors."

Charlie appears to believe what he's saying. Maybe I've become too much of a cynic. Perhaps there are medical students who simply want to heal the sick.

"So you're not here because you want to ace your exams

and get into a competitive residency?"

Charlie hikes up his pants, which have drifted below his chubby waistline. "I don't care where I do residency, so long as I get to have patients of my own I help. That's all I want, to help people."

I consider a snarky reply but stop. This is the first person in my class who's treated me with respect. I should stop being so cynical.

"Well, thank you for supporting me about the PURF, Charlie. That means a lot."

He smiles the broad, wide grin of a child who's just received praise from a parent. "Medicine needs more people like you, Sophia."

I let out another laugh. He's entirely genuine, not a hint of sarcasm. I've found that rare zebra in medical school: a decent soul who cares nothing about grades or class rank or competition.

"Well, uh, thank you," I say.

Charlie escorts me to the library exit that leads to a hallway in the medical school building. He holds the door open like a bell boy. So sweet. Then he waves goodbye and heads down the hallway to the right. I head in the other direction toward the academic entrance where my car is parked outside. I find myself in a surprisingly bright mood, thanks to his comments.

Medicine needs more people like you, Sophia.

I leave the building thinking maybe, just maybe my classmates aren't all so bad.

On my way home, the yellow gas light on my Ford Festiva lights up. I sigh because stopping to fill the tank will delay my return to Anki. Everything now is an obstacle to studying: eating, sleeping, bathing, getting gas.

ANY MINUTE NOT DOING ANKI IS A WASTED MINUTE.

I pull into a Mobil a few blocks from my apartment, the one on the corner of Flatbush and New Park. The other gas pumps are empty; my car is the only one here. Twenty feet away, an attendant looks lazily at his cell phone inside the mini-mart where he's surrounded by lottery tickets and cigarette cartons. I recognize his face. I think his name is Leroy, or maybe Lenny—he went to high school with Jerome. He doesn't look up at me as I step from my car, insert my credit card, then slide the nozzle into my tank. When I pull the lever, gas begins to flow.

Then I get an idea. This doesn't have to be a complete waste of study time. I slide out my mobile phone with my free hand, tap the screen, and pull up Anki. I bet I can get five cards done before the tank fills.

My phone flashes the card: *What pigment found in feces gives stool its brown color?*

Gas rumbles through the hose as I try to think of the answer while not picturing a toilet bowl full of shit. But my thoughts are interrupted by the sound of quick footsteps against the pavement. A man in a navy hoodie and black boots walks hurriedly into the mini-mart. Through the glass window, I watch him approach the register. Suddenly, he begins shouting. He pulls a gun from his waistband and points it at the clerk behind the counter.

My heart lurches. This is a robbery! I fumble with my phone and it falls to the pavement. I grab it quickly, then return my gaze to the mini-mart, where the cashier is frantically handing over bills to the man with the gun, his face trembling with fear. My mind spins as I try to think of what to do. Should I call the police? Or maybe I should run? What if the gunman starts shooting?

Before I can do anything, the man in the hoodie races from the mini-mart. I duck behind my car as he disappears behind the building. Then he emerges on a motorcycle and speeds away. I catch the license plate: 556-WHP.

Inside the mini-mart, the cashier taps at his phone screen, no doubt phoning the police. I should tell him what I saw. I didn't get a great look at the gunman, but I saw enough to estimate his height and build. And I certainly know what he was wearing. Plus, I saw his license plate. My observations could help the police. There's too much damn crime in this city.

I walk toward the mini-mart to offer assistance but then stop abruptly.

My thoughts drift to the work that lies ahead so I can crush the next exam. If I stay to speak to the police, I could spend an hour or more giving a statement and answering questions. If the man is caught, I might be called to testify in court. God knows how much time that'll consume. I have more important things to worry about. My future in dermatology depends on passing my exams. There's $437,000 a year at stake.

That's when I decide to turn around and return to my car. I replace the gas nozzle, slide into the driver's seat, and leave. I'll be home in minutes. I'll wave at Momma, who'll surely be watching television, then head to the solitude of my bedroom to study.

Hooded figures robbing gas stations aren't my problem.

I need to do another 300 Anki cards before I can go to sleep.

12.

A WEEK LATER IN EARLY October, I knock on the front door of a quaint blue townhouse at 41 Woodrow Street. This is the north corner of the city, an area far from my rundown neighborhood. I really don't want to be here. I'd rather be studying in the library, but I have been "voluntold" to travel to this address, the home of a ninety-two-year-old widow named Barbara Dewitt. The school thought everyone in my class should spend the afternoon volunteering for the Senior Friends program, a charity organization that sends young people like me to spend time with old people like Barbara Dewitt, so senior citizens don't get lonely. Supposedly, this will teach us how the older generation lives, a group that one day will make up the bulk of our patients. But this is cutting into my Anki-Video-Question goals for the day. I'll have to work twice as hard as usual to catch up later this afternoon.

I should be ashamed of myself. It's kind of cruel I'd rather study than spend an hour with an old lady who needs a friend. But there's something about success in medical school that works on your brain like a drug. I was crushed with embarrassment over failing my first exam.

But since I aced my enhancement, I've been consumed by the notion of rising to the top. The other students in my class are so smart, and have so many advantages I lack. But now, because of Sebastian, I see a path where I beat them all. I've always been competitive, but med school has brought me to a new level. I see myself graduating at the top of my class, matched into the most competitive specialty, the others gazing at me with a mixture of awe and envy. I want this so badly, everything else seems small.

And this, unfortunately, includes the Senior Friends program and Barbara Dewitt.

The door creaks open, and a hunched woman appears. She wears a faded blue dress with a white shawl, one she probably made herself—she looks like the kind of old lady who knits. Her silver hair is pulled back in a bun, and a pair of inch-thick glasses hang from a chain around her neck.

"Lester?" she says, squinting at me.

Oh, God. If she thinks I'm Lester, I'm in trouble. "Mrs. Dewitt, my name's Sophia. The medical school sent me. We're supposed to spend some time together this afternoon."

A flash of recognition washes over her. "Oh, yes, yes. Come in, Susie. Come in. Yes, they told me you were coming today. Let's have some tea."

I don't correct her for calling me Susie because I want to get this over with. I'd rather be called the wrong name than waste two minutes correcting her.

She leads me into the foyer of her curious little home, which is warm and smells like old people: a weird mix of soups, creams, and ointments. I don't take my jacket off, because I don't want her to think I'm staying long. We cross the creaky floor to her tiny living room. The side tables and walls are decorated with photos of her deceased husband, which is kind of creepy.

I take a seat on the small sofa as Barbara settles into a rocking chair across from me.

"So, you wanna hear the latest?" Barbara asks me.

I glance at my watch. It's 1:34. Maybe I can get out of here by two.

"Uh, latest about what?"

"Well," she says, raising her snowy-white eyebrows. "Mrs. Forty-Two went out of town for the weekend, just like last month. Mr. Forty-Two had that bed bunny over both nights. Same one as before with the high heels and a short skirt. Big headlights like an eighteen-wheeler. They did the blanket drill four times in two days."

This makes no sense to me at first, and I briefly wonder if Barbara has dementia. But then I remember her house number.

"Wait. Did you say Mr. Forty-two? You mean the man who lives across the street?"

"Yes, yes. Mr. Forty-two. Thinks he's Don Juan when the cat's away."

I chuckle. "And you said he did *what* four times?"

"The blanket drill!" She leans in close and squints at me, her face as wrinkled as waste paper. "You know what that is, don't you?"

"I do, but that's not what I expected to talk about." I smile as I picture little old Barbara peering out her window to watch her neighbor cheat on his wife. "And how do you know he did it four times? Four exactly? Not three? Not five?"

"Well, Mrs. Kittery heard them doing the mattress jig when she took the trash out. And you know Jack? Tends bar at the Shamrock? He lives on the corner. He heard them making baskets when he came home. Next night, we heard them again when we were out for a walk."

"That's only three times."

"Two nights ago, I saw him staring out the window about midnight. He was in his birthday suit. Windowsill barely covering his broomstick. He had a look in his eye. Like he'd just fired a shot. I figure that counts as four."

I let out a laugh. "A look, huh?"

"A look. Don't act like you don't know what I'm talking about."

"I have to say, I did not expect a discussion of your neighbors and, er, well . . . sex."

"Why? Because I'm old. I still get mine. You walk two doors down. Find Lester. He'll tell you. He comes over couple times a week to feed the kitty."

I double over laughing, forgetting all about Anki and schoolwork. Moments later, Barbara fetches tea from the kitchen, and we each take a cup as she proceeds to tell me, unprompted, about her love life. She starts at the beginning, when she lost her virginity at age fourteen on a golf course. She states emphatically that she never cheated on her husband, but she thinks he cheated on her. She's had five lovers in the past two years since she lost Dominic.

"I don't sleep around," she says. "But when one dies, I find another. That's how I got to five."

The minutes melt away, and I lose track of time. When I next glance at my watch, it's 2:45 p.m.

Shit, shit, shit.

I've spent over an hour here, and if I don't get back to studying I'll never catch up to my goals for the week.

I rise from the sofa. "Well, I have to go now, Barbara. But it's been lovely speaking with you."

"No, no, no," she protests. "Stay a while longer. We haven't even talked about you yet. Do you have a boyfriend? Are you getting it a few times a week? You're not a virgin, are you?"

I let out a laugh. "Maybe I can come back sometime."

"There're cookies in the kitchen. Go get them, and we'll have a few."

"But I have studying to do."

"Studying for what?"

"I'm in medical school, remember?"

She scratches her wrinkled little chin. "I can teach you about medicine. I've had surgery on both knees and one hip. They took out my uterus when I was sixty, a breast lump at seventy. Birthing three babies stretched my vagina so much, you can stick your head in there and look around if you want. Plus, I take pills for everything. Blood pressure, blood sugar, cholesterol, dry mouth, bad heart, thyroid, kidneys. And my husband had stuff, too, before he died. Bypass surgery. Colon surgery. He had a testicle out as a boy. Didn't affect his performance, though. Whoo-wee! He could go and go and go. I used to call him my one-nut lover."

I chuckle. Barbara probably could teach me a lot about real medicine, but that's not what we're learning. Unless she knows something about the Krebs cycle or bacterial cell walls, she can't help me.

"It's so nice having company," Barbara says. "Just stay for a little while longer."

I feel bad abandoning Barbara over her protests, so I come up with a new plan to get back to my studies. Sitting next to me on the side table is the television remote. If Barbara spends hours at home, she probably passes time with television shows, just like Momma. Maybe I can get her distracted, then slip into the kitchen. I bet I can do some Anki cards right there at the kitchen table, no different than in my bedroom at home. Maybe I can knock off fifty or so, rejoin her for cookies, then excuse myself for the bathroom again and knock off fifty more. I bet I can get two hundred cards done while she's mesmerized by the television.

I click on the TV. "I have to use the bathroom," I say. "Then I'll get the cookies and come back. You want to watch something while I'm gone?"

"Put on CNN," she replies. "That Jake Tapper. He's a fox."

Perfect. She'll be so lost in Jake Tapper's eyes, she'll forget all about me. I scroll the channel listing until I find CNN. Jake Tapper is, unfortunately, not on the screen, but the newsroom host is a young man with broad shoulders and a chiseled chin.

"He'll do," Barbara says. "I bet he's hung."

I leave her to her fantasies as I scurry off to the kitchen, a cramped space with spices on the counter, a bowl of fruit near the fridge. I settle into a creaky chair at the table and get to work, quickly doing twenty Anki cards. About ten minutes pass as the television drones from the living room without a peep out of Barbara.

Then I hear a creak from her chair beyond the doorway. "You coming back?" she calls out. "I need the remote. Wanna see what's on Fox News."

I'm not going back to the living room until I polish off another twenty cards. "I'll be right there," I call out. "Remote's on the table by the sofa."

I turn back to my phone to study an Anki card about sexually transmitted diseases. The card reads: *How does chlamydia typically present in a female?* I should probably ask Barbara about this one.

As I try to come up with the answer, I hear Barbara shuffling across the living room to get the remote.

Then I hear a thud.

"Barbara?" I call out. No response.

My body tenses. I hurry into the living room. Barbara lies sprawled on her back in front of the sofa, her blue dress hiked above her knees.

"Ow!" she howls. The bun in her hair has loosened. Silver strands spill across her cheek.

I squat down on one knee, my heart racing. "What happened?"

"I tripped," she says.

I slide a hand under her back to help her up, but she doesn't move. "Can you sit up?"

"My hip." She looks down her left side. I gently place my hands over her hip. The bones beneath the skin feel askew and the joint is warm. Is that from bleeding? When I press down, she screams.

"Don't do that!"

My pulse skyrockets. I've heard of the elderly having hip fractures after a fall, but I've never witnessed one up close. This is a disaster. I'm going to have to call 911.

Suddenly, Barbara says, "I . . . I feel dizzy." The color has drained from her face.

My heart slams in my chest. Think, think, think. There must be something I can do. I'm a medical student after all. But the only things I've learned so far are biochemistry, renal physiology, and female reproduction. I can describe the structure of Barbara's DNA and I know the amount of sodium filtered by her kidneys. But I don't know shit about hip pain and dizziness.

That's when I call 911. This is serious. I have to get help. Seconds later a female operator answers and I explain—in rushed, hurried speech—what's happened. She says a team is on its way.

"Help is coming," I say to Barbara.

"Don't feel right," she says with a moan, her eyes partly closed. "This . . . this might be the end."

"What! You just fell. You'll be fine."

The hunky CNN news anchor on the television recites the latest changes in the stock market.

Barbara tilts her head to look at him.

"Oh, he's definitely hung." Then her eyes close and she goes still.

"Barbara?" I nudge her but get no response. "Barbara?" My heart pounds so hard, my body shakes. This can't be happening. She can't die now. We were just having tea!

I hear an ambulance siren and run to the front door. Two burly male medics in blue uniforms rush toward the house. I hurry them to the living room, explaining what happened as we go. Barbara still lies motionless on the floor. The medics check for a pulse but can't find one.

No, no, no.

I start to hyperventilate. I've seen people resuscitated when I worked in the ER. There must be a way to get Barbara back. One of the medics begins CPR. He presses his palms to Barbara's chest and compresses her ribs over and over. I hear the crunch of bones as her sternum moves downward, the sound making me wince. This is unreal. I was speaking to her just a moment ago. The other medic readies the defibrillator. He charges the machine, a high-pitched sound emanating from the device. Then he places the paddles on Barbara's chest and sends 200 Joules coursing through her body. She flops like a fish. I cover my mouth to keep from screaming. The other medic checks her pulse again. He shakes his head: still nothing.

As they continue working, my mind spins and spins. She fell walking to get the remote. I'm the one who turned on the television and left the remote across the room from Barbara. If I'd been in the living room with her, could I have prevented this? A nagging thought haunts me: Could Barbara Dewitt die because of my Anki obsession? If I'd been less focused on my daily card goal, she might be eating cookies right now. Instead, she's unconscious on the floor, a victim of my gunner's drive to study. Did I kill her with my crazy study schedule?

But then I shake away these thoughts. She walks through this living room a dozen times a day. It was just dumb luck she tripped when I was in the kitchen. If it didn't happen now, it would have happened later today or tomorrow or next week. She might have fallen when she was alone. At least I was here to call 911.

After two more failed defibrillations, the medic stops his chest compressions. "She's gone," he says.

I feel like I might vomit. "No, no, no. She can't be dead. There has to be something more you can do."

"She's ninety-two. It's sad but we all have to go sometime."

A tear runs down my cheek. No more blanket drills for Barbara Dewitt. Her final words, "He's definitely hung," echo in my head. She lies dead on the floor in her blue dress and white shawl, silver hair spilled over the rug. I think of all the questions I'll be asked about her last moments alive. I'll be sure to tell people she was sweet and funny. I'll tell them she died a quick death from a fall in her living room. But I'll keep the rest to myself. I certainly won't mention that she fell while I was in the kitchen doing my six hundred and fifty-fifth Anki card of the day.

13.

"Oh, my God, Sophia," Dean Weaver says to me the next morning. "Are you alright?"

She speaks these words from behind her desk, her large frame planted in a elegant, wooden swivel chair. I sit across from her, having been summoned to her office as soon as the school heard about the death of Barbara Dewitt. I guess it's not every day a person dies in front of a first-year medical student.

"I'm okay," I say.

This is actually true. I do feel fine. The EMTs took Barbara's body away, and a neighbor—Lester, Barbara's ninety-year-old lover—notified Barbara's daughter, her only child. I went home and sent an email telling the school what happened. I figured better they hear it from me than the police. Then I got back to Anki, knocking out a thousand cards before bed. This settled my nerves. Studying has become like meditation for me, or yoga or a hot bath. It's my escape. After a few hours of Anki and some sleep, I was no longer rattled by Barbara's death. She was ninety-two. Like the medic said, we all have to go sometime.

"I just can't believe she died right in front of you," Weaver says. "That's extraordinary. Do you want to talk about it? Or maybe see one of our counselors? Whatever you need."

What I really need is to get back to studying, but I don't want the dean to think me so callous that a woman dying before my eyes means nothing.

"I think I'll be alright. I just need some time to myself."

"Well, if you change your mind, please let me know."

I nod and start to rise from my chair when Weaver says, "Oh, there's one other thing, if you have a second."

Her tone sends a jolt through me. Something about it seems ominous. I sit back down.

"I understand you've been meeting with Miles Sebastian," Weaver says. "Is that correct?"

Shit. This school is such a small place. Everyone knows everybody's business. The dean told me not to ask Sebastian for help. I wonder if she's angry with me.

"Oh, uh, he just gave me some study advice. That's all."

"I thought I advised you that was not a good idea."

"Well, I ran into him, and he offered some pointers. We just met a couple of times."

The dean stares at me, deciding whether or not to believe me. "I hope that's all. You really should avoid him at all costs. I want to tell you some things about Mr. Sebastian, but you must keep this in confidence. Can you be discreet?"

My stomach twists into a knot as I wonder what she's about to say. "Of course."

Weaver rocks back in her chair, the legs creaking under her weight. "He's been accused of sexual assault. It was by a fellow student. The circumstances were murky, with little proof. Given the weak evidence against him, no action was taken. But his accuser was very credible. I've always believed her. And I don't want to see you end up in a similar situation. I like you Sophia. I'm telling you this because I don't want you to be alone with a person like Miles Sebastian."

My eyes widen as she relays this story. I can't imagine Sebastian assaulting a woman. I've felt completely at ease in his presence. He's never made a pass at me. I've never even caught him staring at my chest the way Dr. Murrow does. But everyone has secrets hidden beneath the surface. You never know.

"Well, thank you for letting me know," I say. "Like I said, we just met a couple of times."

I'm not going to stop getting help from Sebastian, not when I'm gunning for $437,000 a year. If he runs someone over with his car, I'd probably visit him in prison for dermatology advice. Besides, I can handle myself around men.

"He graduates in May," Weaver says. "Hopefully, he'll match at some hospital a thousand miles away. God help me if he matches to the derm program here."

My mind drifts back to my studies. "Is that all? May I go now?"

Weaver raises one of her plump fingers. "Just one more thing. You were studying here last Friday, correct? The librarian said he saw you."

Once again, her tone gives me pause. "Yes, why?"

"Someone used the printer in the anatomy lab that night to print last year's RAT questions. Our IT department has been monitoring the print jobs on campus at my request. Did you see anything unusual?"

More cheating on the RAT quizzes. Someone in my class is in big trouble if they're caught. Of course, I'm breaking rules myself by using pirated materials. It seems lots of us are seeking an edge one way or another.

I shrug. "No," I say. "I didn't see anything unusual."

"Did you happen to see Jennifer Mercer here that night?"

An odd question. "No. Why?"

"She studies in the anatomy lab. But she says she wasn't here Friday night."

I consider this. "A strange place to study."

"There are some tables in the back, and it's quiet. Some people don't mind the dead, I guess."

"Do you think she printed the RAT questions?"

"Highly unlikely," she replies. "But I just wanted to check all the bases."

Man, if Mercer gets caught cheating that would be fantastic. I'd love to see her ass kicked out of school.

"Well, hope you catch whoever's doing this."

"Me, too," Weaver replies. "Trust me when I say this: the punishment will be severe."

I leave her office for the long corridor outside. Now I can finally get some studying done. I head toward the library, but after just a few steps someone calls my name.

"Oh, my God, Sophia," Charlie says, hurrying toward me. "I heard your senior friend died in front of you!"

It occurs to me I should write up the story of what happened and email it to the class. That way no one will ask me about it.

"Word gets around, huh?"

"Are you okay? That must have been so hard to watch."

He seems truly worried about me. What a sweetheart.

"I've gotten over it."

Charlie nods and hikes up his pants. "You know, fall prevention in the elderly is a really important topic. I wonder if your senior friend was properly counseled by her doctor."

More Eagle Scout talk from Charlie. I have no time for this. If I don't study soon, my nerves will unravel. I feel like I'm jonesing for a caffeine fix.

"Look, Charlie, I've got to go."

"Heard you killed an old lady," someone says.

I turn to see Mercer approaching from down the hall. Fuck.

"I didn't kill anyone. She fell and broke her hip." I don't want to sound defensive, but I do.

Mercer stares at me in her bright red T-shirt with a big H on it. I never hated Harvard so much until I met her.

"First of many who'll probably die under your supervision, huh?" Mercer says. "I heard you didn't even do CPR. Waited for the EMTs."

Charlie says nothing. He seems intimidated by Mercer, which is no surprise given his passive temperament.

I ignore Mercer's snide comment—it's hard, but I do. There's no point in arguing with her.

"Is there something you need, Mercer?" I say.

"I was shadowing in derm clinic yesterday," she says. "All the residents were talking about what happened to you. It's not every day a first year kills a patient."

God, I hate her. "Barbara Dewitt wasn't my patient, she was just a friend. And I seriously doubt the derm residents care what happens to first-year medical students. I call bullshit on that story."

Mercer shrugs. "Well, believe what you want. I know what I heard."

"I was actually just talking to the dean about dermatology," I say. This is a lie, but I can't help it. I want to rattle Mercer. "She was saying how first gen students like me—you know, people without a parent who's a doctor—are so impressive. It's a lot harder to do well in school when no one you know is a physician. Since *I'm* first gen, she said this will help me when I apply in derm."

Mercer stares at me for a beat. I can tell I stung her. It's awesome. "Whatever," she says. "I'm off to study. Want to learn medicine so my future patients don't die in front of me." Then she walks away, swinging her ass like a runway model. She is so unbelievably vile.

As she fades from sight, a pit grows in my stomach. *Heard you killed an old lady.* I know people are talking about me. They talk about everyone. Right now, they're whispering about my visit to Barbara Dewitt's home. But one day they'll say something else. They'll gape at me in wonder over the girl from community college who rose to the top of the class and matched into dermatology. I can already see the jealous looks on their faces. I'm determined, more than ever, to do just like Momma said: I will leave them all in the dust.

Charlie sees the expression on my face and looks uncomfortable, like he's not sure what to say.

"Don't worry," I tell him. "Mercer doesn't bother me. I can handle her shit."

Charlie clears his throat. "Well, good. Because you certainly didn't do anything wrong. Calling for help is the first step in an emergency response situation. You did exactly what you're supposed to—"

"Charlie, I've got to go." I think of the work that lies in store for me.

ANY MINUTE NOT DOING ANKI IS A WASTED MINUTE.

"Oh, of course, of course." He hikes up his pants again. "But there's something else I need to tell you."

I quietly sigh. "What is it?"

"I don't know if you know, but I'm a student advisor to the Senior Friends program. Anyway, did Barbara Dewitt tell you she used to be the mayor?"

The mayor? All Barbara talked about was sex.

"She didn't mention it."

"Well, she was. And I don't know if you know, but her grandson is Matt Damon. Like, *the actor* Matt Damon. Anyway, there's a big memorial for her on Thursday. The governor will be there. Plus her kids and grandkids, including Matt. I'm going. You should come. It's a chance to meet a star."

Matt Damon! Momma loves him. She'll freak if I get a selfie. God, I'm a horrible person. I should be mourning for Barbara, not using her demise to meet celebrities. But I can't help picturing the memorial. If Matt Damon comes, maybe other celebrities will be there, too. Could I meet Ben Affleck? What about Jennifer Lopez?

But then I think back to my schoolwork. Our second major exam is this Friday, the day after Barbara's memorial. I have another thousand Anki cards, six videos, and fifty questions to get through before bed tonight. Then I have twice that much work each day until the exam. This time, I'm going to pass on the first attempt. No more enhancement exams for me.

That's when I decide I can't go to Barbara's memorial. Matt Damon is *not* more important than $437,000 a year for the rest of my life. Neither is Ben Affleck or Jennifer Lopez. Besides, Matt Damon hasn't made a good movie since *The Martian*. He was totally lame in *Thor: Love and Thunder*. And *The Great Wall* was a disaster that never should have been made.

"I can't go," I say to Charlie. "It's the day before our exam."

"Oh," Charlie replies, disappointed. I think he was hoping I'd go with him. "Well, if you change your mind, let me know."

"Sure," I say, although I won't change my mind. The reality is that I'm one-hundred percent locked in. I won't let *anything* get in the way of my future in dermatology. Not small talk with Charlie. Not armed robberies at gas stations. Not even Matt Damon.

14.

Two months later, on a dreary Monday morning in December, I enter Dr. Murrow's research laboratory. A cluttered space of microscopes and petri dishes, the lab stinks of acetone and rubbing alcohol, smells I remember very well from college chemistry. As I survey the bench tops and beakers, my mind drifts back to my conversation with Sebastian two days ago at Starbucks. That's when he told me I had to come here today.

"I aced another exam," I tell him in the bustling café. "That's the fourth one where I scored over ninety-five percent."

"Not a surprise. The gunner rules work. All hail the KGB Anki deck."

"I'm in the top ten percent of the class. Mercer is super pissed. I see how she looks at me. It's fucking awesome."

He sips his cappuccino. "Well, now that your classwork is going well, you're ready for Gunner Rule Number Three: ALL RESEARCH IS WORTHLESS UNLESS IT GETS PUBLISHED."

I consider this. "Alright. Explain."

"The places you'll apply for dermatology training are filled with faculty who study cancer cells and skin diseases and

whatnot to get promoted. So they want to recruit dermatology trainees who love research, the kind of people who'll become their scut monkeys and do grunt work in the research lab."

"That's not really me. I've never worked in a lab."

"Doesn't matter. You don't need to like research, it's even okay if you hate research; you just have to pretend. It's all a show. Right now, as a first-year, you have to find a research project. You have to start doing work in a lab, work that'll eventually become published. You want at least fifteen published papers by the time you apply in dermatology. It doesn't matter one lick whether you like the research project or care about the topic. All that matters is that it gets published. When you apply to derm, the publications will make them think you're destined to cure HIV or discover a vaccine or whatever. Then when you get into the program, you can become a plain old private practice dermatologist who makes hundreds of thousands a year and doesn't know PubMed *from* Pulp Fiction.*"*

"Won't they get mad if I say I love research, then change after I'm accepted?"

"Buyer beware. Every derm resident does it. You'll be fine."

"Hmm," I say, "fifteen publications sounds like a lot."

"It is. But I know just the lab where you can easily adhere to rule number three. Believe it or not, it's Dr. Murrow's."

"The creepy old man who ogles all the girls in class?"

"The same. When he's not teaching, he studies cell membrane potentials."

"I don't even know what that means."

"You don't need to. But here's the thing: of all the zillions of cell types in the human body, he uses human skin epithelial cells for experiments. Key word: skin. That means anything you publish with him looks good when you apply for derm."

A hiss from one of the laboratory machines pulls me from my thoughts. There are two people here in jeans and

T-shirts, a man holding a pipette over a bench top and a small woman peering into a microscope. Neither notices me. I don't see Murrow anywhere.

I approach the frumpy guy pipetting liquid into test tubes. "Uh, hi," I say. "I'm supposed to meet Dr. Murrow here."

The man continues his work transferring liquid from a beaker. He has a scraggly goatee and a gut like a blob of jelly. He wears a T-shirt that says, "PhD. Noun. 1. An academic that has learned more and more about less and less until they know everything about nothing."

"Murrow left," he mutters, not taking his eyes from his work.

I check my watch. It's 9:02 am. Murrow told me to arrive at nine. "That can't be. He said to meet him here now."

The man merely shrugs in response. So frustrating. I take note of the double standard: If I'm late to TBL or any other mandatory activity, it's a professionalism violation. But if a faculty member like Murrow is late for something with me? Too fucking bad.

I think back to Sebastian's instructions to me. "Are you Declan?" I say to the man.

He finally looks up from his microscope. "Yeah. Do I know you?"

"No," I reply. "But I heard Dr. Murrow had a post-doc named Declan. Figured it might be you."

From Sebastian: *The reason Dr. Murrow's lab is a hidden gem for gunner research is because of his post-doc, Declan. The guy basically lives in the lab twenty-four hours a day. He cranks out papers every month. If you sign up for a research project in the lab, Declan will do just about all the work. You'll get your name on tons of papers with barely any effort. It's a med student's dream: research publications without work. Pure fucking gold.*

Declan nods at me, then returns to his work. Surveying the lab once more, I spy shelves filled with beakers, flasks, and test tubes. Then one of the far walls catches my eye. A half-dozen pictures are tacked up, printouts on paper from a color printer. They all show women standing in this room. The women are unfamiliar to me until I look at the last photo.

My jaw drops. It's Jennifer Mercer. What the hell? Why is her picture on the wall?

Just then Dr. Murrow scurries into the lab, a pile of papers under his arm. He stops when he sees me, adjusting his glasses. "Oh, Sophia. Yes, yes. I forgot you were coming today."

I'd like to forget to come to a few things in medical school, but that would get me hauled before the dean.

"It's okay," I say, even though it bugs me that he forgot our meeting.

He shoves his papers on one of the bench tops. "Have you met Declan?" he asks, looking toward the man in the T-shirt. "He's my post-doc."

I nod.

"Good, good. And have you met Yuchi, my PhD student?"

On the other side of the lab, a tiny stick of a woman looks up from her microscope. Yuchi nods at me, and I nod back.

"So, you want to study epithelial cells," Murrow says. "Wonderful! The most amazing cells in the human body. "

"They've always fascinated me," I say.

Murrow's face brightens at my words. "I was thrilled to get your email about my lab."

"Cell membrane potentials are the foundation of biology." I don't even know what this means, but Sebastian told me to say it.

Murrow beams at my comments. "Come, come. Let me show you the work we're doing."

Murrow brings me to a fume hood in the back, massive ductwork coursing away from the structure toward the ceiling. Inside the fume hood, several dozen petri dishes hold liquid under the warm, red light. These must be for growing cells—I did experiments in hoods like this in college biology. The smell of the liquid culture media makes me wince. It's a foul scent, somewhere between warm chocolate milk and vomit. Totally gross. If I didn't need to be here for dermatology, I'd run.

The dishes are sorted into groups, each with a label next to it. Beside the far-left group of dishes, I see the label: J. Mercer.

Shit, I think. Now the picture on the wall makes sense. Mercer has already been here. She's working in this lab, too.

"Ah, now, one thing, Sophia," Murrow says. "Before we start, I must get a picture of you. We put pictures of all the students in the lab up on our wall. You deserve recognition for your contributions to science."

Pictures of female students so they get recognition? I'm skeptical. Murrow is the man who gawks at the women during TBL. More likely he enjoys looking at us. Dirty old man.

Murrow pulls out his phone and holds it up. "Come, now," he says. "Give us a smile for the camera."

This whole thing creeps me out. I just want to start working on experiments so I can get publications.

I look at Murrow's camera and give a half-hearted smile.

"Oh, come on," Murrow says. "Let's have a great, big smile. You may win the Nobel Prize for your work someday. Who knows?"

Fuck it. Maybe if I give Murrow a scintillating photo of me, he'll stare at that instead of my body. I arch my back, sticking out my chest, and give a broad, toothy grin.

"Ah! That's it. Wonderful." Murrow snaps a picture.

I pray he doesn't get an erection. That would be super awkward.

"Now," he says, "let me show you the work you'll be doing."

"Bob?" I hear someone say. Dean Weaver is in the doorway in one of her typical stylish dresses and a white coat. "A minute, please," she says to Murrow.

Murrow excuses himself, and I'm left waiting by the fume hood with the petri dishes. Weaver says something to Murrow I can't make out. Her words cause Murrow to react furiously.

"I'm not teaching that!" he yells.

Weaver holds up her hand, signaling him to keep his voice down. "John is in the OR on Fridays," she says. "So he can't teach it."

"That's not my problem," Murrow protests. "No one teaches around here but me. It's bullshit, Sylvia."

Murrow looks super pissed. Sebastian explained to me why the teaching in medical school is so bad. Even though SMS is a learning institution, no one really wants to teach medical students. It's crazy, but the doctors on faculty would rather see patients and do surgery—the things that generate revenue and lead to higher pay. Lecturing a bunch of first years about basic anatomy and physiology is grunt work. It doesn't generate a cent beyond our tuition, which is small potatoes in a world of million-dollar surgeries. The people forced to teach us are the ones like Murrow. They're researchers with PhDs who can't do clinical care. They have little else to justify their job other than us lowly med students.

As Weaver and Murrow continue their heated discussion, I turn my gaze to Mercer's petri dishes in the hood. I can't believe she's already been here. Probably got hooked up with Murrow through her neurosurgeon father.

Next to Mercer's collection of petri dishes, I spy a bottle of acetone. We used this in my college biology lab to sterilize equipment. It kills everything it touches.

Suddenly, an idea occurs to me. It would be so easy to spill some acetone into Mercer's petri dishes. Her cells would die and whatever stupid experiment she's running would be ruined. She'd have to start over from scratch. It's a childish prank, but something about it feels so tempting. Mercer needs to pay for painting "SNITCH" on my car. Plus there's the way she talks to me. *Heard you killed an old lady. First of many who'll probably die under your supervision, huh?* She's so fucking smug. I can't stand how she treats me as her inferior, as if I'm not worthy of being in her presence. She's the epitome of the rich, privileged kids in my class. I'm so sick of them thinking they're better than me.

It's time for Mercer to get some payback.

I can't possibly let this opportunity pass.

I glance at Weaver and Murrow, who are paying no attention to me. Declan and Yuchi are engrossed in their microscopes. I slowly reach out and loosen the cap of the acetone bottle then tip it onto its side. The liquid spills into one of Mercer's petri dishes. Then I lift the bottom, fully emptying the bottle, making sure liquid gets inside each dish next to the label with Mercer's name.

ALL RESEARCH IS WORTHLESS UNLESS IT GETS PUBLISHED.

Well, Mercer won't publish shit from these experiments now.

I slide away from the hood, back toward Murrow's office. No one saw what I did. And they won't suspect me of anything when I'm standing over here, far from the petri dishes. It'll appear to be a random accident.

Fuck you, Mercer.

"Oh, my God!" I hear Yuchi shout from across the room.

She rushes toward the hood, her eyes wide. Mercer's petri dishes bubble over with white liquid. My heart races.

I just wanted to kill her cells, but I somehow kicked off a chemical reaction! The white liquid bubbles and grows, now a massive ball filling the hood, taking over every petri dish inside.

Murrow and Declan rush to the hood. Weaver stays by the door, watching with a concerned look. I can hardly breathe. What have I done?

"Those are my cells," Yuchi yells, pointing to a collection of dishes on the far side of the hood. The growing white ball inches nearer and nearer to her precious work.

Yuchi thrusts her hand into the hood, grabbing one of her petri dishes.

"Don't!" Murrow shouts.

But he's too late. Just as Yuchi grabs a petri dish, the white bubbling ball engulfs her wrist.

She drops the dish and falls to one knee, clutching her forearm. "Ah! It burns!" she shouts, tears in her eyes.

I'm on the verge of puking. How bad is her injury? I won't be able to live with myself if Yuchi dies from my war with Mercer.

Declan speeds to the sink and fetches a wet towel. He hands it to Yuchi. "Wipe it off. Wipe it off."

She does as he says, shoving the white bubbles from her wrist onto the floor. Her forearm has turned an angry red color, the skin sloughed off in some places. I can feel my heart pounding. I just wanted to ruin Mercer's experiments. I never thought I could hurt someone.

Yuchi weeps as Declan consoles her. Murrow examines her arm and says, "It's just a burn. It'll heal."

Yuchi seems unmoved by these words, but to me they're a huge relief to hear. Then Murrow studies the fume hood as the white bubbles begin to pop and disappear, slowly receding. He points at the acetone bottle.

"Who left this here?" he says.

"I . . . I was going to sterilize some stuff later," Declan replies.

Murrow shakes his head. "You never leave acetone near the cell solution. Damn, man. You should know better."

Declan hangs his head as Yuchi continues clutching her arm.

Murrow examines the burn. "You should go to the ER," he commands. "They can clean it and place a bandage."

Declan helps Yuchi to her feet and they exit the lab. Weaver offers to go with them and walks away down the hall.

I stand alone by the hood with Murrow, not saying a word, guilt permeating through my body.

"Did you see what happened?" he asks me. "How did acetone get spilled everywhere?"

This is my chance to come clean. I could tell Murrow I accidentally spilled the acetone. He might forgive me. I'm sure first-year medical students make mistakes in labs all the time. But then I think back to what Sebastian said to me.

There's no place like Murrow's lab. You'll get more publications than a Nobel laureate.

Working here could be the key to my future in dermatology. It could help me become the best in my class. I can't jeopardize that.

"I didn't see anything," I say to Murrow.

He scratches his chin, seeming to accept this.

Hopefully Yuchi will be okay. It's just a chemical burn. Probably heal quickly.

It's not worth risking my dermatology career just to fess up to something like that.

15.

A MONTH LATER IT'S JANUARY, the halfway point of my first year. A sign outside the rotunda reads "First Year Wellness Session." Just seeing these words makes me groan. All first-year students must attend mandatory wellness sessions to help us cope with stress and avoid burnout. Unfortunately, these gatherings make us more stressed, because they take us away from studying. They're usually led by a yoga instructor or psychologist or, in one case, a Nepalese shaman who barely spoke English. The fact that a licensed physician doesn't lead the sessions sends a clear message about how important wellness is to doctors. In fact, the term "mandatory wellness" is the ultimate oxymoron. If these sessions actually produced emotional bliss for medical students, there'd be no need to make them mandatory.

Together with my class I trudge into the rotunda, just one student in a throng that shuffles forward like a battered army. The massive space is cleared of tables and desks and podiums. Dozens of colored yoga mats are aligned on the floor. At the front of the room, a woman in a ponytail and yoga pants smiles at each of us as we enter.

"Welcome, students. Welcome," she says in an overly pleasant voice.

It's killing me to be here. A little piece of my flesh is actually dying each moment I spend in this session. Our next exam is the day after tomorrow. I have an Excel spreadsheet of studying goals laid out for myself: Anki cards, videos, practice questions. My heart winces at the notion that I'm sacrificing precious study time for an hour and a half of yoga mats and Cat-Cow poses.

As our class fans out, each student selecting a mat, my phone buzzes in my purse. I step back toward the door to check the Caller ID. It's Declan, the post doc from Dr. Murrow's lab. A chilling thought grips me: Could he have learned that I caused the lab accident two months ago? Yuchi ended up with a mild first-degree burn because I poured acetone into the culture dishes. I worried for a week afterward until I heard she was completely healed. It seems unlikely he's learned what I did now, after all this time has passed. But could I be wrong?

Then I wonder if he's calling about my experiments. We submitted a paper for publication last month based on my research project, although Declan did ninety percent of the work. Maybe it's been accepted? This would be enormous news. It's only my first year of medical school, and I'd already have one publication.

"Hi, Declan," I say quietly into my phone, lurking near the door. My classmates murmur to each other as they select yoga mats.

"I just got a call from Nature Methods," Declan says. "They *loved* our paper. They want to put it in next month's issue."

My body tingles with glee. This is exactly what I was hoping to hear.

"But here's the thing," Declan continues. "One of the reviewers wants us to make a graph of the membrane potential results on a log scale."

I have no idea what this means. I actually have no idea what our experiment is even about. I go to the lab once a week, squirt some liquid into the petri dishes, and leave. Declan does all the rest.

"They want the new data by tomorrow," Declan continues, "and my son's got a choir concert tonight. I can't crunch the numbers. I need you to do it. I'll email you the spreadsheet with instructions. If you can get this done tonight, you can be first author."

Holy shit! First author on a publication as a first-year student. This is incredible news. My odds of matching in dermatology have just soared.

But then I consider the request Declan just made. Crunch the numbers tonight? If I work on Declan's project, it'll upend my entire study schedule. A first author publication is great, but not if it causes me to fail an exam. I still remember the sting of failing my first test. I can never let that happen again.

"Okay, students," the yoga instructor calls out. "Quiet down. Everyone find a mat."

That's when I decide: I'm getting out of this wellness session one way or another. It's the only way I can do Declan's work and prepare for my exam.

"No problem," I say to Declan. "I'll do it."

I end the call and scurry to the front of the room. The yoga instructor sees me approach and smiles. She's probably about thirty years old. She looks way too happy to be here. She clearly has no idea how painful these sessions are for medical students.

"Hi," she says, extending her hand. "I'm Felicity. Nice to meet you."

Her name is Felicity? Unreal.

"Um, hi, um, Ms. Felicity. I'm not feeling well. I wonder if I could be excused. I need to get some rest."

Her face turns to a pouty frown. "Oh, you poor dear. I'm so sorry. But the dean told me no one can be excused for any reason. We're going to start with some breath work. It's great for relieving negative energy. I think it'll make you feel better."

"I don't know," I say. "I really feel like I might vomit."

Felicity stands before me, places a hand on each of my shoulders, and closes her eyes. "I'll do some quick Reiki to change your energy flow. This should help."

I roll my eyes. A few of my classmates gawk as Felicity tries to make me feel better. It's clear she's never going to let me leave unless I actually vomit in front of her.

After about a minute, she opens her eyes. "There. Do you feel better?"

"A little, I guess. Look, can I just run to the restroom? I'll be right back."

Felicity nods. "Okay, but don't be gone long. We're going to learn the five principles of Yama and Niyama. You'll love it."

I turn and walk away, cursing this woman for making me stay. She is literally standing in the way of my path to dermatology. I quickly leave the rotunda and find the women's bathroom outside. Two other women, secretaries I recognize from the main office, stand at the sinks, washing their hands. The stalls appear empty. I wait for the two women to leave, then begin to plan my next move.

I'd like to run, but I can't. If I leave the building now, I'll get a professionalism violation. But if I go back to the rotunda, I'm stuck for the next hour and a half. That's not an option. There must be something I can do to escape.

I spy a trash can in the corner overflowing with used paper towels. That's when an idea hits me. It's dangerous and risky, but might get me free this afternoon.

I open my purse and find my pack of Marlboro lights, a box of matches tucked inside. I'm not proud of this fact, but I sometimes smoke one cigarette when I'm studying. There's nothing like it to make me wired and focused. No matter how tired I am, after just a few puffs I'm wide awake for at least another two hours. It's crazy that something so unhealthy helps me learn medicine, but it does. Oh, the irony.

I walk to the wastebasket and pull out my matchbook. Last week in histology lab one of the microscopes started smoking and the fire alarm went off. We had to clear the building while two fire trucks came with a dozen men. Our professor ended up sending us home. If I light this trash can on fire now, the same thing will happen and then I can scamper off to crunch numbers for Declan. It's a bold move, way over the line compared to anything else I've done as a gunner. But $437,000 a year is at stake. Money like that can drive a person to do crazy things.

I consider what would happen if I'm caught. I could be kicked out of school. But how would they ever catch me? I glance at the ceiling: no security cameras in the women's bathroom. They'll find the matchbook and know it caused the fire. But they'll never know I used it. Who would think Sophia Abney, dedicated first-year medical student, carries matches around in her purse so she can start bathroom fires?

I look at the matches, then back at the trash can. There really is no other way out of this God-awful mandatory wellness session. And I've got a shot at a first-author publication. That's pure fucking gold.

My thoughts drift to Mercer. A first-author publication would drive her mad with envy. I can already see her face contorted in jealousy and shock. The thought feels glorious.

I strike a match, holding it before my eyes, wisps of smoke rising toward the ceiling. This is my last chance to back out. Am I going too far? But then I think of the next hour and a half. To spend that doing yoga when I could be working on a first-author publication, one that would crush the soul of Jennifer Mercer, is not happening.

I release the lighted match, letting it fall into the trash can.

A paper towel on top instantly catches fire, the flames spreading, smoke beginning to rise. My body tightens with anxiety. This must be some new milestone in gunner behavior: I'm burning things down to match in dermatology.

I turn and leave the bathroom, making sure my steps are calm and measured. I don't want to arouse suspicions by racing back. Inside the rotunda, my class is face down on their yoga mats, all contorted in the Downward Dog pose. I quickly find an empty mat and assume a similar position.

"Remember to breathe, students," Felicity says from the front of the room. "Blow out all that negative energy. Feel the calmness wash over you."

I most certainly am not calm. Any minute now, I expect the fire alarm to sound. My pulse is bounding.

And then I hear it: *Whomp, whomp, whomp. Fire, fire, fire. Please evacuate the building. Fire, fire, fire. Please evacuate the building.*

My class rises from their mats, throwing glances at one another. Felicity's face contorts in worry. The alarm continues for another minute as we wait to see if it'll stop. Then the back door to the rotunda, the door nearest the women's bathroom, opens. Dean Weaver enters, a thin trail of smoke behind her.

"Everyone, go out the other side," she calls. "Please calmly exit the building."

I catch the faint scent of smoke as the alarm blares overhead. I can't believe I did this. I am seriously unwell. But what do they expect? When you put yoga between students and their future careers, something has to give.

My class hurries toward the door on the far side of the room, which leads outside. I walk through the exit, the bright sunlight making me squint as it warms my face. Soon my entire class is huddled in the parking lot, all of us mingling between cars and staring at the tall building as fire trucks and police cruisers arrive. My classmates smile and giggle, no doubt thrilled our mandatory wellness session has been interrupted. No one seems to mourn the disruption.

The funny thing is, though: we *are* all stressed. I don't know shit about yoga, but it might help me if I actually had time to focus on the poses and breathing. But you can't ask a person to learn the endless universe of medical science, then pause for spiritual development. There's simply no time.

"Students, students," Felicity calls out. "Looks like we won't be able to finish today. We'll reschedule for another time."

Poor Felicity. She made a valiant effort, but it was doomed to fail. The fact of the matter is: when you're trying to compete in medical school, there's no time for inner peace.

16.

Three months later it's March as I trudge toward the St. Jude homeless shelter on Flatbush Avenue carrying a cardboard box full of donated shoes. The box is light, but feels like a hundred pounds because I'm so exhausted. Now eight months into my first year of medical school, the gunner rules are taking their toll. I haven't slept past 5 a.m. since last summer. I also stay up late at night staring at my laptop, going through Anki, watching videos, or doing UWorld questions. My dreams are filled with failing hearts, cirrhotic livers, and T cells. Last week, I took a nap on the floor of the library, rolled over into a shelf, and knocked a copy of *Neuroscience 6th Edition* by Dale Purves onto my head. It's 960 pages and weighs over 5 pounds. I still have a bruise.

Tired as I am, I'd rather be back in the library than in this homeless shelter. I'm wasting precious study time by coming here. But Sebastian insisted I do this. He said it was essential I get some community service experience on my application for dermatology.

"Now you're ready for Gunner Rule Number Four: FOR COMMUNITY SERVICE, THE SADDER THE

POPULATION, THE BETTER. When you apply in dermatology, you never know who's going to read your application. You might get a derm attending who's into social justice, health care disparities, or a bunch of other things that don't generate revenue. So you need some community service work on your application. Pick a super needy group to help. The sadder they are, the better the odds of you landing a spot in dermatology. And I've got the perfect community service project for a gunner like yourself. It's guaranteed to yank the heartstrings of anyone who reads your application. They're going to think you're Mother Teresa."

"I'm intrigued. What is it? Suicide hotline? Soup kitchen? Helping the elderly?"

"That's bush league shit. I've got something much better."

He pauses, looking me in the eyes.

"You're going to donate shoes to homeless children with Down syndrome."

The door to the shelter buzzes, pulling me from my thoughts. I walk through into the main living area, a community room with tattered couches and an old television. The walls are grimy and stained. A stuffy, dank smell hits me like a bucket of water over my head. I see a couple of adults and a few children watching the TV. This is a shelter in the barest sense of the word. It provides a roof and warmth, but it's not a place I'd want to live. When Daddy died and Momma became paralyzed, I thought my family might end up on the streets. Luckily, Momma's government checks, plus income from me and Jerome, paid the bills. But we could have easily found ourselves in a place like this if things hadn't worked out. It's a scary thought.

A man approaches from the other side of the room. He must be the man who buzzed me in, the manager of the shelter. He's young, about my age, his arms and neck heavily painted with tattoos. He has piercings everywhere: his ears, his nose, an eyebrow. This guy would never match in derm. Sebastian said clear, unblemished skin is a must. One pimple at an interview could doom your chances. Tattoos and facial piercings like this guy's would probably get you escorted from the building.

"You brought a donation?" he says, pointing to the box.

I clear my throat. "I'm told you have a group of homeless kids here with Down syndrome, right?"

The manager nods. "There're only a few. You must have read that article. They made a big deal of it in the paper."

"Well, this is for them. I figured they might need some new shoes."

I hand the box to him. Sebastian said homeless kids with Down syndrome were "uber sad" and perfect for my application to dermatology.

Here's what you do: First, get about a half dozen cardboard boxes. Use a Sharpie and write 'SHOE DONATIONS FOR HOMELESS CHILDREN WITH DOWN SYNDROME' on each box. Then place them around the medical school. Ninety-nine percent of people will ignore them, but a few of the old Catholic secretaries will throw in a couple pairs of shoes. That's all you need so that on your derm application you can write that you led and organized a drive to collect shoes for homeless children with Down syndrome. 'Led' and 'organized' are key words. Pure fucking gold.

"Well, thanks," the manager says, taking the box in his hands. "Every little bit helps."

"Oh, one other thing," I say. "I need a signature on my community service form. It's so my school can record what I've done." It feels creepy to ask for something in return for a donation to the homeless, but the school won't report this on my transcript without the form.

I slide a piece of paper from my purse. The manager sets down the box, takes the paper from me, and walks to his office for a pen. I'm left alone in the community room, taking in the stench and grime.

Just then, I feel a tap on my side and look down to see a boy, maybe ten years old at most, standing beside me. He has a round face with the broad forehead and wide-spaced eyes that are classic features of Down syndrome. His hair is as blond as sunlight.

"Shoes," he says.

I bend down to his level. "Excuse me?"

"I need new shoes. You said shoes to Brian."

I peer at his feet. His raggedy, scuffed shoes have holes at the top, a few dirty toes sticking out. I reach for the cardboard box and pull it close.

"These are for you. Pick whichever ones you want."

The boy looks inside the box. I wish I had more than nine pairs of shoes to offer, but that's all I collected and Sebastian says it doesn't matter. The little boy rummages through the box and pulls out a pair of old Nikes that appear about his size. He plops down on the floor and rips off his tattered shoes. The stench of nasty feet wallops me in the face. I lean back, waving away the odor in front of me. Then the boy quickly slides on the Nikes, which actually fit him fairly well.

He stands and says, "They good." Then he smiles at me, making my heart lift. This boy is a welcome relief from the drudgery of studying.

The tattooed manager returns with my signed community service form. I take it from him and slide it back in my purse.

He looks at the little boy. "Go on, Roland. Get back to your room."

Roland doesn't move. He points at me. "She give me shoes."

The manager looks at Roland's feet, then up at me. "He's always complaining about his shoes. You made his day."

My heart lifts again as I study Roland. He has such an innocent face. God, this kid is adorable.

"Where are his parents?" I ask the manager.

"His mother's out looking for work. I don't know anything about his father."

Roland smiles at me again, and I think of him spending his day alone at this dingy shelter without his mother. I'd like to stay with him awhile. It feels good to be face-to-face with another human who wants me around, rather than staring at my laptop. But I have to get back to school. We have a major exam in two days. In medical school, there's always a major exam around the corner.

I kneel on one knee. "Well, nice to meet you, Roland." He makes a pouting face because he wants me to stay. So freaking cute. But I just can't. "I'm sorry, but I've got to go."

Still the pouting face and nothing more.

I rise and walk toward the door, my heart stung over Roland. He's cute, he's alone, and I know I could make his day if I stayed. But I simply can't.

Outside, the sky is gray and the pavement wet from last night's rain as I get into my car. Just as I place my keys in the ignition, there's a knock at my window. I turn to see Roland's chubby face and big eyes pressed against the glass. The sight of him startles me. My heart leaps and I jump back.

I roll down my window. "You scared me, Roland. What are you doing out here?"

He doesn't respond. He simply stands beside my car in the parking lot, staring at me with sad eyes. Oh, if only I could stay with him awhile.

I step out of the car and take his hand to walk him back inside. He clutches my fingers tightly, and I wish more than ever that I didn't have to leave. When I press the buzzer to the homeless shelter, the manager appears at the door.

I nod toward Roland. "He followed me to my car."

The manager takes his hand. "Come with me, Roland. You gotta stay inside."

"Bye, Roland," I say.

When I turn to walk away, he begins to cry.

"Aw, it's okay, Roland," I say. "Maybe I'll come back some time to visit you." This is a lie, and I feel horrible to say it when I don't mean it, but his tears are breaking my heart. I'll say anything to make him smile again.

"Come on, Roland," the manager says, "let's go inside."

Roland wails loudly, tears streaming down his face. The manager grips him around the chest to keep him from running after me. "It's because you gave him shoes," he says. "He's been wanting new shoes for a long time."

I study Roland's face, his eyes soaked with tears, his skin red. I could blow off studying for a little while and stay with him. Maybe I could catch up later tonight. Maybe. But the memories of my first exam, the one I failed, flash through my mind. I never want to feel like that again. The next test is in two days. And I have to keep up my grades if I want a career in dermatology.

With a heavy heart, I turn from Roland and hurry toward my car. He cries and cries at my back.

He's just a kid, though. He'll forget about me in ten minutes.

As I drive away, I don't look back at him.

17.

Later that afternoon, I sit hidden behind stacks of books at my library desk, the woody smell of journals and crusty old texts filling the air. I have my earbuds in as a video plays on my laptop, but I'm not listening. I can't seem to focus. My thoughts are consumed with the giant mistake I made a few hours ago after leaving the homeless shelter.

I'm super mad at myself because I knew what I was doing was a bad idea. Sebastian even warned me not to do it, but I couldn't resist. My will crumbled, and I gave in to my curiosity.

I searched the Reddit medical school forums.

Social media is well known for ruining mental health among medical students. Anyone who trained before Facebook, Twitter, Reddit, and Instagram has no idea what it's like today. You can doom scroll through medical student posts about their failures, their successes, and their Herculean efforts to match in derm, radiology, ortho and all the good specialties. When you see how hard everyone else is working, it makes you feel like the competition is infinite, and the chance of succeeding infinitesimally small.

But still, I foolishly did a Reddit search of "Applying in derm" and found the following thread:

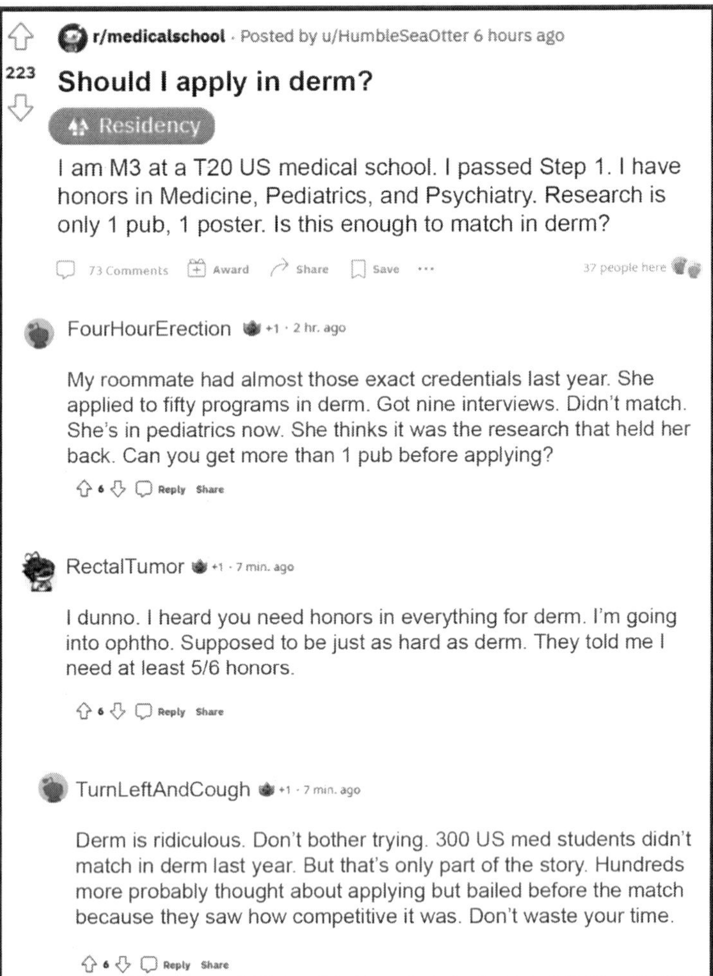
r/medicalschool · Posted by u/HumbleSeaOtter 6 hours ago

223

Should I apply in derm?

Residency

I am M3 at a T20 US medical school. I passed Step 1. I have honors in Medicine, Pediatrics, and Psychiatry. Research is only 1 pub, 1 poster. Is this enough to match in derm?

73 Comments · Award · Share · Save · ··· · 37 people here

FourHourErection +1 · 2 hr. ago

My roommate had almost those exact credentials last year. She applied to fifty programs in derm. Got nine interviews. Didn't match. She's in pediatrics now. She thinks it was the research that held her back. Can you get more than 1 pub before applying?

6 · Reply · Share

RectalTumor +1 · 7 min. ago

I dunno. I heard you need honors in everything for derm. I'm going into ophtho. Supposed to be just as hard as derm. They told me I need at least 5/6 honors.

6 · Reply · Share

TurnLeftAndCough +1 · 7 min. ago

Derm is ridiculous. Don't bother trying. 300 US med students didn't match in derm last year. But that's only part of the story. Hundreds more probably thought about applying but bailed before the match because they saw how competitive it was. Don't waste your time.

6 · Reply · Share

I read each of the 73 replies to the original post. Nearly all of them sent the same message to my brain: matching into dermatology is fucking hard. I should have listened to Sebastian. I wish I'd never read that thread.

The narrator in the video playing on my laptop says, "And that concludes our module on scrotal disorders."

When the video ends, the sudden silence draws me from my thoughts. As I read the replies another time, I start to cry. It's ridiculous to get so down based on comments from anonymous trolls like FourHourErection and RectalTumor, but I can't help it. I bury my head in my arms on the desktop, the tears rolling down my chin. It's not just the thread making me cry. It's this entire year of studying, research, and community service. I'm overwhelmed. And according to Reddit, all my work may lead only to disappointment.

My phone dings with a text from Jerome: *Don't forget - be home at 6p*

I wipe away the tears and glance at the clock in the corner of my laptop screen. It's 5:30. It's a good thing Jerome texted because I'd lost track of time. He's making sure I don't miss dinner for Momma's birthday. I've been so busy with schoolwork, I forgot her birthday was today until Jerome reminded me this morning.

While I've been buried by med school, my brother has somehow morphed into an upstanding citizen. The case against him and Fernando for possession of narcotics was thrown out. Apparently, the police lacked proper cause when they searched for fentanyl in Fernando's backpack. When the charges were dropped, Jerome had a moment of clarity about his life. Since then, he's been on time for work. He's even been promoted to store manager at Burger King. And he's been more helpful with Momma and bills than I've ever seen him. We've changed places, it seems. Now, because of med school, I'm the forgetful one and he's organized.

I reply to Jerome's text, saying I'll be there for Momma's birthday dinner at six. I can't stay long because I need to study, but I'll sing my heart out to "Happy Birthday" for her fifty-fourth year on the planet.

As I start to pack up my laptop, my phone dings with another text, this one from Sebastian.

u in the library?

I reply: *yes but about to leave*

He texts again: *coming have news to tell u*

I text him back with a thumbs up, wondering what he wants. I slide my laptop into my backpack and collect my purse. A few moments later, Sebastian appears. Usually when he meets me, he's in scrubs. But today he has on khaki pants and a button-down shirt. He looks dressed up for something, and even a little bit . . . handsome.

"What are you so happy about?" I say, noting the wide grin on his face.

"You mean you don't know what day it is?"

I think for a second. It's Momma's birthday, but that can't be what he's referring to.

He sees the puzzled look on my face. "March 17th, 2023? Ring any bells?"

I still come up blank. "Wednesday?" I say.

"Aw, God. You are seriously lost in schoolwork if you don't know what today is." He reaches into his pocket and withdraws a white envelope. "Go ahead. Open it. I'm dying to share the news."

I slide a folded piece of paper from the envelope and read:

MILES SEBASTIAN
STATE MEDICAL CENTER DERMATOLOGY PROGRAM

For a second, I'm not sure what this means, but then it dawns on me. My heart leaps with excitement.

"You matched!"

"Yes!" Sebastian says. He makes a fist and pumps it in

the air. "I matched to the program right here at State. I'm going to be a dermatologist. God, it feels so damn good."

My mind scrambles to process this news. Sebastian has successfully navigated the absurd and convoluted match process all medical students must go through. He applied to fifty dermatology programs and was invited to interview at fifteen. He placed those programs in his order of preference, called a "rank list," and submitted them to a mysterious computer somewhere in the clouds. Then, like students all over the country, he learned where he matched today. For some, this day is a disaster. They match nowhere, victims of reaching too high for a specialty that's too competitive. Sebastian was worried that might happen to him. *I* was worried it might happen to him. But it didn't.

My gloom over the Reddit thread suddenly lifts. This isn't just good news for Sebastian; it's great news for me, too. Sebastian came from Midtown, like me. He failed the first exam, like me. And he followed the gunner rules, also just like me. If he can match into derm, I can, too.

"This is amazing," I say.

I feel like I'm the one who matched, not Sebastian. I want to jump for joy. I study Sebastian, noting the glow on his face. He looks so damn happy. What a feeling it must be to have four years of hard work pay off.

Suddenly, he steps forward and kisses me.

This catches me totally off guard, and I freeze. As his lips move over mine, I wonder why I didn't see this coming. I always knew Sebastian wasn't helping me out of pure altruism. He's a guy, and I've been around enough guys to know they all eventually want one thing. On some level, I knew it was a matter of time until he made a pass.

And if he'd kissed me any other day, I probably would have pushed him away. It's not that I don't find him attractive, he's kind of cute, but a physical relationship with him could threaten my studies. The last thing I need is romantic expectations from Sebastian every time I ask for advice on passing an exam.

But something about today is different.

This past year has been a hellish stew of studying and research and Anki and UWorld. I hardly feel human anymore. And then there was the Reddit thread, a thousand-pound boulder dropped on me from above. But Sebastian's match has given me new life. I suddenly feel alive in a way I've not felt for a long time. And because Sebastian is responsible for my new lightness of being, I don't mind that he's kissing me.

And in fact, I start to kiss him back.

We make out for a solid minute, right there behind the book stacks, next to journals M through T. I'm lost in his kiss, all thoughts of studying vanished.

Then I gently push his chest, and he steps back.

"Wait," I say. "I have to ask you something. Did you assault a girl in your class?"

Sebastian's eyes widen. "Who told you that?"

"The dean."

"Figures," he says. He looks down at his feet and draws in a deep breath. I hope he's about to tell me the truth. But if he lies, how will I know? Or does it even matter, when he's been so good to me?

"There's a girl in my class: Deborah," he says. "Maybe you know her? We dated. Anyway, it didn't last long, just a few weeks. She's going into psych, so I should have known she's mental. But when I stopped returning her calls, she got super clingy. Because I ghosted her, she went to the dean and said I assaulted her. It's total bullshit. I showed the dean all her texts. Explained it was a consensual relationship. They took no action, but the dean has me pegged as guilty. Don't know what her problem is."

I study his face closely, looking for evidence of a lie or embellishment. He seems sincere. I've spent a lot of time with him over the past months, meeting in Starbucks or the library. He's never been anything but respectful. It's hard to believe he would assault someone, but you never know.

"You believe me, don't you?" he says.

He desperately wants me to trust him. My thoughts drift over the past year. I was failing before I met him. Now, with him matching, the future for me is bright. I can make a fortune as a dermatologist. Me and Momma and Jerome can get out of that shitty townhouse on Riggs Avenue. And I owe all of it to Sebastian.

I lean forward and kiss him. He places his hands on my face, caressing my cheeks.

Then I stop him again. There's something he has to agree to before we go any further.

"This can only be physical, okay? I can't have a boyfriend in med school."

He considers this for a second. "What do you mean *this*? You mean us kissing?"

"Don't ask questions. Just answer me. Physical only. Nothing more. That okay with you or not?"

"Uh, yeah. Okay, fine."

I'm not sure he really believes this, but at least I've made my intentions clear.

I take his hand and lead him around the corner. Next to the water fountain, there's a utility closet. I open the door and pull Sebastian inside. The door shuts, and darkness engulfs us. I grab his shirt and pull him toward me. He kisses me hard, running his hands up over my chest. I become lost in his mouth, finally feeling something other than the heavy haze of medical school. I'm going to fuck him right here in this closet filled with mop buckets, brooms, and bleach. For at least a little while, I won't think of Anki or UWorld or dermatology. I'll mesh my body with Sebastian's, because sex is the perfect escape from the crushing weight that is med school.

As we tear off each other's clothes, I do not hear the ding of a text on my phone outside.

Later, I'll read it.

It was from Jerome: *where r u?*

18.

The next year passes in a grim tableau of studying, exams and competition with my classmates. It's now May, deep into my second year of medical school. Sitting at my usual library study spot, it's 5 p.m. and my head throbs from staring at my laptop screen since six this morning. I haven't showered in two days, a thin film of grime covering my body. My hair is a mess, and I'm wearing dirty jeans and an old T-shirt. But clean clothes and hygiene don't matter to me right now. That's because tomorrow at 8 a.m., I will travel to a Prometric testing center downtown to take the dreaded Step 1 licensing exam.

I've been studying for this test for six weeks, a time called "dedicated study" where we have no classes. I wake each day at five and grind until nearly midnight with the fear of God inside me. Why am I so afraid? Because last year seven people at SMS failed Step 1. The test can be taken again, but the failure becomes part of a student's permanent record. If I fail tomorrow, my journey toward dermatology is over.

My phone dings with a text from Sebastian: *You got this.*

It's sweet of him to send this. Sebastian graduated last May and is now nearing the end of his intern year. I see him much less than I did when he was a student. He works in the hospital and clinics now, with call and overnight shifts that keep him busy. And even if he had more free time, I've been pounding away at my studies this past year, plus making trips to Murrow's lab. Because of my hard work, I have strong exam grades and several research publications. Everything has fallen into place to make me a solid candidate for dermatology residency.

Everything except Step 1 tomorrow.

I send a heart emoji back to Sebastian.

He replies: *reach out if you need a break.*

This is his way of saying he'll gladly have sex with me tonight. Since our trip to the closet a year ago, he and I have done the blanket drill six more times. I've made it clear I don't want a serious relationship, and he appears to accept this. I hate to admit it, but I basically use him to destress. When the studying gets too much for me, when my mind starts to melt down, I make a booty call to Sebastian. I don't know whether this is healthy or not in the long run, but honestly, it's helped me survive this wretched year of nonstop studying. If I complete my journey into dermatology, I'll owe part of that to sex with Sebastian. Without it, I might have lost my gunner's drive and switched from derm to one of the lame specialities.

I glance at my laptop screen, where my schedule for the rest of the night is carefully mapped out on an Excel spreadsheet. I'll do another one hundred UWorld questions, plus five hundred Anki cards. Then I'll go home at eight, take a hot shower, and try to get to bed early so I'll be rested for the eight-hour monstrosity of an exam tomorrow.

That's when my phone rings with a call from Jerome. I consider ignoring it, but Jerome rarely calls me at this time of day. I can't help wondering if something is wrong.

"Jerome?"

"Soph, something happened to Momma."

My gut clenches with worry. I wait a couple seconds, but Jerome says nothing.

"Well? What happened? You gonna tell me or—"

"She . . . she just left in an ambulance." His voice is shaky. He sounds frightened. "She ain't looked right the last few days. Been tired a lot. Tonight, I couldn't wake her up in her wheelchair. Then she slumped over and slid onto the floor."

I'm suddenly unable to breathe. *She ain't looked right the last few days.* I've been studying so much, I've barely seen Momma. I leave the apartment before she wakes and get home at night after she's in bed. Guilt ripples through me. I should have stopped home more the past few weeks. Maybe I could have seen this coming.

I hear Jerome breathing, but he says nothing.

"Well, what else?" I say, an edge to my voice. I hate to get angry with him, but he's not telling me what I need to know. "Was she breathing? What did the EMTs do?"

"She was breathing. She kinda came to a little bit. Sorta moaned and looked around. But Soph, she didn't look good. She looked real bad. They took her out on a stretcher. I'm . . . I'm worried something's really wrong."

My chest heaves as I try to process what Jerome has said. Suddenly, everything seems small: my studies, dermatology, the Step 1 exam. My instincts tell me this is Momma's cancer. Her oncologist said it could recur, and if it did, the chance of survival was very, very low. I suddenly feel ice cold. If Momma's dying . . . oh, God, I can't even think about it.

To Jerome, I say, "They take her to the ER here?"

"I'm on my way there," he replies. "I'll meet you."

I end the call and rush from my desk, taking only my purse, leaving my laptop, books, and backpack behind. I weave my way through the stacks and out of the library. Then I hurry down the hall toward the medical school exit, so I can cross the parking lot to the hospital.

As I near the anatomy lab, I see a figure sitting on the floor, knees drawn up to his chest. Then I hear whimpering. As I get closer, I see it's Charlie. He has his head in his hands and he's shaking as he cries. I shouldn't stop for anything, but he looks so heartbroken, I can't rush by. I walk up to his huddled body.

"What's wrong?" I ask.

Charlie gazes up and wipes the tears from his face, seeming embarrassed. "Oh . . . uh, it's nothing. I'm fine."

I should accept this and rush to the ER, but I can tell he's lying. I glance at the exit down the hall. I consider hurrying out the door. But then I study Charlie's face. It's red and stained with tears. I decide to stop just for a minute.

I slump down against the wall to sit beside Charlie, placing my hand on his knee. "What's wrong?" I ask again.

He sniffles and looks at me. "The exam tomorrow," he replies. "I'm worried I'm going to fail."

I realize I know nothing about Charlie's school performance. We've spoken many times over the past two years, but he's never told me anything about the grades he gets.

"Well, have you passed the school exams?"

"Barely. I had to retake or, er, enhance two of them. Those tests are so hard. They're nothing like the lectures we get."

Charlie seems to be where I was before Sebastian: trying to learn from the school instead of TPRs. A fatal mistake.

"Well, have you been taking the practice tests?" I ask. The NBME, the licensing board that administers the Step 1 exam, sells practice tests for $60 apiece. I've gotten them for free from Sebastian.

"I did two of them. They're expensive, you know. And my scores weren't good."

Now I see Charlie's dilemma. Bad scores on school exams. Bad scores on NBME tests. And the Step 1 beast looms in the morning. I remember that Charlie volunteers at a retirement home. And he wants to be a primary care doctor. He's probably the exact type of person the medical field needs, yet he's barely getting by and he'll end up making less money than every other person in our class.

"It's not just the test," he says. "I feel like I'm screwing up in a million ways. Like the surveys. I keep sending them in late. I had to meet with the dean. It's a professionalism violation. I mean, if I can't pass the tests, and the school thinks I'm unprofessional, what am I doing here? Maybe I'm just wasting my time."

Twice a month, we're emailed surveys by the school. They ask us about how we study, what we study, and how the school can improve. It's a total joke. Nothing changes based on our feedback, but the surveys are required for the school's accreditation. I can't help chuckling that this is bothering Charlie so much.

Charlie sees me laugh and says, "What?"

"If it's unprofessional to submit a survey late, then we have some rampant unprofessional behavior among the faculty at this school. I'm supposed to meet with Dr. Murrow once a month to talk about research. You know how many times he's showed up? Never. He's missed every single meeting. Always tells me later that something came up. I meet with his post doc instead. The faculty at this school have serious professionalism problems of their own. Don't let them bother you with their double standards for us students. Those surveys are stupid shit."

Charlie's lips turn slightly upward, in kind of a half-smile, a sign that he likes what I've told him. But then he frowns again.

"It's not just that," he says. He slides his phone from his pocket and taps at the screen. "Look," he says. "My peer evaluations. They're terrible."

We're required to submit evaluations of our peers in the class once per month. Why anyone thinks this is a good idea, I have no clue. It's painful to find words to describe your classmates without being offensive to the people you have to work with each day. And the faculty can read the feedback, so we're all careful with what we say. Most of the comments are mundane, inoffensive platitudes. But still, once in a while, someone manages to write something hurtful.

I scan Charlie's peer feedback on his phone screen:

Charlie is a nice guy, but the things he says are obvious and don't add to the discussions in class.

Charlie is too quiet.

Sometimes Charlie gets food stuck in his teeth.

My class is unreal. I can't believe some of them write this shit about decent kids like Charlie. What assholes.

"I have something that'll make you feel better," I say.

I slide my phone from my purse and tap the screen. I show him a piece of feedback I received. It's anonymous, like all the peer evaluations, but I know it's from Mercer.

S*ophia contributes nicely to our TBL group*

N*early every day she arrives ready to work*

I *enjoy working with Sophia*

T*ough concepts do not deter her*

Clearly, she is prepared for class

Her contributions to the discussions are helpful.

Charlie studies it for a second, then laughs. "So childish," he says.

"Honestly, I don't even read most of my feedback. What's the point? Like I care what Jennifer Mercer thinks of me? Or anyone else for that matter? Just ignore that shit."

Charlie sniffles and wipes his nose, his expression seeming brighter. It occurs to me how lucky I am to have Sebastian. He told me long ago that school surveys and peer feedback are nonsense. You don't see practicing doctors doing these types of things, so why should medical students care? But Charlie has no guiding hand like I do.

"Thank you," he says. "You're a good friend."

I suddenly remember what Charlie said to me a long time ago: *Medicine needs more people like you, Sophia.*

I lean over and kiss him on the cheek. "Don't give up. Medicine needs more people like you, Charlie."

Before he can respond, the double doors to the anatomy lab swing open and Jennifer Mercer emerges. She has on no make-up or jewelry, a striking change from her usual appearance. Her hair is disheveled. She looks like shit, but so do I. Like all of us, she's probably overwhelmed by Step 1.

She stops and glances at me and Charlie sitting on the floor. For a second, she seems about to say something. Then she sighs, rolls her eyes, and says, "Seriously?" before walking away.

When she's out of sight down the hall, Charlie says, "Some of the others call her Cersei, you know. As in Lannister. From Game of Thrones."

I consider this for a beat. "Does she sleep with her brother?"

"No," Charlie says, letting out a laugh. "Because she's always scheming to get ahead."

A fitting name for Mercer, but it gives me pause. I, of course, am doing the same thing—scheming to be the best. I wonder what nickname my class has for me.

"Can't believe she studies in the cadaver room," Charlie says. "I'd get sick if I did that."

The word "sick" jolts my memory. Momma! I leap to my feet.

"I've got to go, Charlie," I say. "Good luck on the exam tomorrow."

Then I hurry down the hall, my worries over Momma once again fresh on my mind.

19.

I HOLD MOMMA'S HAND, HER bony fingers ice cold. She looks awful lying here in a curtained-off ER room, her eyes closed as she sleeps, her skin pale as the moon. I can't shake the grim feeling she's dying. Saline slowly drips into her veins as if it's counting the time left in her life. It's maddening I didn't know she looked like this before. If Jerome had just told me, maybe I could have done something.

"You should have said she hasn't been looking right," I say to Jerome from a chair beside Momma's gurney. I know I shouldn't chastise my brother at a time like this, but I can't help it.

Jerome gives me a fierce look. "When am I supposed to tell you, Soph? When, huh? We never see you anymore. You basically live at that library." He shakes his head and slumps back in his seat at Momma's feet. He has on the same Burger King uniform I've seen him wear for years, only now the name tag reads "Manager."

"You could have texted me," I say.

"And say what? Momma looks tired? Momma's not eating as much as usual? You know she gets like this when her mood ain't right. If I'd told you, you would have just told me to stop bothering you while you're studying. That's all that matters to you now: studying."

The words make my head throb. It's been almost two years since I started medical school, and in that time, I've hardly seen my family. And while I've been lost in my studies, the world has changed. Jerome's become a responsible adult. Momma's had dozens of moods come and go, none of them known to me. I've missed birthdays and dinners and lots of other things that used to be regular occurrences.

I stroke Momma's arm, my eyes filling with tears. "She's dying," I say to Jerome.

"Don't say that. We don't know that."

I want to believe this, but I can feel it in my bones: Momma's cancer is back.

The curtain whooshes open and Dr. Miller appears, the same petite woman in scrubs and a mask who cared for Momma the last time she was in the ER. Jerome and I sit up straight and lock eyes with her. She must have news on Momma. My heart braces for what she's about to say.

"Just wanted to give you an update," she says, her tone measured, not grim. A hopeful sign. "Your mom's severely anemic. Looks like when she was here a year and a half ago, she had a low red count, but she left AMA before we could work it up. Now, it's gotten much, much worse."

Momma promised to go to her regular doctor for the anemia a long time ago. I've been too busy with school to check up on this.

I look at my brother. "You took her to Dr. Reynolds, right?"

"Of course," Jerome replies. "Momma said it was all better. That's what she told me."

"Yes, but didn't you talk to Dr. Reynolds yourself?" I say. "You know Momma doesn't tell us things."

"I don't go in the room with her," Jerome replies, super defensive. "That's Momma's business. She told me everything was fine."

I let out a frustrated sigh. Momma hates doctors and ignores her health. I wonder if she even told her regular doctor about the anemia. This is another consequence of my absence from my family. I used to take Momma to her appointments. When I did, I always went in the room with her and asked lots of questions. Now, because I've been so busy, Momma's had anemia for over a year that hasn't been evaluated. What if it's too late now?

I look at Dr. Miller. "Do you know why she's anemic?"

"We're going to run some tests," she replies.

I'm so deep into studying for Step 1, a thousand causes of anemia race through my mind. "Well, what's her MCV? Her ferritin level? Does she have reticulocytes on her blood smear?"

"I've called the hematologists," Miller replies. "They'll look into those things."

It drives me crazy not to have more information. I could make a diagnosis for Momma if I just had some test results. "Don't you at least know her MCV? That's the standard test in a patient with anemia."

"Like I said," Miller replies, "we're still looking into it. Meanwhile, we're going to give her a blood transfusion. That should make her feel much better. I'll be back when I know more."

Then she scurries from the room, closing the curtain behind her. It's exasperating to have so little information about Momma's illness. On UWorld questions, all the data is given instantly to make a diagnosis. In real life, the medical system grinds out information one tiny grain at a time.

Jerome looks at me, the medical expert in the family. "That's good news, right? She'll get better with the . . . uh, what's it called . . . transfusion?"

"Maybe," I say. I hate to burst my brother's enthusiasm, but grim thoughts fill my mind. "But they have to figure out why she's anemic. That's the most important thing."

Among the scores of causes of anemia, one looms in my thoughts. "It could be her cancer," I say. "If it's back and it's spread to her bone marrow, that's bad. That's what I'm afraid of."

Just saying this aloud floods my eyes with tears that roll down my cheek. I clutch Momma's hand in mine and weep. Jerome's expression turns bleak. He slides his chair next to mine and puts an arm over my shoulders. Together we huddle beside Momma, praying these aren't her last moments on Earth.

I tap my phone to check the time: it's 10:20 p.m. I should be in bed asleep so I'll be well-rested for the Step 1 exam tomorrow. Instead, I sit at Momma's bedside watching a third unit of blood drip slowly into her veins. Step 1 feels a thousand miles away right now. All I care about is Momma.

Jerome is nodding off in a chair in the corner. The room lights are out so Momma can rest, the neon glow from her heart monitor lighting the space. Beyond the curtain, the ER buzzes and hums with activity.

Suddenly, Momma stirs beneath her blanket, shifting her weight on the gurney.

I jump to my feet, peering down at her over the guardrail. "Momma?"

Jerome hears this and opens his eyes. He sees me beside Momma and hurries to the other side of her gurney, gripping her hand.

Momma blinks a few times. "Soph?"

The sound of her voice is so good to hear. "It's me," I say.

"I'm here, too," Jerome says.

She shifts her gaze from my brother back to me, taking in her children. "What happened?"

Jerome quickly tells her about how he found her at home and brought her here. I tell her about the blood tests and her anemia. I point out the blood transfusion going into her veins.

When I finish, Momma looks around the room, her eyelids still heavy with sleep. Then her lips turn down in a frown. Some horrible thought has gripped her, I can tell.

"I'm dying," she says, a tear welling in her eyes.

Jerome clutches her hand with both of his. "They're still running tests, Momma. We don't know anything yet."

I wish I felt like Jerome does, but I have the same fear Momma just spoke aloud, a fear that pierces my insides like a knife. The weakness, the pale skin. She had all of this when she first got cancer. It must be back. I hold Momma's hand even harder. It occurs to me that I may not be able to hold her living body much longer.

She shifts her gaze from me to Jerome and back, her eyes swollen with tears. "I ain't been right for weeks. I should have told you both, but I didn't want to see you worry." She looks at me. "I knew you had your big test tomorrow. I didn't want you unsettled by me."

Momma's trying to explain herself, but her words only make me feel sad and guilty. If not for medical school, she might have told me she was sick a long time ago. My studies not only kept me from noticing Momma's decline, they kept her from telling me about it, too.

"Maybe it'll be something that's not serious," I say. I don't believe this, but I say it anyway. I'll do anything to keep Momma's spirits up.

"This feels just like when I first got the cancer," she says, gazing up at me from the gurney, her long brown hair fanned over her pillow. "I'm so tired. I thought it was the cancer come back weeks ago, but I didn't want to say anything. What's the point? They said if it came back, that was the end."

My body aches with grief. This is exactly what I feared. Jerome holds Momma's hand but says nothing as he tries not to cry. We both stand over Momma, her words like a hammer to our hearts.

After a long huddle of silence, Momma asks, "What time is it?"

"Ten-thirty," Jerome says.

Momma turns her weary head toward me. "You should get to bed. You got your test tomorrow."

"I'm not taking that test," I say.

"What?" Momma says.

"I don't know if I'm even going back to that school."

Jerome and Momma both glare at me. "You serious?" Jerome says.

I look down at Momma. "I don't know if I can when you're sick or . . . dying."

"Why not?" Momma asks.

I take a second to think. It's hard to express myself with Momma looking so poorly. I search for the words to explain my feelings. "When I study, I have this vision in my mind. I see you and me and Jerome in a big house in the suburbs. It's our own house, and nobody else's. We don't have old Mr. McKernon upstairs, walking over our heads. We don't pay rent to Ms. Banbury and crazy Lenny. We have a yard with grass. And we have new cars. No more crappy Festiva for me. No rusty pickup for Jerome. But most of all, we have freedom. No more worries over money. We have all we need."

"You can still get that if I'm not here," Momma says.

"I don't know," I reply. "So much of that dream is you, Momma. I love you so much. And I know you've had a hard life. It's not fair that Daddy died so young. It's not fair you got cancer so young. I wanted to give you something good for once. Something truly good. Me and Jerome can get by. But it was you, Momma. It was always you I wanted to see living the good life. I . . . I just don't know if I can drive myself so hard if you're not here."

Outside the curtain, someone yells something, and I hear hurried steps. It sounds like there's a cardiac arrest down the hall. Momma and Jerome are silent, processing what I've said.

After a long moment, Momma says, "Promise me you'll keep going if I'm gone. I want you to promise. I don't want you to give up because of me. You're my brilliant little girl. If I leave this Earth, I wanna leave knowing you're headed for the top. You get out of the city. You get that house you want. Promise me, Soph. Promise me."

Tears stream down my cheeks. I wipe them away, then gaze into Momma's eyes. The truth is, I can't go on if she's dead. I'll drop out of school the minute she breathes her last, even though it means I have to pay back my scholarship money. But I don't want to say this to her now. I don't want her to think her baby girl is a quitter.

"Alright," I say. "I won't give up. I promise." Then I lay my head on Momma's chest, both of us crying while Jerome looks on, trying to be stoic but on the verge of tears himself. God, I am such a fool to have abandoned Momma these past two years. If I'd known she was going to leave me, I never would have set one foot in that medical school.

Suddenly, the curtain whooshes open again, and Dr. Miller appears. "Ms. Abney," she says, "I have some news."

My body stiffens. This is it. They must have found

that her cancer is back. This is when I learn that my mother is dying.

"You have a vitamin deficiency," she says. "You're not absorbing vitamin B12. It's a condition called—"

"Pernicious anemia!" I interject.

My spirits suddenly lift. I know everything about this diagnosis from my studying. Common among women in their fifties—just like Momma—pernicious anemia occurs when the intestines can't absorb B12. Without the vitamin, red cells can't grow, causing anemia. This is an easily treatable condition. Momma can be cured!

"That's right," Miller says. "And the treatment is—"

"A vitamin B12 shot!" I exclaim. I leap from my chair. "Oh, my God, Momma. This is fantastic news. You're not dying. Well, I mean, you are dying from pernicious anemia, but you won't be for long. This is completely reversible!"

I turn to Miller. "And the cancer . . . the cancer isn't back?"

Miller shakes her head. "This is all B12. That's the entire problem. Everything is going to be fine."

I'm floating on air. The fatigue of my studying for the last six weeks vanishes. I'm suddenly wired from the news that Momma will live. It occurs to me that if she'd followed up with her regular doctor two years ago, she would've been diagnosed as B12-deficient and never gotten as sick as she is now. But none of that matters. She's going to live. She's not dying. I want to leap for joy.

And then something hits me: this is medicine. This is what it's all about. The very medical knowledge I'm cramming for the Step 1 exam has just saved my mother's life. Sebastian may be right that doctors produce a lot of documents, but they also save lives. I'm going into the greatest profession in the world. I can't believe I thought of dropping out. What was I thinking? I'm halfway through medical school, at the midpoint of a degree that'll allow me to help others and earn millions. Could there be any better profession on the planet?

I glance at my watch. It's 10:45 p.m. The library closes in fifteen minutes. I have to grab my laptop and then get home to bed.

Tomorrow morning, at 8 a.m., I am taking the Step 1 exam.

20.

When I return to my study spot in the library, my laptop is missing.

Where could it be? I search behind the small desk and under the chair, but no computer. I think back to my exit from the library six hours ago. I grabbed my purse but left my backpack and laptop. The backpack is still here, hanging off a corner of my chair, but the laptop, including the power cord, has vanished. Could it have been stolen?

The lights flicker telling me I have five minutes until closing. Shit, shit, shit. I need my laptop tonight. It has dozens of study sheets I typed up over the course of my Step 1 studying. It holds everything I plan to review tomorrow morning, just before the exam. It can't be gone! Frantically, I race up and down the aisles of books and journals, checking everywhere. Could I have dropped it? Could I have set it down on some random shelf? But everywhere I look: nothing.

"We're closing," someone says.

I glance up to see the librarian, a squat little man with a bald head. He shuffles down an aisle toward me.

"I can't find my laptop," I reply, my eyes scanning up and down, searching for my computer.

"Did you leave it unattended?"

An extremely unhelpful question. I drop to my knees to peer under the desk again. "It was here a little while ago. Did you see anyone come back here?"

"No, but you'll have to look for it tomorrow. We're closing now."

I'm going to lose it on this guy. My Step 1 exam is in nine hours. My laptop has vital information.

"Well, I'm not leaving until I find it."

The librarian huffs. "I can call security if you'd like. You can report it stolen. But I wonder if a friend of yours took it for safekeeping? Did anyone know you were studying back here?"

I climb up from my knees. Who knew I was here? I saw Charlie on my way out of the building. Could he have taken it for me? Unlikely. But he's the only student I saw . . .

Then it hits me: Mercer.

She saw me talking to Charlie outside the anatomy lab, her bizarro study spot. She knows I study back here. She's seen me walk into the library stacks with my backpack many times. It would be just like her to take my computer the night before Step 1. That bitch. If she took it, I'll kill her. Like, for real, kill her. I will literally turn her into a cadaver for the M1s to dissect.

"Did you see one of my classmates in here tonight?" I ask the librarian. "She has blonde hair. Wears a Harvard sweatshirt."

"Ms. Mercer," the librarian replies. "Yes, she was just here an hour or so ago. Do you think she may have your computer?"

I glance at my watch. It's 11:01 p.m. Mercer has the exam tomorrow, just like me. She could be studying in the anatomy lab. If she's there, she and I are going to have a talk.

"I have a hunch where my laptop is," I say to the librarian.

Then I sling my backpack over my shoulder and jog out of the library.

When I open the anatomy lab doors, the smell of formaldehyde overwhelms me. The room is cold and dark, but I can make out the dim outlines of dead bodies, each lying on a metal slab and covered in plastic. In a far corner of the room, a light shines over a small desk where Mercer sits before her glowing laptop screen. She has headphones on and doesn't hear me enter.

I slowly snake through the dead bodies toward Mercer. When I reach her desk, I stop and stand over her from behind. She stares at her screen, no idea I'm there. I study her closely, noting her blond hair, her skinny shoulders and arms. I don't think I've ever hated anyone as much as her.

I scan her desk for my laptop but don't see it anywhere. Maybe it's in her backpack by her feet?

I muster all the courage I can and yank her headphones from her ears.

She gasps, then spins around in her chair, eyes wide as saucers.

"Where's my laptop?" I demand.

Mercer's eyes dart around the room. "What are you doing in here?"

"I said: Where's my laptop?"

Mercer stands from her chair, facing me just a few feet away. "I don't know what you're talking about."

"Someone took my laptop from the library tonight. I know it was you."

"You're wrong."

I glance around the room, noting the dead bodies. "Why do you study in here anyway? It's creepy."

"It's quiet, and no one comes in here . . . well, usually no one."

"I bet you're the one who printed RAT questions in here. The Dean knows about that. She's gonna bust your ass for it."

Mercer lets out a laugh. "God, you're clueless. I *don't* cheat. And didn't you hear? It was Collins. He got the RAT questions emailed to him from a third year. He goes before the AAC next week. He's fucked."

Randall Collins, the perpetual wearer of scrubs from my TBL group, the one Mercer's been fucking since first year. *Of course* it was him. The kid is gung-ho on becoming an orthopedic surgeon, but he's dumb as a rock. Like Neanderthal dumb. Barely passes his exams. It fits perfectly that he'd cheat to get ahead on the RATs.

But I still find it hard to believe Mercer is innocent.

"You mean to tell me your boyfriend had the RAT questions, but you didn't use them yourself?"

Mercer rolls her eyes. "Aren't you listening? I don't cheat. Besides, don't you know anything? We broke up awhile ago. You are so out of the loop."

Although I didn't know this until now, it actually makes sense. As much as I hate Mercer, she's orders of magnitude smarter than Collins. She's indeed an evil genius like Cersei Lannister in *Game of Thrones*. Collins, on the other hand, is just marginally smarter than a turd from one of the dragons. God help his future patients if he somehow manages to become a surgeon.

"Now get out," Mercer says. "I need to finish what I'm doing before the test tomorrow."

"I'm not leaving without my laptop."

"Well, I don't have it."

I lunge toward her backpack on the floor. That's got to

be where she hid my computer. Mercer grabs my arm and pushes me away.

"Keep off my stuff, you bitch. I don't have your stupid laptop."

"I'm not leaving until you show me what's inside your backpack."

"Fuck off. I don't have to do anything you say."

Again, I lunge for her backpack. She grabs my arm, then pushes me hard in the chest. I stumble backward into one of the cadavers. My elbow plunges into the plastic over the body and sinks into the dank abdomen. I get back on my feet and glare at Mercer. She stares back at me, with a satisfied grin. God, I hate her so much.

I should turn around and leave this room. I know she took my laptop, but she'll never admit it, so what's the point in fighting with her? The angrier I get, the harder it'll be to fall asleep tonight. My exam is in less than nine hours.

As I mull my options, Mercer says, "Why are you doing derm anyway?"

Here it comes. I can feel it. She's going to unload all her anger at me now. Every bitter thought she's had about me since I told her I was going into dermatology.

"You're fucking everything up for me," she says. "There were twelve people in our class doing derm, but they've all given up because their class rank is shit. Everyone but you. Do you know how great it would be if I was the only one going into derm? Fucking fantastic. I'd get all the attention from the faculty. No competition for research or clinic time or recommendations. But you're in my way. I know you're doing derm just to piss me off. So stupid. You're not derm material. Go into family med or internal medicine, like the other poor kids who want to open free clinics or whatever."

The other poor kids? Oh, now I'm mad. Like, really mad. I want to throttle her skinny little neck. But fighting with her won't help anything. It'll just ruin my exam tomorrow, because I'll be too agitated to sleep tonight.

But then I look at her face in the dim light, the high cheekbones, the painted lashes. My first two years of medical school could have been great if not for her. She's so rich and so smug. She's everything a poor kid like me hates about the world. She painted "SNITCH" on my car, I know it. And I know she took my laptop.

That's when I decide: I can't walk away.

My mind fills with a rage so strong my temples pound. I lunge at Mercer with lightning speed, her eyes widening in surprise. I grab her stupid Harvard sweatshirt and hurl her onto the floor. I stare down at her, shocked at what I've done, but incredibly satisfied. This is the last thing I need to be doing the night before Step 1, yet it feels so good. Mercer looks up at me with a fiery rage in her eyes, a look that sends a chill through me. She leaps at my legs tackling me onto the cold, hard floor. She grabs my hair, yanking with all her strength, searing pain coursing through my scalp. I push at her face with my hands, scrunching her cheeks against her jaw. Then I pull my knee up hard, slamming it into her abdomen.

Mercer howls in pain, then rolls over clutching her stomach.

I slowly rise to my knees, my chest heaving as it takes in rapid breaths. Mercer looks a mess on the floor, her hair in shambles, her sweatshirt in disarray. I must look the same way myself.

Then I spy her backpack, now unprotected by her desk. I hurry toward it and kneel to reach the zipper.

Suddenly, I feel a harsh tug at my shoulders. Mercer stands over me, yanking me away from her backpack. I leap to my feet and turn to face her. She swings a fist wildly toward my head, the blow just missing my jaw. I grab her hands and we push each other back and forth, our bodies a tangle of limbs, grunts, and thrusts. Then I lose my footing and start to stumble. Mercer shoves me hard and I careen backward slamming into one of the metal cadaver tables.

The table tips over, the metal crashing loudly, one of the dead bodies spilling onto the floor with a thud.

Mercer and I both freeze. We gape at the cadaver, a skinny male, his glassy eyes fixed, his chest cracked open with the lungs removed. The sound of the table overturning was so loud. If someone heard and comes into this room, we're both screwed.

I sprint to the exit, swinging the door open. The hallway outside is dark and quiet.

"Is anyone coming?" Mercer says, her tone grave.

"No," I reply.

"We have to clean this up," she says. "If they find this room trashed, we're both screwed."

She's right. We have to fix this. I walk toward the table and the corpse. The body must weigh at least a hundred and fifty pounds. It will take all of our combined strength to get him back on the table. It's quite the paradox that we need each other now because of our fight.

Suddenly, a thought occurs to me.

"Wait," I say.

Mercer looks at me cautiously.

"I'm not cleaning this up unless you give me back my laptop."

"Are you insane?" she says. "We can't leave this here. I don't have your laptop."

"You'll never get this stiff off the floor by yourself. You need my help."

She considers this. "If you don't help me, I'll tell them you knocked it over."

"And I'll say you pushed me into it. We'll both be in

big trouble. Is that what you want? Give me my laptop back, and I'll help you get this room like it was."

Mercer says nothing, her eyes taking me in, her brain turning. I know she has my laptop.

Finally, Mercer sighs and looks down. Then she strolls to her desk, bends down toward her backpack, and reaches inside. A second later, she slides out my laptop.

I knew it. That bitch took my computer.

"I wasn't going to keep it," Mercer says. "I was going to put it in the library lost and found after my exam tomorrow."

She's probably telling the truth. She doesn't need a stolen laptop. She just needs to rattle me so I fail Step 1. A part of me is impressed. If her plan had worked, and I had failed my exam, she'd be the lone student in our class headed for dermatology. That's like being the only runner in the Boston Marathon.

I take the laptop from her. "You ever steal something of mine again, I'll kill you. They'll send me to jail, but it will be worth it."

Mercer rolls her eyes and sighs. "You're insufferable. I pray to God I don't see you again after Step 1. If the school puts us in the same group for rotations, I'll flip."

"If we're in the same group, you and I will go to the dean together to ask for a change."

"At least we agree on something," Mercer replies.

Mercer and I walk to opposite ends of the upturned table. We bend down and heave the metal contraption back to an upright position. Then we take positions around the cadaver, Mercer near the feet, me at the head. God, this man is going to be heavy to lift. It will take all our strength to raise him to the table. I nod at Mercer and she nods back. Then I slide my hands under the shoulders, the dead, pale skin cold to the touch. With a grunt, I lift the torso as Mercer raises the legs and pelvis. My muscles strain against the weight. I just manage to get the head on the table. Then I slide down the body, raising the abdomen as Mercer lifts both feet. Finally, we push the rest of the body onto the metal surface. Mercer places the plastic cover over the dead man as I use paper towels to wipe slime from the floor. Then we both wash our hands to rid them of the sticky grime of dead flesh.

Moments later, I marvel at the good job we've done. The room looks as it did when I first walked in. No one will ever be able to tell that two women in their twenties, both medical students at the top of their class, both gunners for dermatology, had a savage fight in this room that spilled a dead body onto the floor.

This makes me wonder if other crazy, violent fights among medical students have occurred that are now kept secret? If there's been a murder at some point it wouldn't totally shock me. Maybe there's a dead body of a medical student gunner buried in the woods somewhere. And maybe there's a practicing dermatologist in this world who knows exactly where to find it.

When I glance at my watch, it's 11:30. Oh, God, it's so late. I have to get home and get some sleep.

I take Step 1 in eight and a half hours.

What a way to spend the last night before the biggest exam of my life.

21.

"This year, we are placing a renewed emphasis on professionalism," Dean Weaver says from the podium at the front of the rotunda.

I shift my weight to get comfortable in my stiff, wooden chair. Beside me, Charlie fiddles with his glasses, wearing a crisp white shirt and tie, his khakis so new they still have creases in them. My entire class, all eighty-nine of us, has assembled here for our first day as third-year medical students. Everyone has dressed in sharp new clothes, ready for the second half of medical school. Finally, we're done with lectures and labs and TBLs. Now we venture into the clinics and hospital wards to see real patients with real diseases.

But first we have to listen to Dean Weaver's speech.

"I don't need to tell this group that we have a major issue with professionalism at this school," she continues. "We have identified one individual who violated the code of conduct by obtaining RAT questions in advance. This person will be repeating a year of school as punishment. But I know there are others who did the same thing and are still at large. Remember what I said last year: anyone who comes forward with information about this will not be punished. But if we learn that you had knowledge of these crimes that you did not disclose, the penalty will be severe and may include expulsion."

Some of my classmates cringe, but I'm barely listening. All I want is for Weaver to finish her speech so I can get my schedule for the upcoming year. I'm dying to know where I'll start my clinical rotations. Will I be sent to inpatient surgery? Or maybe the emergency department? Or could it be the outpatient pediatrics clinic? So many exciting possibilities.

My phone buzzes with a text from Sebastian: *Good luck! Tell me what rotation you get first.*

This reminds me of how far I've come thanks to his guidance. I finished my first two years in the top 10% of my class. I also have five research publications through Murrow's lab and the help of his post-doc, Declan. And perhaps most important of all, I passed Step 1. Sebastian's KGB Anki deck was my salvation. Not only did it get me through the first two years, it also contained an entire block of cards called "Morning Of," which I reviewed just before walking into the Prometric testing center to take the Step 1 exam. Pure fucking gold. It flashed a dozen facts at me that came up in nearly every section of the exam. I have no idea which Russian spies collected that information, but I owe each of them a debt of gratitude, even if they were communists trying to undermine the United States government.

Dean Weaver goes on. "We've also had lots of problems in recent years with professionalism violations during third-year rotations: students skipping teaching conferences, arriving late to rotations, leaving early, and even, in one case, stealing food from a patient's tray. This year, I am putting a stop to all of this. I'm announcing a new online form you must complete: the Professionalism Security Sheet. Each week, you will submit the time you arrived each day, the time you left, and all the conferences you attended. We will share your responses with your supervising attendings. Any disagreement between you and your supervisor will result in an immediate professionalism violation. This will then require a hearing before the academic advancement committee."

Groans and rumbles arise from the room. I shake my head. Such a waste of time. One more stupid survey we have to complete. Filling in the boxes each week will only take time away from my studying. Another example of school getting in the way as I try to learn medicine.

"Why would anyone want to leave their rotation early?" Charlie quietly mutters to me.

A classic Charlie statement. He'd never cut out early from a rotation to study. Charlie does everything by the rules. He passed Step 1 by a single point, a result that would have devastated me but doesn't seem to bother him at all. I, on the other hand, scored in the upper tenth percentile, but I'm still nervous today. Why? Because if I don't excel in the next twelve months, I'll never match in dermatology.

I recall Sebastian's advice: *Remember, you're only halfway through medical school. In third year, you enter a critical new phase as a gunner. Each rotation of third year is one to two months long. At the end of each one, you'll receive an evaluation of your performance. You have to crush these, which means you have to make the supervising attendings love you. This year will be brown nose city for you. Besides the evaluation, you'll take a test on each rotation called a "shelf exam." Don't ask me why they call it that. No one really knows. But the shelf exam plus the evaluation determines your grade. You can earn one of three grades: pass, fail, or honors. To match in dermatology, you have to get honors in as many rotations as possible, ideally all of them. That means for the next year, you must be at the top of your game each day.*

"I wonder if we'll be in the same group," Charlie whispers, pulling me from my thoughts.

Our class is divided into groups of four that cycle through the rotations together. I don't really care who's in my group, so long as it's not Mercer.

"We'll find out whenever Weaver stops talking," I reply.

"When you are at your rotation sites," Weaver proclaims from the podium, "remember that you represent this school. We expect impeccable behavior. Anything less will be dealt with severely."

God, this is going on forever. Will it ever end?

Weaver says, "You may now proceed to the back of the room, where you'll find an envelope with your name. In that envelope is your schedule and the members of your team."

Finally.

Everyone rises from their seats at once, the room shuddering from the movement. I scramble along with my classmates to the back of the rotunda, toward envelopes laid out on a large folding table. As others open their envelopes, the clamor of voices grows louder. Everyone is abuzz with their new schedules and group assignments.

I weave my way between bodies to get to the table. As I search for my name, Charlie taps me on the shoulder.

"We're in the same group!" he says, clutching his open envelope, a wide grin on his face.

"I still haven't found mine," I say, scanning the table. The envelopes are sorted by last name. I need to find the As and I'm standing near the Zs.

"We start with surgery," Charlie says.

I nod in reply as I inch my way toward the other end of the table. Starting with surgery sends a twinge of worry through me. It's notorious as one of the hardest rotations. I guess I'll be diving right into the deep end.

Finally I see my name on a white envelope, which I grab and tear open. It contains a single sheet of paper. At the top is my schedule for third year, which starts with surgery, just like Charlie said. Then I'll rotate through internal medicine, neurology, psychiatry, pediatrics, and Ob/Gyn.

But what I really care about is the other members of my group, the people who'll be with me through the entire year. I already know Charlie's one of them, but who are the other two?

At the bottom of the page, I read the following:

Group K
Sophia Abney
Celia Chalas
Jennifer Mercer
Charlie Phillis

My heart plummets. They put me with Mercer! God, this is going to make my life so much harder. We'll be competing for the good graces of our supervising attendings. Even worse, she could try to make me look bad. There are dozens of ways to undermine a fellow student on a rotation.

A tap on my shoulder pulls me from my thoughts. I turn to see Mercer standing beside me, her golden hair perfectly straight, as if it was just cut. She wears a stylish skirt and crisp white blouse, the entire outfit reeking of money. For once, she doesn't have an H across her chest. Seems odd to see her that way. It's like if Jerome forgot his Burger King shirt at work.

"Just so you know," she says, "I tried to make sure we weren't in the same group."

"Well, it didn't work."

"My father asked the dean, but they wouldn't make any special exceptions."

Mercer can't seem to go one minute without mentioning her father. "I guess he's not as important as you think."

Mercer glowers at me. "Don't get in my way this year. I'll ruin you if you do."

I start to think of a snide comeback, but then reconsider. Talking to Mercer's a waste of time. Now that I know I start with surgery, I can begin organizing my studies to ace the shelf exam at the end of the rotation. That's all that matters: crushing my exams and earning honors in every rotation. I won't let Mercer or anyone else stop me.

I look down at the paper in my hand. I need to arrive at the surgery clinic in one hour for orientation. If I leave right now, I can stop for coffee and do a few Anki cards before then.

"I mean it," Mercer says. "Stay out of my way."

I ignore this and leave the rotunda, heading toward my car outside.

22.

Two weeks later, I say to Mercer, "I'm not leaving."

"Well, one of us has to, and it's not going to be me," she replies.

The two of us stand in the corridor leading to the operating rooms of the hospital. I'm in my blue scrubs, ready to join Dr. Canning on a case from the ER: a splenic laceration in a man hit by a car. But Mercer seems to think it's her case, not mine.

"You did the gallbladder yesterday," Mercer says. The sharp white lights above are like a spotlight on her face. Her blonde hair is back in a bun, but she still wears lipstick and eye shadow. Leave it to Mercer to doll up for the OR when she's dressed in scrubs.

"I went down to the ED to see this case with Canning," I say. "That means I get to scrub in."

Dr. Canning is the site coordinator for our surgery rotation. He's the one who completes our evaluations. A chance to operate with him on an emergency case is pure fucking gold. I'm not letting Mercer take this away from me.

Mercer grabs my arm. "Damn it, Sophia. Get out of here, now."

I yank my arm away from her. Crazy bitch. "I'm not leaving."

The OR doors beside us swing open, and the head nurse emerges. Her name is Georgeanne, a sixty-something woman with gray hair pinned back and large, drooping breasts like bowling bowls in a sock. She scowls at us in a way that seems to make the temperature drop a few degrees.

"Which of you two is doing this case?" she demands.

"I am," Mercer and I say to her in unison.

She narrows her eyes at us and takes a step closer. "Only one student, and if you can't decide, you can both get out of here now."

I look at Mercer, who looks back at me. I'm not backing down. I'd rather both of us get sent away than lose this case to her.

"Well?" Georgeanne says. Her tone implies we have about one more second before she sends us both away. I'm not budging. Either Mercer leaves or we both do.

"Arrh!" Mercer exclaims. Then she turns and stomps away down the hall. I've never felt so happy to see her backside. She's probably going to complain to her father about this, but it doesn't matter. I'm getting the case with Canning.

"Get scrubbed!" Georgeanne commands once Mercer is out of sight.

I turn toward one of the sinks to wash my hands and forearms when I hear someone call, "Sophia!"

Walking down the hall toward me is Dr. Canning. I'm not surprised to hear him call my name. He's taken a liking to me on this rotation—another thing that's been driving Mercer nuts. He calls her "Ms. Mercer" and calls me "Sophia," something I can tell pisses Mercer off. His attention has been wonderful, because Sebastian gave me clear instructions that I need to impress him to earn a grade of honors.

OK, now you're ready for Gunner Rule Number Five: NOTHING MATTERS ON A ROTATION EXCEPT THE ATTENDING. You'll meet a zillion people on rotations: nurses, techs, interns, residents. But only one person matters: the attending. That's who'll complete your evaluation, which needs to be strong. But here's the catch: attendings hate completing evaluations. They get so many of them, not just for med students, but also for nurses, interns, residents, fellows. Not a week goes by that they don't have at least five of these stupid online forms to complete. So when your evaluation comes up, they're going to zip through it at a hundred miles an hour so they can get back to their patients, their kids, cheating on their spouse, playing Candy Crush, whatever. Believe it or not, your future as a dermatologist depends on whether some overwhelmed attending, in a split-second decision, gives you a three out of five or five out of five for questions like, "Does the trainee display sufficient knowledge of medical systems?" But this is the way it is. Bottom line, you have to make a very strong impression that sticks. That way, your attending clicks mostly fours and fives, not threes. Fours and fives lead to dermatology. Threes lead to primary care, emergency medicine, and psychiatry. And you don't want any of that miserable shit.

Dr. Canning walks up to me in his blue scrubs and long white coat. He's tall, with a neatly trimmed goatee. He's handsome for an older man. I'd guess he's in his fifties. The residents say he's an excellent surgeon.

"Will you be scrubbing in on this case?" he asks.

"Absolutely," I say. "I've never seen a splenic laceration."

"Well, when you become a surgical resident, you'll see dozens of these."

At the start of the rotation, I lied and told Canning I'm definitely going into general surgery. From Sebastian: *Rule Number Six: THE ATTENDING'S SPECIALTY IS YOUR SPECIALTY. On every rotation, tell the attending you're going into their specialty. They always pay more attention to students going into their own field. So on pediatrics, you'll love kids. On Ob/Gyn, you'll love the vagina. And on general surgery, say you eat, sleep, and breathe gallbladders and hernias.*

Canning props open the OR door and sticks in his head. Over his shoulder, I see the patient anesthetized on the table, nurses and residents scurrying around him to prepare for the case.

"How long?" Canning asks.

"Five minutes," I hear Georgeanne call back.

Canning lets the OR door swing shut. "Come with me," he says. "We can chat before the case."

I suddenly feel lighter than air. One-on-one time with the site director who'll write my evaluation. I couldn't have wished for a better opportunity to make a strong impression.

I follow Canning down the hall into the surgeon's lounge, a large room with a sink, refrigerator, several sofas, and a television. There's no one here but us. I've never been in this room before. Even the residents don't come in here; it's for attending surgeons only. I feel like I've been escorted into the king's chambers of a castle.

"Here, sit," Canning commands as he slides onto one of the sofas.

I take a seat beside him, still unable to believe I'm getting such precious alone time with the site director.

"Have you thought about what kind of surgeon you'd like to be? Strictly general surgery? Or will you specialize in colorectal or vascular or some other field?"

Luckily, Sebastian prepared me for this very question. *Canning is a general surgeon. He lives for the basic stuff, like appendicitis and hemorrhoids. He gets shit from the specialists who do more complex procedures, like transplants and heart surgery. They treat him like a glorified grease monkey who does the scut work no one else wants to do. That's why he's in charge of the medical students. No transplant surgeon is going to waste time teaching lowly third years how to hold a retractor. That shit falls on Canning. Keep this in mind when you talk with him.*

"I'm definitely going to do general surgery," I reply.

"Oh? I'm surprised. Most of the medical students I meet want to do transplants or hearts or something."

"Oh, no. Not me. I think the scope of the general surgeon is fascinating. I was just reading a paper about advances in hemorrhoidectomy. I think it was in *Diseases of the Colon and Rectum*. It seems the Ferguson has better outcomes than the Milligan-Morgan, according to the recent studies."

Canning's eyes widen. "I wrote that paper!"

"You did? I had no idea. I should have looked at the authors more closely."

"So, you found it interesting, huh?"

"Oh, yes, very interesting. There's just as much science behind hemorrhoids as colon cancer or liver transplants or whatever. It's fascinating stuff."

Canning smiles at me and slides a few inches closer on the couch. "We get so few women interested in general surgery, you know. It's nice to see a young, attractive female like you taking a liking to the field."

Young, attractive female? Dr. Canning just flirted with me. Sebastian warned me the male attendings would ogle my body and maybe even hit on me. He said I could use this to my advantage.

They'll stay away from Mercer, since her dad is the chief of neurosurgery. And you're much better looking than Celia. Of the three women on your rotation, you should draw the most attention from the Y chromosomes. Use that to your advantage. Don't wear a T-shirt under your scrub top. That way, you'll show a little cleavage at the V neck. Also, wear a pink bra in case it peeks out on your shoulders. Those colored straps attract male attendings like flies.

Before I can reply to Canning, the lounge door opens, and Georgeanne pops in her head. "We're almost ready," she says. "But his pressure is low. You should probably get in there now."

"Did he get the two units?" Canning asks.

"Second one's almost done now," she replies.

"Alright," he says. "I'll be right there."

Georgeanne pauses and gives him a look. She seems unhappy he's not jumping up to follow her into the OR. The patient, George Flores, is a forty-two-year-old man who was struck by a car while crossing the street. He has a pelvic fracture and collapsed lung, in addition to his splenic laceration. He arrived in the emergency department unconscious and was placed on a respirator. When the CT scan showed bleeding from his spleen, they took him to the OR. He's quasi-stable, meaning his blood pressure isn't plummeting and his oxygen levels are normal. But he's still losing blood internally. It seems risky for Canning to sit around the lounge when the head nurse wants him in the OR.

"Where are you from, Sophia?" Canning asks once Georgeanne has left us alone again. He seems totally unconcerned with his patient's bleeding spleen down the hall. "Tell me more about yourself."

"I grew up right here in the city. On Riggs Avenue. It's on the south side."

Canning places his hand on my thigh. "A city girl, huh? We don't get a lot of those around here. Seems all the other students are from the suburbs."

I'm in a delicate spot. I'm certain Canning is hitting on me, which is gross—he's married with two kids. But I need to hold his interest so I get a strong evaluation. I also don't want him making a move on me. Then I'll have to push him away, and he might get angry. I'm walking a tightrope.

Georgeanne sticks her head in the lounge door again. "You need to come now," she says. "His pressure's dropping."

Canning narrows his eyes at her. "I'll be right there, damn it. Tell anesthesia to handle it for just a second more."

Georgeanne looks at his hand on my thigh. She sighs and rolls her eyes. Canning has clearly done this sort of thing before.

When she's out of the room, Canning slides even closer. "Sophia, this may seem a little forward, but I wonder if you'd like to meet for a drink this evening? We can talk more about your future career as a surgeon."

Shit. This is what I was afraid of. He's making an official pass. Luckily, I planned for this.

"I'd love that," I say. A total lie. I'll email him later that some emergency came up and I can't have a drink. Then I'll flirt with him each day in the hospital and keep making excuses about after-work encounters. Once I get my evaluation, I'll ghost him completely.

"Terrific," he replies. "We can meet at—"

The overhead speakers suddenly blare: "Code Blue, OR Room Four. Code Blue, OR Room Four."

"Shit," he says, leaping to his feet. My body tenses. OR Room 4 is where Mr. Flores lies unconscious, awaiting surgery. I race behind Canning from the surgeon's lounge.

Seconds later, we burst through the doors to OR Room 4, where Mr. Flores lies on the operating table, unconscious beneath a drape. At least a dozen people have gathered around him, some calling out orders, others rushing to grab equipment. The anesthesiologist, a tiny woman in blue scrubs, has mounted Mr. Flores's legs on the table as she administers chest compressions. I glance at the screen in the corner. The heart rhythm shows a flat line.

"He's bleeding out," Canning says. He looks at the anesthesiologist. "Get off the table, now! We've got to open him up."

"Oh, now you want to help," the anesthesiologist replies. "Where have you been, Sam?"

Canning grabs a surgical gown and thrusts it over his body. To the anesthesiologist, he says, "Jeanine, so help me, I will shove you off the patient if you don't get down right now."

At this, she hops from her straddle of Mr. Flores, resuming her chest compressions from the side of the table with the help of a small stool one of the nurses has placed on the floor.

In a flash, Canning has on a mask and gloves. He's changed his outfit like Superman in a phone booth. As chest compressions continue from the side of the operating table, others in the room stand back to let Canning near the abdomen. I slide into a corner to watch, not wanting to get in anyone's way.

Canning calls for a specific type of scalpel. I don't understand the terminology, but the nurses do, and in an instant, they hand him a tool. With expert quickness, he slices open Mr. Tores's abdomen. At the same time, he calls out for doses of epinephrine to be administered. One of the surgical residents retracts the skin, and soon Canning shoves his hands deep inside the belly.

"He's still flatlining," someone calls out as chest compressions continue.

"Give him more blood," Canning says as he moves his hands around the abdomen.

"Fourth unit going in," Georgeanne announces loudly to the room.

Surrounding her, a dozen onlookers watch in hushed silence as Canning works.

Canning calls for more tools. I can't see what he's doing exactly, but he appears to be severing something in the abdomen. Seconds later, a large, globular structure emerges from Mr. Tores in his hands. It's the spleen, its surface a dusky color, with blood spattered everywhere.

Canning plops the organ into a tray held by one of the nurses. Then he reaches back into the abdomen, his hands again moving with expert quickness. The surgical resident brings sutures, and moments later I see Canning tying knots.

"Bleeding's stopped," he says to the room as he continues twisting sutures around his fingers.

I glance up at the monitor. The flat line changes to show the blip of a single heartbeat. Then it returns to a flat line for a few seconds, but then another blip appears. Soon, a series of rapid blips stream across the screen in neon blue.

"He's got a pulse," Georgeanne says, her hands under the drape.

"Stopping compressions," the anesthesiologist calls out, stepping back from the patient.

A second later, the blood pressure reading on the monitor changes to 94/66.

Several others in the room let out audible sighs. I'm in awe of Canning. I don't think he even broke a sweat. Soon he has the abdominal incision sewn up. The wound is covered in a bandage by Georgeanne. Moments later, Canning removes his gloves and gown. Some of those who'd gathered for the Code Blue filter out of the room. All that remain are Canning, Georgeanne, myself, and a few others.

"Well, that was exciting," Canning says, walking toward me.

I vibrate with nervous energy. It's hard to find words. "Er . . . yes. Um, amazing."

"So, anyway," he says. "I've got a professionalism committee meeting at four, but we can meet right after that for a drink. Where would you like to go?"

23.

A MONTH LATER, I SIT in the dermatology residents' room, a narrow space near the clinic with a table and computers. There's no one here but me as I wait for Julia, one of the residents. I'm on my one-week elective rotation between surgery and medicine. We're allowed to choose any specialty we like for this week. Of course, I selected dermatology.

To pass the time while I wait, I decide to listen to the voicemail Dr. Canning left on my phone earlier this morning. I've been avoiding it for hours, but I suppose I should hear what it says.

Hi, Sophia. It's Sam. Uh, I'm not sure if you've gotten my messages or not, but I've been trying to get in touch with you. I still really want to take you for that drink. Look, I'll be totally honest here. I mean, cards on the table, okay? You're an extremely attractive woman. I feel this . . . lust when I think about you. I just can't get you out of my mind. My wife is . . . well, let's just say things aren't good. We're going to separate soon and then get a divorce. But I think you and I . . . we could really have something special. So, please, call me back. You can call me anytime, day or night. Doesn't matter. Hope to hear from you soon.

Gross. Now that my surgery rotation is over and I've received honors, I want nothing to do with him. I select his voicemail on my phone, then tap Block this Caller. Hopefully I never run into him again.

That's when the door to the residents' room swings open and Julia sticks her head inside.

"Are you coming?" she asks.

I hop to my feet and scurry from the room, following her down the hall. I've been assigned to the mole clinic here in the outpatient pavilion. I wanted the melanoma clinic, but they couldn't accommodate a student this week. But at least I'm not in Mercer's shoes. She was assigned to the blisters and pus clinic. I'll take moles over that any day.

Julia stops outside room four. She's a second-year dermatology resident, probably about thirty years old with a pretty face and long, dark hair. Her most striking feature is the enormous rock of a diamond on her left hand. According to Sebastian, she's married to a cardiology fellow. Their combined salaries in the future could be close to a million a year. As Sebastian put it, "Skin rashes plus dying hearts equals serious cash."

Before entering the room of our next patient, Julia says to me, "This guy is seventy-five years old. He has some SKs we're watching, but none of them look too bad."

SKs are seborrheic keratoses, common skin lesions in older people. They're benign, but must be distinguished from similar-looking lesions that are cancerous. Not exactly a thrilling case, but this is the mole clinic, so I don't expect much.

"Just stay behind me and keep quiet," Julia says as she opens the door.

This seems to be her mantra today; she's said it to me about a dozen times. I'd hoped this week would give me some face time with the dermatology attendings. I'll need recommendations from them when I apply to residencies. But mostly I've been following around the derm residents, like Julia. I've hardly spoken to the attendings at all. I wish Sebastian were here to make introductions, but he's assigned to a different clinic across town this week.

Even worse, I learned yesterday that Mercer is writing a case report with one of the derm faculty. Earlier this week, she and her attending saw a baby with a super-rare skin condition, Harlequin ichthyosis (which, I have since learned, has nothing to do with romance novels). Mercer plans to publish a case report about the baby in the *Journal of Newborn Rashes*, then present it as a poster at the regional derm conference in two months. This generates *three* publication credits from a single case: one for the journal article, one for the poster, and one for the abstract book at the conference. Med students call this the "Triple Crown." It's a legendary accomplishment, basically like winning the Nobel prize for gunners. I am so fucking jealous.

"How *are you*, Mr. Cohen?" Julia proclaims as she enters the room, her tone sugary sweet.

Mr. Cohen nods at her from the exam table, wearing only his tighty-whities. All the patients in mole clinic strip to their underwear so we can easily examine their skin. A balding, elderly man with a belly like a glob of Jell-O, Mr. Cohen has dozens of SKs over his hairless chest. They're dark spots, some waxy, some with scales like a lizard. I pray to God I never get these things later in life. They're nasty. And they're useless to me. I'm not going to win a Triple Crown from an old man with a bunch of boring SKs.

"So, how have you been?" Julia asks.

She doesn't introduce me, which is no surprise. She hasn't introduced me to a single patient this morning. I am literally her shadow, a nebulous form that floats behind her, unacknowledged.

Julia chats with Mr. Cohen for a few moments, then examines the multitudinous lesions on his skin. I peer over her shoulder trying to get a closer look.

Mr. Cohen clears his throat a few times. "Uh, nurse," he says to me. "Could you get me some water, please?"

Nurse? Seriously? I was called "nurse" dozens of times in the hospital during my surgery rotation, but then I was dressed in scrubs. Today, I'm wearing a fitted blouse and skirt with my white coat. You'd think that might send a message, but it doesn't.

Julia asks me to get Mr. Cohen a cup of water from the kitchen down the hall. Just terrific. She doesn't introduce me, doesn't correct Cohen when he calls me nurse, and now I'm sent for water like a waitress. This one-week rotation isn't turning out the way I'd hoped.

Moments later, I return to Mr. Cohen with his drink. Soon, Julia leaves the room, with me following behind. We walk to the conference room down the hall, a large space with huge windows looking down onto the city.

Seated at the conference room table is Dr. Lillian Allen, an elegant woman in her fifties who is the program director for the dermatology residency. Since Julia is a resident, she must present Mr. Cohen's findings to an attending dermatologist like Allen.

It's nearly impossible for me to avoid gawking at Dr. Allen's beautiful skin. I cannot identify a single blemish on her complexion, a porcelain canvas that defies the ravages of time itself. Surrounded by glossy, chestnut hair, and centered with two sparkling blue eyes, her face practically shimmers in the light. It's no secret that she devotes herself to the art of skincare, like da Vinci to the Sistine Chapel. Her daily facial regimen is legendary among the dermatology residents, described as "worthy of the Gods." I don't completely understand all the things she does, but it involves chemical peels, laser therapy, and microdermabrasion plus infinite creams and hydrating lotions. They say she spends an hour a day on her eyelids alone.

Dr. Allen raises her majestic eyes from her laptop computer on the conference table when Julia approaches. Just being in Dr. Allen's presence gives me star-struck shivers. She's the person who decides which medical students to take into the derm program here. There's no one more important to impress, yet I've barely spoken a word to her all morning.

I try to pay attention as Julia presents Mr. Cohen's case, but my mind wanders. It's so boring to stand around watching with no important role to play. What I need is a chance to present a case of my own to Dr. Allen, but that seems unlikely to happen.

Suddenly, Julia's phone buzzes from the pocket of her white coat. "It's the nursery," she says to Dr. Allen. "I'm sorry, but I need to take this."

Allen nods, and Julia answers the call. I hear murmurs from the phone. Then Julia says, "When?" and "Okay" and "I'll be right down."

"My daughter fell," she says to Allen after ending the call. "She's downstairs in daycare. I just need to run down for a minute, if that's alright. I'll be right back."

Allen agrees to the request, and Julia dashes away. I suddenly find myself alone in the conference room with the prestigious Dr. Lillian Allen. This is the chance of a lifetime.

I muster all the courage I can find. "Uh, Dr. Allen, can I ask you a question about Mr. Cohen's case?"

Allen looks up from her laptop. "Of course. Here, sit down."

Sebastian told me Dr. Allen is very nice, so I'm not afraid of her. I just don't want to say anything dumb. I have only a few precious moments to make a good impression. My future in dermatology may hinge on what I do next. Medicine is a crazy field.

I slide into a seat at the table. "How do you decide when to biopsy an SK?" I ask.

Allen launches into a long explanation of the criteria used to distinguish benign from malignant skin lesions. I focus my eyes on her thoughtfully, but it's hard to pay attention because I'm so overjoyed that she took my question seriously. We're discussing dermatology like two practicing physicians. My mind spins to think of a follow-up question, one that'll make me look even more perceptive and bright.

When Allen stops talking, she says, "Tell you what. While Julia's gone, I'll go finish up with Mr. Cohen. Why don't you see the next patient yourself and present to me?"

I sit perfectly still, but inside I'm jumping for joy. I have to consciously suppress an urge to pump my fist. This is a golden opportunity.

I agree to Allen's wonderful offer—who wouldn't?—and she glides from the room to see Mr. Cohen. I quickly sit before a computer in the corner and open the clinic list in the electronic medical record. The next patient is Arthur Hickey, a seventeen-year-old kid with acne. It's strange that he's in the mole clinic, but then I read in one of the notes that he's the nephew of Dr. Allen. He requested an urgent visit and was scheduled for today. I can't believe my luck. A family member of Dr. Allen? I'll make this kid love me so much, he'll sing my praises to Allen at every summer barbecue.

Moments later, I enter a room where Arthur Hickey sits on the exam table, wearing only his boxers. He's a lanky teenager with toothpick arms and legs. His face is covered in acne.

"Hello, Arthur," I say. "I'm Sophia, a medical student. Dr. Allen asked me to come talk to you today."

Arthur stares at my breasts, then catches himself and looks up at me. "Oh, uh, hello," he says. He keeps darting his eyes from me. He seems nervous to be in the presence of a woman. I guess if I had to strip down to my underwear at seventeen for a man, I'd be nervous, too.

"It's my acne," he says. "It's exploded in the last week. You have to do something."

The skin of his face has lesions everywhere, some bursting with pus. It's gnarly stuff.

"Do you mind if I take a closer look?" I say.

Arthur darts his eyes at me, then looks away. "Sure . . . sure. It's fine."

I walk closer and lean in, carefully examining his left cheek. In my mind, I try to come up with the perfect way to describe his skin to Dr. Allen. My future in dermatology may depend on the words I choose to characterize zits in this seventeen-year-old kid.

Suddenly, Arthur raises his hand and grabs my breast, giving it a firm squeeze near my nipple.

I push his arm away and step back.

"Aw, shit," he says. "Shit, shit, shit. I didn't mean to do that."

"What do you mean, you didn't mean to do that? You just felt me up."

I glance down at his boxers, where he has an erection, his engorged penis poking out from the flap like a soldier at attention. This can't really be happening. I've aroused this kid simply by standing near him. Arthur sees me looking at his crotch and glances down. Then he quickly tucks his erection into the waistband of his underwear.

Of all the things I thought might happen today, this was nowhere on my list.

Arthur looks at me with a pleading expression. "Please, please don't say anything. My mom will kill me. You don't understand. I can't help myself. Last week with my piano teacher, I did the same thing. My mom . . . she thinks I'm a deviant. She's trying to get me a therapist. But she'll flip if she hears about this. You can't say anything."

Arthur's mom is right: this kid is a deviant, and he does need a therapist. But my problem is deciding how to handle this with Allen. My first thought is to tell Arthur it's no big deal and say nothing. He's Allen's nephew, after all. The last thing I want to do is get in the middle of family dynamics around Arthur's libido.

But then I see an opportunity.

"I'll tell you what, Arthur, I won't say a word about this—"

"Oh, thank you, thank you, thank you. I'm really sorry. I don't get close to girls much, you see. It was just so hard to resist with you standing right beside me."

"But here's the deal," I say. "I need something in return."

"Oh, anything, anything."

"When I come back in here with Dr. Allen in a minute, I want you to tell her that I'm the nicest, kindest, smartest person you've ever met in health care. You tell her I have a great bedside manner. You say I was professional when I examined your skin. And you also tell her that I put you at ease about your acne by telling you we have lots of treatments. Make her think I'm the best medical student on the planet."

Arthur takes only a nanosecond to consider this. "Sure, sure. I'll do anything you want. Just don't tell my mom."

Moments later, I'm back in the conference room, presenting Arthur's findings to Dr. Allen. I carefully choose my words, trying to sound as dermatological as possible. I manage to work in fancy terms like "acne vulgaris," "erythematous base," "sebaceous glands," "follicular," and "papules." I'm very proud of myself. I sound like a seasoned dermatologist. The words roll off my tongue like poetry.

Dr. Allen takes notes as I speak, and I hope she's writing something like, "this kid is great," although she's probably not. When I finish, she goes over the management of acne with me, speaking as if I'm a derm resident already. It's awesome.

We return to see Arthur, whose erection, thankfully, has resolved. From the exam table in his boxers, he delivers an outstanding endorsement of me to Allen, even saying, "You should make her a resident here; she's phenomenal." He may be an awkward teenager with unchecked hormones, but the kid gives one hell of a performance when properly motivated. Who would have thought zits and a horny teenager could be the key to a residency spot in the coveted State Medical derm program?

When we leave his room, Allen says to me, "Oh, one more thing, Sophia." I'm floating on air. I didn't think she knew my name. "I'm having a dinner for the residents at my home in two weeks. I'd like you to come."

I blink a few times. I can hardly believe what I just heard. A dinner in Dr. Allen's home! This morning, I wasn't sure she knew my name. Now I'm her dinner guest. Mercer is going to shit her pants when she hears about this.

"Oh, of course. I'd love to come. Thank you for inviting me."

"Well, I like to get to know the students applying in derm. I've also invited Jennifer Mercer. I told her about it yesterday. You can get my address from her. Dinner's on

Thursday the twelfth at six o'clock. You two can carpool if you'd like."

I feel like I've been punched in the gut. I thought I was getting a special invitation as appreciation for my performance with Arthur. I gave him a pass for groping me, after all. Surely that deserves a reward. But this is a routine invitation, something she probably does every year for students going into derm. I'll be stuck with Mercer all night. I wonder if Mercer and I will be seated at a separate little table, like children at Thanksgiving.

Suddenly, Julia appears. "I'm back," she says. "Nothing serious. My daughter just got a little bump on the head."

Allen nods and heads toward the conference room. My opportunity to impress her is over. Whether or not I match in dermatology may depend entirely on my presentation of a single patient, Arthur Hickey, a pimple-faced seventeen-year-old who fondles random tits. Now I'm back to being Julia's shadow.

"Come on," Julia says to me. "Let's see the next patient. Just stay behind me and keep quiet."

24.

THAT AFTERNOON WHEN I OPEN the door to the dermatopathology lab, Julia says, "Oh, finally. Did you get the diapers?"

I lumber into the room, balancing a tray of Starbucks drinks in one hand, a CVS bag with diapers in the other. Julia watches me from her seat in front of a microscope. Next to her are two other derm residents, a lanky guy named Oliver and a short woman named Loryn. None of them gets up to help me.

I plop the drinks down on the table next to Julia's microscope. "They didn't have strawberry," I say to her. "So I had to get you vanilla."

She takes a drink out of the carrying tray. "Ugh, fine. I'll let it slide since you got me the diapers."

Oliver and Loryn grab their drinks and take sips. No one says "Thank you," even though I just walked two blocks to Starbucks, then another block to CVS for the diapers that Julia's daughter needs. Sebastian warned me that the residents treat medical students like errand monkeys. I basically have to do whatever they ask. A good word from them to Dr. Allen could get me a spot in dermatology. A bad word and I'm finished. It's not like I'm going to refuse a drink run when $437,000 a year is at stake. Honestly, if they asked me to wash their cars and massage their feet, I probably would.

I set the diapers down next to Julia, then walk to the corner of the dermatopathology lab, a small room with a dozen microscopes used to examine skin biopsies. Julia, Oliver, and Loryn have a stack of specimens to go through from actual clinic patients. In a half hour, one of the attendings will arrive to review their slides and generate a formal path report, one of the precious "documents" Sebastian says drive the medicine world.

I, on the other hand, have been assigned to read through a book called *Skin Microscopy Atlas*. It's 500 pages and weighs about eight pounds. I'm supposed to read as many chapters as I can before the attending arrives.

"He's so skeevy," Julia says to the others, apparently continuing a conversation that began before I entered the room.

I slide into a chair and listen. I'm not interested in reading through the skin atlas at all. It's not like it will help me get into dermatology.

NOTHING MATTERS ON A ROTATION EXCEPT THE ATTENDING.

Loryn says to Julia, "You know Dawn? The medical assistant who works Mondays and Thursdays? She went on a date with him. He tried to maul her in his car. It was date-rapey. She had to shove him away and run into her apartment."

"What?!" Oliver replies. "Did she report him?"

Loryn shakes her head. "She should have. But he's a resident, and she's a lowly MA. She didn't want to risk her job."

"Unreal," Oliver adds. "Jenny at the front desk said he asked her out. She's married, of course. But he said she should leave her husband for him because he's going to make millions when he finishes residency."

I try to decipher the conversation. Clearly, some resident in dermatology assaults women and tries to break up marriages. It occurs to me they may be talking about Sebastian, a thought that makes my stomach clench.

"They never should have taken a single resident," Loryn says after sipping her drink. "He's the only one of us not married. With so many applicants, why take someone who's just going to hit on the nurses and assistants?"

"There are plenty of single people I know who behave themselves," Julia says. "The problem is not his marital status. It's his wandering eyes and hands."

The residents then become quiet as they each peer into a microscope at biopsy specimens. I'm dying to know if they were talking about Sebastian.

He tried to maul her in his car.

It was date-rapey.

She had to shove him away and run into her apartment.

Could these comments be in reference to the man I've been sleeping with? Believe it or not, I know very little about Miles Sebastian. He's given me school advice over the past two years, of course. And we've had sex about a dozen times. But because I've said "No" to a serious relationship, he roams the world outside my view, doing whatever he wants. For all I know, he could be selling drugs or working for the mob. He certainly could hit on the staff in derm clinic without my knowledge.

I find myself torn over what to do. I could ask the residents if they were talking about Sebastian, but then I'd have to reveal that I know him. If he's the "skeevy" one

Julia's referring to, they might think less of me for associating with him. But if I say nothing, I'll forever wonder if Sebastian is the date-rapey, marriage-busting resident of today's conversation.

I decide that I have to know.

"Um, were you guys just talking about Miles Sebastian?" I ask.

The three residents turn from their microscopes to look at me. "Do you know him?" Loryn asks. "Has he mauled you, too?"

You could say Sebastian actually has mauled me during sex, but I'm not about to admit that.

"He went to the same college as me," I say.

"You went to Brown?" Julia asks.

"No, Midtown College."

The three residents laugh. "Sebastian did not go to Midtown College. Where did you hear that?"

The hairs on my neck stand up. Did Sebastian lie to me?

"Oh, er, maybe I'm mixing him up with someone else, then," I reply, trying to save face. I don't want to admit that I fell for a lie from Sebastian.

"It's hard to confuse him with anyone else," Loryn says. "He hits on anything with a pulse and breasts. He also assaulted a woman in med school. She's the younger sister of a friend of mine. When she tried to break up with him, he pushed her down on the couch. She kicked him in the balls and ran out of his apartment. Honestly, I'm amazed he matched here."

My heart pounds. This is the same thing Dean Weaver told me when she warned me to stay away from Sebastian.

"Dr. Allen had to sit him down last month," Oliver adds. "The nurses complained about him making sexual comments in clinic. He could get kicked out if he doesn't stop."

A cold shudder runs through me.

Dr. Allen had to sit him down last month.

I've been planning to ask Sebastian to put in a good word for me with Dr. Allen. But that's totally off the table if he's a problem resident. It's bad enough that Sebastian is a creep with women, but it's much, much worse if he has a reputation that could ruin me with the program director for dermatology.

It occurs to me that I've been a fool to sleep with a man I hardly know. He's helped me get through school, something I'll always be grateful for. But if he's a threat to my derm career, I can't be seen with him anymore.

That's when I remember that he texted me this morning.

When the residents return to their microscopes, I tap at my phone to pull up Sebastian's message from earlier today: *see u tonight?*

Then I see my reply: *yes, of course.*

I can't do that now. In fact, I can never be seen with Sebastian again if I want to match in dermatology.

Quickly, I compose a text to Sebastian: *Something came up. Can't make it tonight.*

I press send. I may not be able to avoid him forever. But I'm going to have to try.

25.

On the last day of my elective week, I have to leave my dermatology rotation to attend a mandatory clinical skills assessment, a painful requirement for all third-year students. It's one o'clock in the afternoon and I'd rather be with the derm residents seeing rashes and boils, but instead I'm in a narrow waiting room at the medical school. I sit with the others in my group, all of us in our white coats with stethoscopes slung around our necks: Charlie, Celia, and, of course, Mercer, who's still angry at me for taking the splenic laceration case with Dr. Canning three weeks ago. Shortly, we'll be instructed to march outside to the examination rooms down the hallway. In one of these, I will interview and examine a "standardized patient" or SP—a person recruited from the community and trained to act as a patient with a medical problem. Based on how I conduct the interview and physical exam, my performance with the SP will be assigned a grade.

I didn't always hate these exercises like I do now. As a first year, I loved clinical skills. I needed practice with fake patients before I ventured into the world of true illness.

But now, as a third year, it *pains* me to attend this clinical skills session because I miss an afternoon of chances to impress, sway, or otherwise schmooze the dermatology attendings. And I can't use this time to my advantage. The assessment is pass-fail—there are no honors awarded in clinical skills, no way to perform that increases my chances of matching in dermatology. And besides, I know how to interview and examine patients. I've already been doing it for months as a third year.

My group thumbs through the manila folders we were handed moments ago, reading about the SPs we'll soon meet.

"I got a lady with shortness of breath," Charlie says. "Could be something serious."

"I got an old man with constipation," Celia chimes in. "Ugh. Just kill me now."

Mercer says nothing as she studies her patient folder in silence.

I open the manila folder in my lap and read about M. Smith. His name is not M. Smith, of course. The SPs are given fake names, fake illnesses, and fake symptoms. They use a script to describe their medical problems, then assess us with a checklist of things we're supposed to ask and do. It's really a game. I have twenty minutes to ask as many questions as I can, and examine as many body parts as possible, hoping I hit every item on the checklist. Forget to ask about loose stools? Lose a point. Forget to examine the armpits? Minus another point. The almighty checklist determines who passes and fails.

From the information in my folder I learn that M. Smith came to clinic today with a complaint of erectile dysfunction. I groan to myself as I read this. Why couldn't I get shortness of breath like Charlie? I can't wait until I'm a dermatologist. Then I'll never have to work up the many problems of the male equipment again. Good riddance to erectile dysfunction, delayed ejaculation, or swollen testicles once and for all.

My goal today is simply to pass, even if I just squeak by. If M. Smith fails me, I have to attend enhancement sessions then repeat today's exercise with another SP. That means time away from my rotations and less chance to impress attendings. No fucking way am I letting that happen.

Finally, we're told the SPs are ready for us. We file out of the waiting room into the hallway. Moments later, I knock on the door to room three and hear, "Come in."

I swing open the door to see a figure I recognize immediately and my heart plunges. It's Miles Douglas, a guy who graduated ahead of me in high school. He lives a few blocks from me in the city. Sitting on the exam table, he stares at me wearing a gown and boxers.

Three years ago just before I started medical school, Miles and I dated briefly. He took me to dinner once and a movie another time. I kissed him, but I wasn't interested in a relationship. I don't like to lead men on, so I told him on the phone how I felt. He got angry and ended the call. I haven't spoken to him since.

I consider aborting this assessment because of my history with Miles. I could walk out to tell our instructor that Miles and I know each other. I won't be expected to discuss erectile dysfunction with an old boyfriend.

But then my session today will be canceled. All the other SPs are with my fellow group members right now, and once my group finishes, the SPs will be seen by other groups throughout the afternoon. I'd probably have to come back another day meaning time away from my next rotation. That would suck.

But then I think: Maybe it will be fine? He's being paid $25 an hour to act like a patient. Maybe he'll just do his job. And our brief romance—if you can even call it that—was years ago. He's probably moved on. Besides, he's got a script to follow. He'll probably just answer my questions as he's been told.

I decide to stay.

"Hello, Mr. Smith," I say with a smile. I could acknowledge that we know each other, but that might get weird, so I elect to simply act as if we're strangers. "My name is Sophia. I'm a medical student here to meet with you today."

Miles nods his head, seeming a little surprised I played my part without mentioning we know each other. He pauses briefly then says, "Nice to meet you." Apparently, he's going to play along.

I wash my hands which is always one of the checklist items, then pull out a chair and slide it before his perch on the exam table. He looks just as I remember him. He's clean shaven with thick black hair. He has broad shoulders—I think he played football back in high school. I again notice he's wearing only boxers under his gown. We were told not to do genital and rectal exams today—those require special SPs who get an extra $10 an hour, a bonus we call "probing pay." Thank God for that. No way would I *ever*, not in a million years, examine the testicles of someone I used to date.

I open with a bunch of questions we're required to ask as part of the checklist: "How do you prefer to be addressed?" "Can you confirm your name and date of birth?" I've never, not *once*, seen a real physician say these things to a patient, but clinical skills assessments are not reality.

"So, what brings you in today?" I ask.

Miles clears his throat. He looks at me, then lowers his

gaze to the floor. "Uh, er, I've been having some problems in the bedroom with my wife."

Oh, God, this is going to be super awkward. Maybe I should break character and ask for another SP? But I'm twenty minutes away from getting this exercise behind me. I've got to push through.

"I see. Can you tell me more?"

I actually feel bad making Miles tell me about his penis glitching during sex. It's going to be difficult for him to talk about this with me. I don't know what's written in his script, but I hope he memorized it cold because improvised answers wouldn't be easy.

Miles keeps his gaze pegged to the floor, unable to make eye contact while he answers my questions. "I'm able to get an erection, but I can't maintain it during sex." He speaks the words robotically, clearly reciting his script.

I shift in my seat. This conversation is so uncomfortable. "And how long has this been going on for?"

Miles fidgets on the exam table as he manages to eke out an answer. Then I ask for dozens more super embarrassing details of his fictitious sexual dysfunction. I don't know how we manage, but Miles and I somehow get through questions about bloody ejaculation, masturbation, and whether or not he can penetrate his make-believe wife, Mrs. Smith. After each one, I think how stupid I was to do this. I should have asked for a different SP no matter the consequences.

Finally, I complete my interview and move on to the physical examination. This part is actually okay since I stand next to Miles with no eye contact. As I listen to his lungs, I admire his muscular shoulders, then silently chastise myself for checking him out when he's playing a patient. I drift back to our brief relationship. The problem wasn't his looks. He told his mother *everything* I said to him on our dates. He even told her we kissed. Momma is friends with his mother so I heard about it all. I didn't want a boyfriend who shares my every word with his mother. It felt weird.

I complete my examination then leave the room. Once I get outside and shut the door, I fall back against the wall, place a hand on my chest and let out a breath.

Thank God that's over.

I return to the waiting room where the others in my group slowly file in once they've finished with their SP. After a few moments, we're instructed to return to our SPs to receive feedback on the interviews and examinations we conducted.

Seconds later, I shut the door to room three behind me and take a seat in a chair by a small counter near the sink. Miles, now changed into jeans and a sweatshirt, sits beside me holding an evaluation form in his hand.

"Hi, Miles," I say.

"So, you do remember me?"

"Of course I remember you."

"Well, you didn't say anything when you walked in. I thought maybe you'd forgotten who I was."

"I was just playing my part. That's all."

Miles nods. "Alright. Well, how do you think you did in our session?"

The SPs always open with this question. It's part of their training. I hate it because it's a formality. All I want is to know that I passed.

"I thought it went fine," I say. A bland answer just to keep things moving forward.

"Well, let's look at the evaluation form together."

I can't believe Miles Douglas is evaluating me. Momma told me he got fired from his job at Jiffy Lube for smoking weed in the bathroom. Where do they find these SPs anyway?

Miles pushes the first page of the evaluation form toward me. It lists clinical questions I was supposed to ask, like things about his erectile dysfunction plus other clinical items like "History of HIV?" and "Any fevers?" and "Loss of appetite?" The box is checked next to nearly all of them. No surprise there. I *know* how to evaluate patients.

"You did pretty well with all of these," he says. Then he flips to the second page of the form. It's titled "Interpersonal skills."

"But you need some work in this area," he says.

Nearly every box is unchecked. My jaw drops. He's taken off enough points to make me fail! I scan the questions. "Did the student put you at ease?" "Did the student make enough eye contact?" "Did the student listen as you spoke?" Every one is totally subjective.

We've been told never to argue with the SPs. If we disagree with their evaluation, we're supposed to appeal to the clinical skills director, not squabble directly with the fake patients.

But, God damn it, I know Miles did this to get back at me for dumping his ass.

I tap the evaluation form. "This is wrong. You know how hard it is to ask someone I used to date about his penis? But I was professional, polite. And no eye contact? That was you! You couldn't look at me once, you were so nervous."

I see a slight smile crack at the corner of Miles's lips. This is exactly what he wanted. Damn it! I should have walked out. He's going to get even with me for dumping him by failing me in clinical skills.

"Sophia," he says in a condescending tone, "I do this job every week. Compared to other students, you really need to work on your interpersonal skills."

His words make me so angry, I clench my fists, holding back the urge to punch that smirk off his face. "Every week? You were working at Jiffy Lube not six months ago. My momma talks to your mother all the time, you know? They've been friends forever."

Miles shows no reaction, still smiling his creepy smile. He's loving this, absolutely loving this.

"Would you like to *calmly* discuss this? I can give you some feedback on how to improve your bedside skills with patients. That is, if you can handle it."

I want to punch him in the nuts so he actually does get erectile dysfunction, but all I can do is take his shit. I'm going to have to tell our instructor that Miles and I know each other. Hopefully, they'll let me repeat this evaluation without going through enhancement sessions. But they might think I'm complaining just because I got a bad evaluation. Oh, God, what if they *do* make me go through enhancement. I could miss days and days of my next rotation. Mercer will fawn over the attendings in my absence. This could cost me honors. This could cost me dermatology!

"Miles, stop it," I demand. "You're doing this because I wouldn't keep dating you."

He scrunches his face at me. "Pfft. That's ridiculous."

"How stupid do you think I am? This is not my first time in clinical skills. No SP has ever trashed me like this."

He shrugs. "Take that up with the director if you want. This is my evaluation and I'm not changing it."

"I could get you fired for this. I'll tell them you trashed me to get even."

"Oh, yeah? First question they're gonna ask is: why didn't you stop the session right away when you recognized me?"

Shit. He's right. If I rat him out it could get messy. My mind races for an escape from this mess. Miles looks so pleased with himself. I'm tense with anger. How the hell can I let this mama's boy sabotage my career?

That's when I get an idea. It's a bold move but it's all I can think of.

I reach into the pocket of my white coat and slide out my phone.

"What are you doing?" Miles asks.

I tap the screen, turn on the speaker, and listen as the phone trills. I pray that this idea works.

Miles suddenly looks worried. "Who are you calling?"

"Hello?" I hear Momma's voice say.

"It's me," I reply, my eyes fixed on Miles. "You remember Miles Douglas? A boy I went on a few dates a while back?"

"Yeah. Lilly's son. Why?"

Miles swats at my hand, but I yank it away. "What are you doing?" he demands. "Put that phone down."

"Who's that?" Momma asks.

"It's Miles," I say into the phone. "I'm here with him now. He got a job at the med school. He's trying to make sure I fail a test."

"What!" Momma exclaims. "I thought he wasn't working. Lilly said he hardly leaves the basement since they fired him at Jiffy Lube."

"Well, he got a job here somehow."

"Doing what?"

"He has to pretend he has erectile dysfunction, like a patient for us students."

Cackling laughter comes over the phone. Miles looks furious. He rises from his chair, placing his hands on his hips. "End that call now, Sophia. You end it, damn it."

Now he looks like *he* wants to punch me. But all he can do is stand and watch. It's awesome.

Finally, Momma stops laughing.

"Miles is gonna fail me for bad bedside manner," I say. "He says I didn't make eye contact. Wasn't polite, didn't listen, all that stuff."

"You?" Momma exclaims. "No damn way."

"Mrs. Abney, please," Miles says, leaning forward toward my phone. "I'm just trying to do my job. Sophia's being very difficult."

I ignore him and say to the phone, "Momma can you call Lilly? You tell her Miles was pretending to have erectile dysfunction and tried to fail me for not being nice."

"Do *not* do that, Mrs. Abney," Miles pleads. "Don't call my mother."

There's a pause over the phone. I watch with glee as Miles fidgets nervously, waiting for a response from Momma.

"Boy, you better pass my girl on her test," Momma says. "Or so help me, I will call your mother and she'll let you have it."

I look at Miles who stands frozen, his mind slowly turning. He can't let his mother find out he faked a limp dick with Sophia Abney then gave her a failing grade. Lilly Douglas is a talker. The whole neighborhood will hear about this. He's already embarrassed that I told Momma. He clearly did not think through the consequences of trying to fail me.

Miles holds up his hands. "Okay," he says to me. "I'll change the eval. Just please, please, don't say anything to my mother."

I'm reminded of Arthur Hickey, the teenager with acne in the derm clinic. He begged me not to tell his mother that he grabbed my breast. What is it about these men who fear their mothers so much? Seems I can get them to do anything so long as I keep their secrets from the women who brought them into this world.

"I'll talk to you later, Momma," I say then end the call.

Miles returns to his seat and starts checking boxes on the evaluation form. He looks pissed that I forced him to give me passing marks, but I ignore this. He was trying to sabotage my medical career for refusing a third date. No way I was going to let this pass.

Thank God for Momma. If not for her, Miles might have succeeded. She's always there when I need her. She saved me when I broke down after Mercer wrote "SNITCH" on my car. Now she's done it once more. She'll probably save me again and again before she leaves this Earth.

Of course, I shouldn't need saving. It's crazy that someone like Miles Douglas gets to grade me on ambiguous aspects of a doctor-patient interaction. I wouldn't mind if he simply gave me his opinion of my bedside manner—I'm always interested in how I'm perceived by others. I do mind that he gets to ding me on a checklist that could impact my career. One person's opinion of whether I put them "at ease" should not alter my standing as a student.

In fact, the whole exercise of grading an encounter with a point system seems wrong. Can you really define an interaction between a doctor and a patient with a checklist anyway? Who thought that was a good idea in the first place?

26.

"Sophia, will you present Mrs. Fielding now?" Dr. Taylor asks me.

Two weeks have passed since I received my invitation to Dr. Allen's home for the dermatology dinner. I'll be heading to her mansion in the suburbs later tonight. Meanwhile, I'm in the computer room on the general medical ward of the hospital. Now on my internal medicine rotation, I'm here with my team: Charlie, Mercer, Celia, two interns, a resident, and our attending physician, Dr. Lana Taylor. But of course, Dr. Taylor is the most important person in the room.

NOTHING MATTERS ON A ROTATION EXCEPT THE ATTENDING.

She's a blonde woman in her fifties with heavy mascara, her skin aged in a way no dermatologist would find acceptable. She wears a white coat, scrubs, and stylish sandals, her pink painted toenails visible for all to see.

My team is "rounding" in the modern sense of the word. We don't actually walk around to see patients—that sort of thing died when the medical records went electronic.

Instead, we discuss cases while sitting in front of computers so we can scan the patient data, those golden documents like lab results, X-ray reports, and daily progress notes.

These rounds are the only time I expect to see Dr. Taylor today. She appears in this room every morning, plants herself in a chair to discuss the cases with my team, then vanishes to places unknown, only available by phone. It's rumored that she's going through a divorce and spends all day complaining to her sisters about her husband, or on Tinder looking for men. Wherever she goes, she never sees the patients, instead relying on us to describe to her their symptoms and exam findings. This is a violation of hospital policy and, probably, numerous state and federal laws—attendings are supposed to personally examine each patient and confirm the clinical findings of trainees. Nevertheless, the medical school, in its grand wisdom, appointed her chair of the professionalism committee last year.

I clear my throat and sit up straight, recalling gunner rule #7: NAIL YOUR PRESENTATIONS. Dr. Taylor's presence is so fleeting, I see her an hour a day or less. Patient presentations are one of the few times I hold her undivided attention. I have to be perfect. I must know every key piece of data about my patients, from weight to blood pressure to potassium level. Plus, I have to speak with authority. A shaky voice, "Um"s and "Er"s—these things could sink my dermatology career. I actually write out my presentations the night before and practice them in front of my mirror. The other night, Jerome heard me say, "Breast tenderness" to myself and made fun of me, but who cares?

I begin my presentation to Dr. Taylor in a commanding voice. "Mrs. Fielding is an eighty-two-year-old woman admitted with sepsis and dehydration."

I move my eyes from one team member to the next as I speak loudly and clearly. Mercer gives me a sinister glare, hoping to make me nervous, but it won't work. I'm too polished. I even sprinkle in little details just for Dr. Taylor. She has an obsessive worry about kidney failure because she had a patient die when no one noticed the kidneys were shutting down. So, I make a point to emphasize things like the urine output and the renal lab values. Her eyes light up when I do this.

When I finish presenting, Taylor says to me, "Sounds like she's improving. We should switch her to oral antibiotics for when she goes home. Does she have any allergies?"

This question brings to mind gunner rule #8: KNOW YOUR PATIENTS. I know *everything* about Mrs. Fielding. There's no question Dr. Taylor could ask that I cannot answer. Any recent travel? No—I made sure to check. Sexually active? Yes, even at 82. Good for her. History of rheumatic fever as a child? Another no. I even made a point to write down her shoe size (seven-and-a-half), city of birth (Miami), and eye color (hazel), just in case. You never know what might be important to the attending.

"She reports an upset stomach when she takes ibuprofen," I say. "And Tylenol once made her dizzy. Otherwise, no adverse reactions to meds."

Mercer scowls as I say this. She was hoping I wouldn't know this information. Wrong!

Taylor nods at me. "Let's give her Azithromycin, then."

"Oh, but I checked with her insurance company," I say. "Azithro is tier three, so her co-pay will be twenty-five dollars. If we give her levofloxacin instead, she'll have no co-pay. Levo is tier one."

Taylor looks at me for a beat. I can tell she's impressed.

God, I'm killing it on this rotation. Mercer clenches her jaw in frustration, knowing I just scored big with my comments. There's nothing she can do but watch. It's awesome.

"OK, fine," Taylor says. "Levofloxacin, it is."

"I'm putting in the order now," Dolores, our team's resident physician, says, pecking at the computer. She's a frumpy woman in her thirties who wears faded green scrubs. She wants to go into primary care, a career path she boasts about by claiming, "It's not as bad as everyone says."

"Make sure to send the script to the CVS pharmacy on Flatbush Avenue," I say. "Her grandson drives by it each day, and he's the one who picks up her meds."

Taylor raises an eyebrow and nods, clearly impressed. I love swaying her with my words. She's like putty in my hands.

"Let's move on to Mrs. McMaster," Taylor says.

A melancholy look falls over the faces on my team. Mrs. McMaster is the second patient I'm following. She's ninety-one years old and dying of heart failure. Yesterday, our team had a meeting with her family—the only time I've ever seen Dr. Taylor actually in the room with one of our patients—and Mrs. McMaster was placed on hospice. We expect her to die sometime today.

"I checked on her this morning," I say. Since Mrs. McMaster's dying, I don't need to give a formal presentation. But I still want to convey to Taylor that I'm on top of everything. "She's very sleepy. Only said a few words to me, then nodded off. She reports no pain whatsoever."

I speak in a sorrowful tone, trying to convey my sadness that Mrs. McMaster is fading. But the reality is that her demise has been pure fucking gold for me on this rotation. End-of-life patients consume lots of time. Family members have endless questions. Sometimes a distant relative flies in from out of state and insists on speaking to the doctors. For a gunner like me, this is an opportunity to be the liaison with the relatives. Mrs. McMaster's family *loves* me. I'm practically an adopted daughter at this point. I've spent so much time with them that Dr. Taylor's hardly been bothered. Not even Mercer has been able to do something like this. She'd probably love to have one of her patients go on hospice and die, but she hasn't been so lucky.

"Will you update the family this morning?" Taylor asks me.

"I've already texted with John and Sarah," I reply, emphasizing the word "texted." I want to be sure Taylor knows I gave my phone number to the family, something only a superstar medical student would do. "They went home late last night, but they'll be back in soon. I'll text them if there's any change in status."

Taylor gives me a satisfied nod. The group discusses a few other random items regarding patients, then the team disperses onto the medical floor. I notice Mercer leave with a sour look on her face, a sure sign I did great on rounds.

As I get up to leave, Dr. Taylor says, "Sophia, will you stay for a moment?"

My body stiffens, wondering what she wants as I slide back into my seat.

"You're doing an outstanding job," she says. "Really impressive. Keep up the good work."

These words dance across my ears like sweet music. I knew I was doing well, but it's wonderful to hear it straight from Dr. Taylor.

"Thank you," I say. "I'm just glad for the opportunity to help the patients."

"You're going to make a great hospitalist," she says. "I can't wait to see where you end up for your internal medicine residency."

I would literally die if I had to do residency in IM, but I don't say this. I let Taylor go on believing the lie I told her about my future as an internist just like her. "Maybe I'll wind up here. It would be great to keep working with you."

Dr. Taylor smiles at me and starts to say something, but then her mobile phone rings. She takes the call, and I scurry from the room, my spirits soaring over her praise.

As I walk down the hallway, a nurse steps from Mrs. McMaster's room. A stocky man with a yellow mask over his thick black beard, I think his name is John, but I'm not sure.

"She may have just died," he says to me. "She's not moving much."

This is the moment I've been waiting for. I nod at the nurse, then enter the room to confirm what he said. As I approach the bed, Mrs. McMaster lies perfectly still, her mouth open, eyes closed. Her long silver hair spills over the pillow under her head. When she transitioned to hospice yesterday, all her IVs and EKG leads were removed. Now she looks peaceful tucked under her covers, without lines and electrodes anywhere on her body.

If she has indeed died, I'll spring into action. First I'll notify Dr. Taylor, being sure to express my sadness over the loss. One of the criteria on my evaluation is: "Does the trainee display compassion for the suffering of others?" Mrs. McMaster is sure to get me a five out of five on this one. After I notify Taylor, I'll call the family to break the news—a task no one likes to do. By eagerly taking it on, I can stand out once again in Dr. Taylor's eyes.

Studying Mrs. McMaster carefully, I don't see her chest rise or fall. She certainly looks dead. I step toward her and rub her sternum, but she doesn't respond.

"Mrs. McMaster?" I say, inching closer to her still figure. "Sheila?" Still nothing.

I take her arm, the skin cool to the touch. I feel for a pulse but find nothing. She's gone.

Quickly, I leap into action. I leave the room and take a seat at the nurses' station outside. Then I make a call from my phone.

"Hi, Dr. Taylor. It's Sophia. I . . . I wanted to let you know that Mrs. McMaster passed." I purposely speak with a slightly shaky voice, keeping my evaluation in mind.

Does the trainee display compassion for the suffering of others?

"Oh, that's very sad," Taylor says. "You sound a little upset. Is this the first patient you've lost?"

"Yes," I say. The truth is, I had two patients die on my surgery rotation, but I'm not going to mention that. "It's so hard. Do you ever get used to it?"

"It's never easy, but it does become easier. Would you like to come talk about it?"

"Uh, no. I'm okay. I want to tell the family. Sarah and John. They're such sweet people."

"They really seem to love you. Do you feel up to calling them?"

This is what I had hoped she'd ask me to do. "It'll be hard, but I want to do it. I'll call Sarah right now."

Does the trainee display compassion for the suffering of others?

The call ends, and I immediately phone Sarah, Mrs. McMaster's oldest daughter.

"Oh, no," Sarah says when she answers. "Has she gone?"

"I'm afraid this isn't good news," I say. "She . . . she's passed. I'm very sorry to have to call you about this."

I hear a wail over the phone, then sobbing that continues for at least a minute. A wave of sadness washes over me. I've been viewing Mrs. McMaster in terms of my grade on this rotation, but I'm not completely without a heart. I know she's a mother to Sarah. I know she means a lot to many people. It's crazy, but medical school reduces patients to challenges. My goal has been to navigate Mrs. McMaster like some turn on a racecourse. But Sarah's tears remind me that she was a human being who's left this world.

Finally, Sarah composes herself. "The whole family is here," she says over the phone. "Most of them got in last night. Can you keep mom in her room? We'll all be over shortly. Stanley, her grandson; he's a preacher. He wants to say a prayer for her with all of us in the room."

"Absolutely," I say. "I'll make sure no one moves her."

"Thank you, Sophia. You've been wonderful. I don't know how we could have gotten through this without you. You're a beautiful person. You're going to make a great doctor someday."

This is a nice compliment, but it means little if Dr. Taylor doesn't hear it. I make a note to myself to try to get Sarah to repeat this later in Taylor's presence.

The call ends, and I text Dr. Taylor that the family is on their way in. Then I hurry to Mrs. McMaster's room to fix her hair and tuck the covers so she looks super peaceful when the family arrives.

Once again, I approach the bed and study Mrs. McMaster as she lies still. I pick her silver hair up off the pillow and tuck it behind her ears. It's sad that she's gone, but she was ninety-one. What did that paramedic say to me when Barbara Dewitt died?

We all have to go sometime.

At least Mrs. McMaster died peacefully. She didn't suffer in the end.

Suddenly, the figure on the bed sits bolt upright and swallows a massive, noisy gulp of air.

I cover my mouth and scream, stumbling backward. What the hell is this? She's risen from the dead.

Mrs. McMaster looks around the room, her eyes glassy and distant. I take a slow step toward the bed. "Sheila?" I say. "Can you hear me?"

She stares straight ahead with a creepy, zombielike expression on her wrinkled face. My mind thinks of *The Walking Dead*. Is this the start of a zombie apocalypse? Then she collapses backward on the bed and closes her eyes. Her chest goes still for a few seconds before she takes another big gulp of air.

The nurse with the beard, John or whatever his name is, enters the room. He eyes Mrs. McMaster, watching her chest rise and fall.

"I guess she's not gone yet," he says. "Sometimes at the end they stop breathing for a little bit, but they're still with us."

"She can't be alive," I say. "I was in here a minute ago. She didn't have a pulse."

"You sure you checked right?" He steps toward the bed and grabs Mrs. McMaster's wrist, sliding his fingers up and down. "She's got a pulse. It's faint. Kind of thready. But it's there."

I press my palms against my temples. This can't be happening. Mrs. McMaster lives. Shit, shit, shit. I told Taylor she was dead. How could I have misdiagnosed death? I should have listened to her heart with my stethoscope. I should have checked for pulses everywhere, not just one flimsy arm.

Then it hits me: the entire family is on their way in. And I just told them she's dead.

"I'll come back in a few minutes to check on her again," John says. "I'll text you when she dies. You don't have to hang around here if you don't want."

John departs the room, leaving me alone with the still-barely-alive Mrs. McMaster, the woman I believed dead just minutes ago. She lies still for long stretches of time, then gulps down huge breaths of air. I've read about this pattern of breathing. It's called agonal breathing, a sign of a person near death. I'm certain Mrs. McMaster is close to the end, but will she go before the family arrives?

As my heart hammers in my chest, I think through the repercussions of my mistake. I should call Dr. Taylor right now to let her know Mrs. McMaster still lives. But will this hurt my evaluation? It was an honest mistake. I *really* thought she was dead. But what kind of medical student can't tell a living person from a corpse?

And then there's the family. If they arrive to pray over her body, they'll flip on learning she's still alive. Sarah was bawling on the phone. Who knows how she'll respond when she learns she was misinformed about her mother's death. She might go nuclear. She might complain to the hospital administration. This could cost me a grade of honors or get me sent before the dean. Oh, my God, this could be a total disaster.

My only hope is for Sheila McMaster to leave this life in the next few minutes before anyone arrives. I watch her wrinkled body on the bed as she takes gulps of air every twenty seconds or so. I see her hands twitching. She's so close to death. She has to die before they get here. They can't see her like this.

I glance at my watch. It's been about ten minutes since I called Sarah.

We'll all be over shortly.

They live just minutes from the hospital. I quickly do some math to estimate their time of arrival: get in the car, drive to the hospital, park, walk in the building. They could be here as soon as ten minutes from now.

God, I am a horrible person for thinking this, but: *please, Mrs. McMaster, just die!* If there is a God, He needs to take this woman's soul post fucking haste. My future career as a dermatologist hangs in the balance. I could lose out on $437,000 a year if this woman lives another twenty minutes.

Then a dark, sinister thought occurs to me: the pillow under her head.

I could slide it out, place it over her face. She'd be gone in seconds.

For reasons I cannot explain, an image of Momma lying unconscious in a hospital bed pops into my thoughts. I see myself in this very room, holding a pillow over Momma's face, suffocating the life from her.

A jolt of panic runs through me, and I gasp. What am I thinking? Am I actually considering murder to get a grade of honors? No, I can't do this. I could never do this. But it horrifies me that, even for a brief moment, I contemplated homicide so I could become a dermatologist.

I step backward to the corner of the room and slide down to the floor, pulling my knees into my chest. Tears begin to flow. Look at what I've become. The death of another human being is little more than an exam I have to pass. I bury my face in my palms and weep.

The nurse walks into the room again. He sees me on the floor and says, "Oh, has she gone?"

I look up at him, wiping tears off my cheek. I realize he presumes I'm crying over Mrs. McMaster. Which I am, but not for the reasons he thinks.

He walks to the bedside and takes Mrs. McMaster's wrist. I notice her chest is still now.

"No pulse," he says. He places his stethoscope in his ears and listens to her heart for a few seconds. "Heart's stopped. She's gone."

Suddenly, my spirits rise. I've been saved by Mrs. McMaster's death! But then my mood sinks again. That I feel relief only reminds me of how sick I've become. What a messed-up world I live in where my dead patient is cause for celebration. But think of the stakes. If she had lived, it might have cost me my grade, and maybe even a career in dermatology. Because she died, I could go on to make millions. Medical school is insane.

I hear footsteps outside. Sarah and John and about ten other people enter the room. They see Mrs. McMaster lying dead. A few gasp, others cry.

Sarah notices me slumped in the corner with swollen cheeks. "Oh, Sophia!" she says as she walks toward me.

I rise to meet her, and she gives me a big hug. I squeeze her back with all my might. This time, for once, there's no pretense in my actions. I'm not doing this to earn a better grade. I'm embracing her because I genuinely need comfort over the trauma of this loss. Not the loss of Sheila McMaster, although that's surely a sad thing. But I've lost my soul. Somewhere along the way in medical school, amid the exams and evaluations and grades, I have become a cold, callous gunner.

27.

"Where's Mercer?" I say to Charlie the next morning as he sits at a computer on the medical ward.

He looks up at me. "Haven't seen her. Why?"

"Because I'm going to kill her."

I stomp away from him, prepared to search every corner of this hospital until I find that bitch. I'm furious because she made me miss the dinner at Dr. Allen's house last night. She told me the address was 8 Waterville Lane. I dutifully put this into my phone, which directed me to a street in the suburbs far outside of the city. When I arrived, 8 Waterville Lane was a dusty lot that held nothing more than wooden scaffolding of a house under construction. I carefully checked the address I wrote down, but there was no mistake. She said 8 Waterville Lane.

That's when it dawned on me that she'd given me the wrong address.

I attempted to look up Dr. Allen's address on the web but couldn't find it. I called Sebastian, but he didn't answer because his phone was in his car, outside the dinner party. He saw my messages when the event was over. He phoned me, but I sent the call to voicemail. By then I was in no mood to talk.

Glancing at my watch, it's 7:30 a.m. We round in thirty minutes with Dr. Taylor, but before then I'm going to find Mercer. I march down the corridor, glancing into each patient room I pass. I can't seem to spot Mercer anywhere. Then I round a corner and spy her blonde hair in front of a computer at a workstation.

I walk up and slam my fist on the table next to her. She recoils in surprise and looks at me.

"You gave me the wrong address," I say. "And I know you did it on purpose."

A slight smile forms at the sides of her mouth, then she turns serious again. "I don't know what you're talking about."

"Eight Waterville Lane. That's not Dr. Allen's address."

"You must have heard me wrong. I said 'eighty-eight Watertown Lane.' That's where she lives."

This is total bullshit. She most certainly did *not* say 88 Watertown Lane. "You're gonna pay for this," I say. "You better watch your back."

Dolores, our resident, appears at the nurses' station. "You ready?" she asks Mercer.

"Ready," Mercer replies, rising from her chair. She looks at me. "I'm putting in a central line on my patient," she says. She's gloating since students rarely get to do procedures.

As she walks away, I find myself hoping she screws up and maims her patient. But then I quickly regret this thought. After yesterday, when I considered suffocating Mrs. McMaster, I vowed to change my ways. I planned to truly focus on the patients and stop worrying about grades. But thanks to Mercer, I'm pissed off and already wishing for horrible things to befall her patients so she fails the rotation. Medical school has a way of turning sick people into pawns.

That's when I notice Mercer's white coat slung over the back of a chair. She left it behind when she went with Dolores to place the central line. At first I consider throwing it in the garbage, but that would be childish and do little more than annoy her. Then I see her badge clipped to the lapel.

Suddenly, a better idea occurs to me.

I slide into the chair where Mercer was just sitting. I grab her badge and swipe it over the badge reader. The screen before me unlocks, an electronic medical record appearing with the words "USER: MERCER, JENNIFER" in the top right corner. I quickly glance left and right, but no one is around. I feel a ripple of excitement. I'm in the system as Jennifer Mercer.

What can I do to get Mercer in trouble? I could order something ridiculous for one of the patients. Maybe an enema for the man who already has explosive diarrhea. Let her explain that to Dr. Taylor. But a patient order might hurt someone, and I don't want to do that. I only want to hurt Mercer.

Then I consider the progress notes we write for our patients each day. The only person who reads the student notes is Dr. Taylor. She checks them for accuracy, co-signs them, then adds her own addendum. What if I write something preposterous in a progress note?

Mercer is following two patients, both their names listed on the screen. I click the first one, a seventy-five-year-old man with blood in his stools. At the end of her note, it says: "Plan: Colonoscopy later today." Then I click on her second patient, an eighty-two-year-old woman with a stroke who's paralyzed on half of her body. At the bottom of Mercer's note, I read: "Plan: Physical therapy later today."

Using the mouse, I quickly cut and paste the plan from the first patient into the note of the second. Then I take the plan from the second patient and paste it into the note from the first. It'll appear that Mercer mixed up her patients when writing her notes. When Taylor reads that Mercer wants the stroke patient to have a colonoscopy, she'll throw a fit. Because Taylor never sees the patients herself, she cares deeply that our notes are polished and perfect lest someone start looking into what she does all day. One of her mantras is "Everything in your notes must be accurate." This error could cost Mercer honors. If nothing else, it'll rattle her and hopefully ruin her day.

Satisfied with what I've done, I sign out of the computer and return Mercer's badge. Then I rise and walk away to find my own patients in preparation for rounds.

"So, the plan for today is physical therapy, with possible discharge tomorrow."

Mercer says these words confidently as she stands before our team in the computer room. We're rounding, and she's just presented her patient Florence Gilbert, the elderly woman with a stroke. I hate to admit it, but Mercer's presentation was good. Just like me, she knows how important it is to speak with confidence and authority. Apparently, I'm not the only one who follows gunner rule #7: NAIL YOUR PRESENTATIONS.

Dr. Taylor gives a satisfied nod. "Okay, good. And her blood sugar? Has it been stable?"

"Last three readings were one-twenty, one-thirty-five, and one-ten," Mercer quickly responds. She seems proud of herself to have answers to Dr. Taylor's questions at the ready. Evidently, she also follows gunner rule #8: KNOW YOUR PATIENTS.

"Great," Taylor says. "She seems to be making progress after her stroke."

Dolores turns from the computer screen in front of her. To Mercer, she says, "You wrote that she needs a colonoscopy?"

Mercer gives her a puzzled look. "What?"

"Your note," Dolores replies. "In the plan, you wrote, 'Colonoscopy later today.'"

The eyes of our group turn to Mercer, who hurries to the computer screen and bends forward to read. "No, no, no. That's not right. That's the plan for my other patient, Mr. Franklin."

"Well, you wrote it under the plan for Gilbert," Dolores says. "You are aware colonoscopy isn't part of the management of stroke, right?"

Mercer shoots a concerned look at Dr. Taylor, who scratches her chin, then says, "You have to be careful in the EMR. It's easy to write something in the wrong patient's chart. What am I always saying to you guys? Everything in your notes must be accurate."

I'm gleeful. Mercer is in deep shit. That's what she gets for giving me the wrong address to Dr. Allen's home.

Mercer darts her eyes from Taylor to the screen, clearly flustered. "Can I sit here?" she says to Dolores. "I want to fix this right away."

Dolores moves to let Mercer take her seat. Taylor scribbles something on a piece of paper in her lap. I wonder if she's writing a note to herself about Mercer's screwup. My plan is unfolding perfectly.

Suddenly the overhead speakers announce, "Rapid response, second floor, room two-fifteen. Rapid response, second floor, room two-fifteen."

I sit up straight in my chair. Room 215 is just down the hall. I think it's the room with Mercer's stroke patient.

Dr. Taylor rises to her feet and hurries from the room with our entire team—me, Mercer, Charlie, Celia, Dolores, and our two interns—following behind. As we approach room 215, a stretcher is overturned in the hallway. Beside it, Florence Gilbert, a frail woman with snowy-white hair, lies sprawled on the floor. Two nurses in blue scrubs huddle beside her.

"Ow!" Mrs. Gilbert howls, clutching her arm.

Dolores and our two interns kneel to the floor, tending to Mrs. Gilbert.

"What happened?" Taylor asks as we reach the overturned gurney.

One of the nurses, a young woman with red hair, looks up with a tear in her eye. "They called for the patient for colonoscopy, so I got her on the stretcher."

"But she's not going to colonoscopy," Taylor replies.

"I read in one of the EMR notes about a colonoscopy, so I thought she was going," the nurse says, wiping her eye.

My body turns ice cold. This nurse read Mercer's note and acted on it. I never thought anyone but Dr. Taylor read our notes.

The other nurse, an older woman with gray streaks in her hair, replies, "She got the wrong person, but before we fixed it, the patient rolled over on the gurney and the guard rail wasn't up. We tried to catch her so she wouldn't fall, but then the whole thing tipped over." The nurse shoots a glance at the redhead, then looks back at Dr. Taylor. "She's new. In case you can't tell."

The red-haired nurse looks at Mrs. Gilbert's crumpled figure on the floor, tears streaming down her cheek. "Oh, my God. I can't believe what I've done."

My stomach feels like a ball of lead. I never thought a

nurse would actually read a student note.

Mercer looks at Dr. Taylor, her face pale, her eyes welling with tears. "I'm so sorry," she says. "I don't know how I could have mixed up the two patients."

Dolores calls out from the floor, "I think her arm's broken."

Mercer shudders. Dr. Taylor turns to her with fury in her eyes. "This is a major screwup. This is not some computer game. Those notes you write are part of the permanent medical record."

"But there was no order for a colonoscopy," Mercer pleads. "She never should have been taken from her room just because of my note."

Dr. Taylor glares at the redheaded nurse, who's kneeling on the floor by Mrs. Gilbert. She's new. She read the student note and saw the plan for colonoscopy. What a disaster.

Mercer covers her face, crying. Taylor, too pissed off to care, walks away to assess Mrs. Gilbert. Soon, others arrive because of the rapid response announcement: residents, attendings, nurses, even security guards. Mrs. Gilbert is transferred back to her gurney. Plans are made to X-ray her arm, which is red and swollen at the elbow—almost certainly broken.

I watch the commotion in stunned silence as my body quivers with guilt. My prank caused harm to Mrs. Gilbert and drove a nurse to tears. All I wanted was for Mercer to get in trouble with Taylor, nothing more. But if I say anything about what I did, it'll end my medical school career. They'll kick me out for falsifying the medical record. No more dermatology residency. No $437,000 a year salary. And I'll have to pay back three years of tuition and stipends I received for my scholarship.

I can't do that. It's not my fault there was a new nurse on duty, one who didn't know enough to ignore a med student note.

Finally, Mrs. Gilbert is taken away. The nurses, residents, and security guards slip back to their duties. Dr. Taylor tells the team to work on our patient-related tasks. Rounds can continue later in the day. I return to the computer room to write notes.

But for at least ten minutes, I simply stare at the screen.

All I can think is: It could have been worse than a broken bone. What if she'd died?

28.

"THANK YOU," I SAY TO the waitress as she places my drink on the table, a Long Island Iced Tea.

It's 5:30 in the evening, a half hour after Dr. Taylor dismissed my team for the day. Normally, I never socialize like this. Most days after rotations I head for the library to study for my shelf exams. But for some reason, tonight I felt like doing something different. So when Charlie and Celia invited me to join them for a drink, I agreed. It's very out of character for me. In fact, when I said, "Yes," Charlie replied, "Holy shit!" and he almost never swears.

The three of us stand at a pub table at the Tavern, a city bar not far from the hospital. Since I rarely come to places like this, it feels strange to be among the after-work crowd. I have on a skirt and blouse, which seems to fit right in with the corporate attire of the room. The smell of whiskey floats through the air. Overhead, speakers blast the Rolling Stones: *But, she'll never break, never break, never break, never break . . . this heart of stone. Oh, no, no, this heart of stone.*

The waitress places beers on our table for Charlie and Celia, then flutters away. Charlie takes a slug of his drink, getting beer on his upper lip, a dollop spilling onto his shirt. Celia daintily sips from her glass. I flash back to how she sat at my table during TBL in first year. She's forgiven me for the PURF I filed back then. Unlike with Mercer, she and I have made peace. Thank God. One archenemy is enough.

"So, what's happening with your professionalism thing?" Charlie asks Celia, pushing his glasses up his nose.

Celia rolls her eyes. "Ugh. Seriously? I don't know if the dean is ever going to let this go."

I gulp my drink, no idea what they're talking about.

Celia sees the perplexed look on my face. "I lied on my PISS form."

"PISS form?" I ask.

"The Professionalism Security Sheet," Celia says. "You know, that stupid email we get every week? The one that asks about our rotations. Like when we arrived and when we left each day."

I nod, now understanding what they're referring to. I didn't know it had been dubbed the PISS form. Appropriate.

"So what happened?" I say to Celia.

She runs a finger around the rim of her beer glass. "I left early one day on surgery. There was *nothing* going on. All the patients were tucked. So I ducked out to record a new TikTok. I have followers, you know. I have to do these things."

I'm reminded of Celia's self-proclaimed status as a med student influencer. I haven't seen any of her posts in years—it's not my thing.

She continues. "I wrote on my PISS form that I stayed until five. But you know that weird intern, Dwayne? The one with the earring who's always picking his nose? He saw me leave early. Apparently, he snitched to Canning. Next thing you know—bam! I get an email to go meet the dean."

"Why didn't you just stick around until five?" Charlie asks.

"Ugh. Come on, Charlie. It's boring sitting in the hospital with nothing to do."

Charlie shrugs. "I usually read when there's downtime."

"Of course you do," Celia says. "You have, like, five followers on Insta. Do you even have a TikTok account? You don't understand the pressure to make content."

Celia turns to me. "Nothing bad happened because I left early," she explains. "And the attendings and residents leave early all the time when it's slow. Why the hell are we monitored like prisoners?"

I drain the last of my Long Island Iced Tea. "One of the many paradoxes of med school," I say. "So, what was your punishment? Stoning? Crucifixion? It was a professionalism violation, after all."

"I have to write an essay," Celia says, twirling her hair. "About the importance of professionalism to the medical world. Can you believe it? What a stupid topic. I was supposed to hand in the essay last week, but I didn't. The dean sent me a nasty email yesterday."

The alcohol floats through my body, making my head buzz. This is just what I needed. Some drinks and a bitch session about medical school. I'll go back to studying tomorrow night. For now, I want to let it all out. I want to have fun! I don't want to think about attendings or grades or dermatology. And I certainly don't want to think about Mercer and Mrs. Gilbert.

"So, was that crazy or what?" Charlie says. "That thing that happened with Mercer's patient this morning."

My spirit dips. Just the topic I want to avoid. I signal the waitress for another Long Island Iced Tea. Charlie and Celia have only drunk half of their beers.

"I asked Mercer to come out for a drink, but she ran off," Celia says.

"Probably too upset to do anything social," Charlie replies.

"You know the nurse?" Celia says. "The one who put the patient on the stretcher? She got fired today. Dolores told me. Security came and walked her off the premises. Hard-core shit."

My entire body stiffens. I really need another drink to settle my nerves. Why are we talking about this?

"Well, she did make a big mistake," Charlie replies. "Can't take a patient to colonoscopy without an order."

"Yeah, right," Celia says. "A nurse should know better than to read the med student progress notes. No one should take anything I write in the chart seriously."

I feel my buzz fading. I want to change the subject but can't think of anything to say. I look for the waitress with my drink order but can't find her anywhere. Then I see Randy, Jerome's boss at Burger King, on the other side of the room with a girl. His eyes fall on me for a moment, probably surprised I'm here. God, I wonder if Jerome will come to meet him. My brother will freak if he sees me out.

"Think this will affect Mercer's grade?" Charlie asks Celia.

"No way she gets honors now," Celia says. "And if the derm people hear about what she did, it could hurt her chances to match."

My shoulders grow tense from this discussion. "Oh, come on," I say. "It was an honest mistake. She apologized. I can't believe she'll get screwed for it."

Celia shrugs and sips her beer. "She was crying in the residents' room today. She said she called her father and he went off on her. He told her she'd ruined her career."

Mercer's father sounds like a dick. I guess it's not all sunshine and rainbows in their family. I still can't believe Mercer is in for anything more than a bad evaluation from Dr. Taylor.

This conversation is ruining my buzz. I don't want to talk about Mercer or Mrs. Gilbert. Our waitress is nowhere to be found.

"I think I see someone I know," I say to Charlie and Celia as I peer over their shoulders at the bar. This is a lie. I just want to get away. "I'll be right back."

I glide away from our table, glad to escape the conversation. When I reach the bar, I take an empty seat next to two men in business suits. They look a little older than me. Probably just got off work.

I order another Long Island Iced Tea, which the bartender begins mixing in front of me.

"I've always liked the name of that drink," the man beside me says. He sits alone now, his friend having slid down the bar to talk to someone else.

"It's a stupid name. It has no iced tea."

The man raises an eyebrow. "Did not know that." He pauses. "I'm Jack," he says.

Not only do I rarely go to bars like this, I *never* talk to random guys when I'm out. But once again, I'm feeling wild tonight.

"Sophia," I reply.

Jack explains that he's an accountant who works for an investment firm in the city. He's twenty-eight years old and moved here from California for his job. I down my second Long Island Iced Tea and order a third as we chat.

"So, what do you do?" he asks me.

"Medical student."

Jack takes a swig of his beer. "Interesting. What specialty are you going into?"

"Dermatology."

Jack scrunches his face. "You like rashes and boils and stuff like that?"

I take a gulp of my drink. "Actually, I don't. I mean, not really. It is kind of gross. But dermatology *pays*."

Jack considers this. "What about surgery? That pays well, doesn't it? Cut people open. Save lives."

"Too much work," I say. "Would you want to get up at two a.m. to drive into the hospital for a gallbladder? There's stuff on weekends, too. I'd burn out."

"What about a pediatrician, then? Work with cute little kids all day."

"Pay is shit. Parents are psycho. Teenagers are all depressed. No way. Trust me, I've considered this from every angle. Dermatology is the holy grail of medical specialities. Nothing comes close."

I realize I sound like Sebastian now. I can spout the arguments for dermatology from memory. My conversion from innocent first year to gunner is complete.

Jack and I move on to other topics, the booze swirling through my brain. Charlie and Celia come over to see if I'm okay, but I send them away. I like talking to Jack. He's not in medicine. He knows nothing of Mercer or Mrs. Gilbert or rotations. I feel lighter in his presence than I've felt in a long time.

When I finish my third Long Island Iced Tea, Jack says to me, "How did you get here? Did you drive?"

"Uh, yeah, why?"

"Can we go outside to your car? There's something I want to show you."

I take a second to think. It's pretty clear Jack likes me. I suspect he wants to get me somewhere alone so he can make a move. Leaving a bar with a man I just met is another thing I never do. Yet somehow, on this night, just like everything else, it seems reasonable.

I take Jack by the hand and leave the bar with him. Outside, the sun has set and streetlamps light the sidewalk. My crappy Ford Festiva is parked near the corner. Ordinarily I'd be embarrassed to show it to someone like Jack, but with three drinks in me, I don't care. I slide into the driver's seat, and Jack gets in the passenger side.

He reaches a hand into the breast pocket of his suit jacket and pulls out a small plastic bag filled with powder.

"Have you ever done meth?" he asks.

This catches me by surprise. Back at the bar, I didn't take Jack for a user of hard drugs. I'm reminded that I barely know this man. I should end this now, before it goes any further. But once again, tonight is different.

"I've smoked weed, and once I did cocaine," I say. "But I've never tried meth."

Jack opens the bag and places a small amount of powder on his fingertip. Then he quickly snorts it up his left nostril.

He hands the bag to me. "Try some," he says.

The powder could be spiked or concentrated or God-knows-what. I should walk away right now. But tonight, I feel like playing with fire. I want to forget my life. The booze has helped, but I need more. I want to float away from this world for a while. And I'm willing to take chances to make that happen.

I take the bag and place some powder on my fingertip, just like Jack did. Then I snort it up my nose.

I suck through my teeth and shudder. "Ah, it burns."

"That'll go away in a second." He takes the bag from me and slides it back into his suit jacket.

Slowly, the burning sensation fades. Then the car seems to spin around me. God, I'm wasted.

I turn toward Jack and see him gazing into my eyes.

Then, in a blink, we're kissing.

As his hands run over my chest, it occurs to me that what I'm doing is reckless. I'm in my car with a strange man. I'm drinking and taking drugs. But I no longer care. I'm not sure anything matters anymore except grades. I didn't really care about Mrs. McMaster, who was dying. She was just an instrument to help me get ahead. And then there was Mercer's patient, Mrs. Gilbert. I altered her medical record with no regard for her as a person. The truth is, none of them are people to me. This is the price of becoming a gunner. The patients are just devices made of flesh, only useful if they make me look good in the eyes of the attending. And you can't treat patients as objects for long without becoming one yourself. It was only a matter of time before my outlook reflected onto me. Now, I don't even care about myself.

Jack climbs over the gear shift and places his weight on top of me, his tongue sliding over my neck. Through the windshield beyond his shoulder, the city lights blur into a tapestry of shimmers. Maybe it's the meth, but suddenly my car seems to move like it's rolling end over end. My stomach lurches and bile rises in my throat.

I push Jack off me, back toward the passenger seat. Then I shove open the door, turn to my left, and puke. Vomit hits the asphalt with a splat. I step out of the car, but my legs wobble and I fall to my knees, vehicles passing me by in the street.

Jack climbs out the passenger side and hurries around the car to me. "Are you okay?"

As I look up at him, a wave of vertigo consumes me and I fall to my side. I roll over on my back, the hard asphalt pressing my shoulder blades. I feel another wave of nausea. I twist onto my side and puke again, the putrid smell of my half-digested Long Island Iced Teas filling my nostrils.

Jack looks at me. "Come on," he says. "Get up. Someone's going to call the cops."

I can't move. My limbs weigh a thousand pounds. I lie on the street, praying the night will stop spinning around me. Cars motor past, some just inches from my face. No one stops to help me. Why would they? I'm nothing but a soulless vessel.

Jack sees me making no effort to rise. He glances left and right, then rushes away down the sidewalk.

A truck rumbles past just inches from my face, and I wonder if I'll die here. I should be panicked, but the alcohol has dulled my senses. The next vehicle in the street could easily crush me. For some reason, I flash to Mrs. McMaster, lying dead in her hospital room. What was it like for her world to blink away? Am I about to die like her? Maybe this is where my gunner life has led me. Maybe I deserve this fate. I've become nothing more than a piece of garbage on the city street.

Suddenly I feel strong hands under my shoulders.

"Soph," someone says. I look up to see my brother kneeling beside me. "Come on. You gotta get up."

My vision still wobbly, I sit up, my brother's hands guiding me. Jerome! I can't die. Not here. Not now. Not with Momma and Jerome in my life.

"How did you know I was here?" I ask, my words slurred.

"Randy texted that he saw you. Come on, get up."

I think for a second, the spinning lights slowing before me. "Why'd you come looking for me?"

"You weren't answering your phone."

He pauses, as if reluctant to speak his next words. A distant ambulance siren wails in the night air.

"We gotta get to the hospital," he says. "Momma's sick again."

29.

Two days later, I sit at Momma's bedside in the hospital.

"Mrs. Abney, please," says the nurse, a rail-thin young woman about half of Momma's age. "I need you to roll on your side, or I can't change your dressing."

Momma pushes up in her hospital bed, propping her back against a pillow. "Well, I am *not* rolling over."

Momma has a pressure ulcer on her rear end, a deep breakdown of the skin from sitting in her wheelchair all day. What's more, the wound is infected, and bacteria have spread to her bloodstream. She's on antibiotics and needs the dressing changed twice a day. But dressing changes are painful, and Momma doesn't like random nurses causing her pain.

"Why you gotta change this thing so much anyway?" Momma says to the nurse. It's an accusation, not a question. "Just leave it be and let me heal."

I rise from my chair, unable to watch in silence any longer. "Damn it, Momma," I say. "You know the bandage gets soaked. It can't be left like that. Why do you have to put everyone through this every time?"

Momma narrows her eyes at me. "I need some rest, Soph." She points to the nurse. "I can't rest with these people rolling me over twice a day and poking fingers around my ass."

Before I can respond, the door to the room slides open, and Jerome appears. He sees the look on Momma's face. He sees me and the nurse glaring at her.

"Dressing change time, huh?" he says.

"I'm not doing this now," Momma says to the nurse. "Maybe later. I'll think about it."

"So help me," I say, "I will wrestle you onto your stomach myself if you don't do what this nurse asks."

Jerome walks to Momma's side across the bed from me.

"You should go home and rest," Momma says to me. "Jerome's here now. He'll stay. You look like you ain't slept for days."

"That's because I've been here making sure you get better."

I ask the nurse to give us a moment alone with Momma, and she exits the room. Jerome and I stand on either side of her bed, gazing down on Momma under the covers in a hospital gown. She looks pale and weak. After we treated her vitamin deficiency three months ago, her spirits seemed better. She had more energy and started to put on weight. This infection is a major setback.

I open my mouth to argue with Momma again over the wound dressing, but then I stop. I can't force her to comply. She has to want it herself. "Look, I love you, and I want you to get better. What can I do so you stop fighting with people? I want to get you through this and get you home."

Momma's eyes study my face. "I know I got to do what they say. But damn, Soph, they come in here whenever they want. They ask me to roll over like some dog. I'm not having that."

Momma wants some control, that's all. It's no surprise. She's not one to be pushed around.

"I can ask them to give you a warning. To not come in here unannounced. Maybe they can tell you what things you've got to do for the day?"

Momma considers this. I can see it in her eyes: she likes my suggestion. "Look at you. Little Miss Peacemaker."

"I just want you to get better. And you can't get better if you're agitating the doctors and nurses."

"You want me to stop fighting, huh?" Momma says. "Okay, then. I'll make you a deal. I'll go along with these people if you tell me why you were on the street two days ago."

I glare at Jerome. "You said you wouldn't say anything!"

Jerome holds up his hands. "I'm sorry. I'm sorry. Look, Soph, I was worried about you, is all. Momma and I got to talking about you, and I told her. Come on, now. You were nearly passed out drunk on the street."

I press my palms to my forehead. I guess it was stupid of me to expect Jerome to keep this from Momma. He cares about me too much. But I'm too ashamed of myself to talk about the circumstances that led to my inebriation two nights ago. It's hard for me to admit to myself what I've done, let alone admit it to my family.

I look at Momma and shrug. "I just drank too much. That's all. I'm sorry if you thought your daughter was a saint, but I'm not. From time to time, I overindulge. I smoke cigarettes once in a while, too. I've also jaywalked and double parked before. Now you know everything."

Momma rolls her eyes and scoffs. "You expect me to believe that? You ain't a drinker, girl. I can count on one hand the number of times you been drunk. Something *made you* want to drink. And that's what I want to know."

Most people with a life-threatening infection would gladly accept treatment. Momma, on the other hand, wants me to bare my soul, or she'll let the wound on her backside fester and rot.

"If I tell you this," I say, "no more arguing with the doctors and nurses?"

"I'll be so nice, they'll pray for me to get sick enough that I can stay here forever."

Seeing no other way to move forward, I nod at Momma and Jerome. "I don't even know where to begin," I say. All they know, all I've ever told them, is that I'm doing well in school. They don't ask for details, and I haven't provided any. They don't know about Sebastian or Mercer or dermatology. It occurs to me that I've kept this from my family because I fear what they'd say if they knew.

Knowing this is a long story, I slump into the chair beside Momma's bed. Then I tell Momma and Jerome the tale of my life at State Medical School. I tell them about skipping lectures and sabotaging Mercer's research experiments and lighting trash cans on fire. I admit to lying to my attendings about what specialties I like. I tell them I let Dr. Canning gawk at me and allowed a seventeen-year-old kid with acne to grab my tits. And then I reveal my thoughts about Mrs. McMaster: that I considered suffocating her, so she'd die quicker. And finally, I tell them about Mrs. Gilbert's fall from her gurney, a gurney she never would have been on if not for me. As I speak, my words become more and more animated. It's a catharsis to tell them everything, like I'm baring my soul to a priest in confession. It's a grand purge, and I realize how sick it's made me to do these things and keep them bottled up inside, like some dark secret.

"Wait a minute," Jerome says when I finish. "Why do they have lectures if no one wants to go to them?"

Momma looks at him. "*That's* the part of her story that shocked you? Seriously? How about the patients like me? Shit, there's probably some medical student thinking about me right now. Probably wondering what they can do to me so they get noticed? I'm a prize at the county fair they're trying to win."

"You don't understand," I say. "There's a lot of money at stake. Four hundred thousand a year! Think of what we could do with all that."

"Why do you think medicine is the only way to make that kind of money?" Momma says. "Who told you that? Where did you get that silly idea?"

"I'm making seventy-five thousand now as store manager," Jerome says. "I can make more if I get to district or regional."

"That's a long way from four hundred thousand."

"Yeah, but I'm not hurting anyone to get there. Damn, Soph. You wanted someone to die so you could get ahead. An old lady fell on the floor and broke her arm. It's messed-up shit."

It's funny how normal the crazy world of medical school can seem from the inside. By revealing the truth to outsiders like Momma and Jerome, I see just how sick the system is. I've been playing a game, but lives are at stake.

A tear wells in my eye. "I was only trying to make money," I say. "I wanted a better life for us. I hate our apartment. I hate that we live on a shitty street in a rundown city." I look at Momma. "It's not fair you lost Daddy. It's not fair you can't walk. I want you to have something good."

"I'm glad you want to see us move up in the world," Momma says. "But you don't have to do it this way."

"So what then? You want me to quit?""

Momma looks at me for a minute, her soft eyes studying my face. "You want to know why I don't like doctors?" she says. "I mean, they cured me of cancer, right? I should be grateful, right? Well, I am grateful, but I still don't like doctors. Want to know why? Because I'm vulnerable when they're not. They can be kind or rude or thoughtful or dismissive. But I can only be sick and vulnerable. I went to a dozen doctors for my cancer. Too many times, they failed to notice how exposed I was. How defenseless. They left me to wait for them. Or they brushed me off when I asked questions. Or they just didn't pay attention when I was baring my soul about how bad I felt. They have the luxury to do this, but I don't. I can only sit there and take what they give, no matter how much I want more. I lost my legs, Soph! I can never walk again. I don't expect my doctors to shed tears over this, but they can at least treat me with respect for my condition. Your stories about med school only prove what I've known all along: too often, I'm not their priority. I matter to them, but not the way I want to matter. And I can feel that every time I'm in a hospital. I can *feel* my insignificance. And I don't want you to be a person who makes other people feel that way."

I weep as Momma's words strike deep. I think of Barbara Dewitt, the old woman who died in her living room while I was doing Anki. She wanted my attention, but I ignored her. I think of Roland, too, the adorable kid with Down syndrome. He cried for me to stay with him a while, but I wouldn't. I'm already putting myself before others. When I become a doctor, will it be any different?

"Come here," Momma says to me.

I get up and walk to her bedside. She takes my hand in hers, the warmth of her fingers surrounding mine.

"You should leave," she says. "It's not worth it. There's lots of other ways to make money."

My shoulders tighten. Momma has just spoken aloud a thought I've had myself the past few days. It's probably the thought that led me to drink and take meth at the Tavern. Medicine is rotting my soul. And I should leave while there's still some humanity left inside me. But if I leave, I'll bury my family in debt.

"I can't quit," I say to Momma. I look from her to Jerome, then back. "It's my scholarship. If I quit, I have to pay it back."

Momma and Jerome stare at me as they process my words. I should have told them this before. I thought if I did, they'd tell me not to go to medical school. Maybe that would have been better.

"Well, then," Momma says. "We've gotta find a way for you to become a doctor without turning into a monster."

Yes, I think. That's exactly what I have to do. I've let the money and competition consume me. When I arrived at medical school, I knew nothing about class rank or research publications or honors. And I certainly didn't know the average salary of a dermatologist. Now these things monopolize my thoughts. I want to go back to the innocence I had at the start.

But is it too late for that? I've done so many terrible things. Can I ever, with a clear conscience, be someone's doctor? Does a person like me deserve that kind of status and authority?

And then a sickening thought occurs to me. I shudder as I consider it.

Would I want someone like me taking care of Momma?

Or to put it another way: once you become a gunner, is there any turning back?

30.

Having bared my soul to Momma, she finally agrees to a dressing change then promptly falls asleep. Jerome leaves for work. I'm alone in the hospital, left to my own thoughts. That's when I decide it's time for me to read through Momma's chart.

It's been nagging at me for days, this need to see what's being written about her care. I'm used to seeing illness from the doctor's perspective. I can't stand being on the other side, knowing only the things the doctors and nurses choose to share. With the halls outside quiet, this is my chance to find a computer and read through the daily progress notes.

A moment later, I'm down the hall from Momma's room. I creep into the nurses' workstation, a box-shaped area of countertops with computers. Quickly glancing left and right, I see no one. With hurried movements, I slide into a seat before one of the locked computer screens and wave my badge over the reader. The screen flickers, then displays the words "Enter Patient Name." It's against hospital policy to read the medical records of family members.

If I'm caught, I'll be sent before Dean Weaver for a professionalism violation and God-knows-what punishment. But it's a risk I'm willing to take. I have to know what the doctors are thinking and doing.

I enter Momma's name, and her medical record blinks into view before my eyes. There are nearly a dozen notes in the chart just for today. I see dozens more going back to her admission two days ago.

The purpose of modern medical care is to produce documentation.

Momma has generated enough verbiage to fill a small library.

Ping. Ping. Ping.

A cardiac alarm chimes overhead. Those things are constantly going off on this ward, usually due to a false alarm when a patient knocks the leads off their chest. Seconds later, a nurse emerges from the break room across the hall and hurries to a display of heart monitors in the corridor. She's just a few feet away from me. If she turns to look in this direction, she'll see me for sure, and she might ask me what I'm doing. I duck my head below the computer screen to keep out of sight. She scans the cardiac alarm panel, then clicks something using a mouse. Abruptly, the chime stops. A moment later, she disappears back into the break room.

I let out the breath I was holding and return to the computer screen. Quickly, I scan the notes in Momma's electronic chart. I find a plethora of documents from interns, residents, and attendings. I also see notes from floor nurses and wound nurses, physical therapy, and social work. She also has consult notes from surgery, cardiology, oncology, and infectious disease. So much documentation.

"Hi, Sophia," someone says.

I jump in my seat. I spin around to see Charlie standing over me, his eyes peering at me through his glasses.

I place a hand over my chest. "Oh. You scared me."

"Didn't mean to startle you," he replies. He motions toward the screen. "Whatcha looking at?"

I quickly close Momma's record with my mouse. "Nothing," I say. "Just need to send an email to the dean. I'm going to miss a few more days of our rotation."

The old Sophia never would have taken time off from school. She would have kept gunning for honors day and night, no matter what. But when Momma got sick, things changed. I can't leave her side until I know she's okay.

"How's your mom doing?" Charlie says in a heartfelt tone. It's sweet that he asks about her.

"She's getting better," I say. "The ulcer is healing. Thanks for asking."

"I'm so sorry for you and your family. I hope she gets better really soon."

A part of me wishes Charlie could be assigned to Momma's case. He cares so much. And he never worries about grades or honors or residency. I don't think there's a single gunner bone in his body.

It occurs to me that Charlie is alone, his team nowhere to be found. "Where is everybody?" I ask.

"Mercer hasn't been here for two days, just like you."

"What? Why?"

"It's the thing with Mrs. Gilbert. It really rattled her. She had to go see the dean. I heard she asked to take some time off."

This is stunning news. I didn't know Mercer was so shaken over Mrs. Gilbert. For so long, I've wanted to see her brought low. But now that she is, I feel badly for her. God, look at what I've done. Mrs. Gilbert broke her arm because of me, and Jennifer Mercer's spirit was crushed.

"Everyone else is in the break room across the hall," Charlie says. "Dr. Taylor's been promoted. She's going to be the new Assistant Dean of Students. She'll be in line for Weaver's job in a few years. It's a big deal. The staff made her a cake."

My face scrunches with surprise. "Taylor's getting promoted? But she never sees the patients? Nobody even knows what she does all day."

Charlie shrugs. "Apparently, her brother is on the school's board of directors."

I guess it pays to know the right people. No one in my family will ever help me get a promotion unless I go to work at Burger King with Jerome.

"You could come for cake if you want," Charlie says. "I mean, you're still part of the medicine team, even if you're taking time off."

The old me would have jumped at the chance to congratulate Dr. Taylor over cake. I probably would have fawned over her, proclaiming that she deserved the promotion more than anyone else in the school. But now I only care about seeing Momma get through her illness.

I decline Charlie's offer, then he waves a hand and walks away. I watch him open the door to the break room across the hall and vanish inside.

I'm alone again, just me and a computer screen. My stomach is tense, probably from lingering guilt over Mercer. But I push this aside and return my attention to Momma's medical records. I click on the first note, one from the cardiology attending.

The patient is a 50-year-old woman with prior spinal malignancy and paraplegia . . .

My stomach turns as I read. I hate that they call her "the patient," as if she's not a real person with a name. I do this too in my notes. Everyone does it. But now that Momma's sick, it feels cruel and insensitive. Maybe that's why I'm not supposed to read her chart. Maybe they don't want family members to see how impersonal medicine can be.

Suddenly, a popup window appears in the bottom right corner of the screen. NEW TEST RESULT AVAILABLE. When I click the box, it takes me to an echocardiogram report describing the appearance of Momma's heart by ultrasound. At the bottom of the report, I read the following language:

LARGE BACTERIAL VEGETATION ON MITRAL VALVE. CONSIDER CARDIAC SURGERY CONSULTATION.

I clutch my chest, suddenly feeling like I may puke. Momma has bacteria on one of the valves in her heart! She may need open heart surgery. I can hardly breathe. Her case has gone from a simple skin ulcer to something much more serious.

For she's a jolly good fellow! For she's a jolly good fellow!

A chorus of singing voices wafts from the break room. It's the celebration of Dr. Taylor's promotion. The sound sickens me. Momma has an infection in her heart! Who can sing at a time like this? I want to run across the hall and scream at everyone gathered for cake. How can they be so insensitive! This ward is filled with suffering patients. It's no place for singing the stupid Jolly Good Fellow song.

Then I think of Momma. She doesn't like to roll over for dressing changes. How will she react if she needs open heart surgery? I see the terrible path that lies in store for her: major surgery, excruciating post-op pain, and months of rehab. That's all assuming she doesn't die of some complication along the way. My hands begin to tremble.

Ping. Ping. Ping.

Another annoying cardiac alarm chimes overhead. It continues on, all the staff gathered for cake and unaware. I ignore the noise and rise from my chair. Suddenly, I don't want to read Momma's chart anymore. It hurts too much to see her described as "the patient" with "paraplegia." And I don't want to read about ominous findings on her imaging tests. I want only to be at her side and hold her hand.

Ping. Ping. Ping.

I step into Momma's room and gaze at her as she lies in bed, her eyes closed. Should I wake her up to tell her about her heart? The imaging report just came back. Her doctors don't even know about it yet. Maybe I should wait until they have a plan?

Ping. Ping. Ping.

I glance up at the heart monitor, the small screen in the corner of Momma's room. It shows only a flat line. Her leads must have fallen off her chest, I think. I walk to Momma's bedside and look down at her face. Her lips are pale. Her chest isn't moving.

That's when it hits me: the flatline could be real. Momma could be dying.

I quickly yank off her blankets. The EKG leads are securely attached to her chest! This is not an equipment problem. My skin turns ice cold. I feel for a pulse on her neck. Nothing.

Ping. Ping. Ping.

My stomach lurches. Those are not false alarms! Momma's heart has stopped beating.

My mind scrambles to think of what to do. Should I start CPR? But I don't even know CPR. I've only seen it in movies and TV shows. They haven't taught it to us yet. It's crazy, but third-year medical students only know biochemistry and pharmacology. We know nothing of actually saving a life.

"Help!" I shout, but no one comes. Through the door, I see the hallway outside is empty. "Help!" I shout once more, but still no one comes. Then I remember: everyone is in the break room to celebrate Dr. Taylor's promotion. The staff is eating cake, while Momma is having a cardiac arrest. I clench my fists in rage. I'd like to strangle them for missing the alarm, but there's no time for that now.

I race to the break room down the hall. When I swing open the door, about twenty heads turn to look at me, all with paper plates in their hands, some forking cake into their mouths. I see Charlie and Celia, both gawking at me with puzzled expressions. I see Dr. Taylor looking at me quizzically.

"My mother's heart isn't beating! She's flatlining!"

Then I turn and race from the room back to Momma. Within seconds, Dr. Taylor arrives with a gaggle of nurses behind her. A resident hurries to the bedside and begins compressing Momma's chest, slamming it into the mattress with all her might.

What happens next is a blur. The room spins around me as a horde of unfamiliar faces gathers by the bed.

An overhead speaker blares, "Code blue, room two-eighteen. Code blue, room two-eighteen."

A nurse wheels a cart into the room, a defibrillator sitting on top. Oh, God! Are they going to shock Momma? I don't know if I can watch that. But Dr. Taylor waves off the machine. Momma's heartbeat is a flatline, completely asystolic. This can't be treated with a defibrillator. She's too sick to be revived by an electric shock.

And then Jerome appears at my side. He gawks at the melee in the room. "I . . . I forgot my bag," he says, his voice shaky. "What's . . . what's happening?"

"Her heart stopped," I say.

I bury my head in my brother's chest as he puts his arm around me. I can't watch, but I hear the words: Epinephrine. What's the rhythm? Is there a pulse? Bag her. We need a central line. More epi.

I know what the words mean. I've learned about them in school. But they never hurt me like this before. They were always abstract and impersonal. Now they mean something different. They mean Momma is dying.

And then I turn from Jerome to look upon the scene, unable to keep my eyes away any longer. I see Momma's body lying on the bed, her eyes glassy and lifeless, her lips white as stone. But then, suddenly, she begins to change before me. She sits up in bed, no longer a fifty-four-year-old woman lying in the hospital. She's forty-four, the mother of two teenagers, the one who smiles at me when I hop off the school bus, the one who sent Jerome to his room for smoking a cigarette but then squeezed him to her chest later and said "I love you." That woman, now many years gone, somehow sits in the bed, smiling at me. Then she changes again. She's thirty-five years old, long, dark hair falling over her shoulders, her skin smooth and youthful. She's the woman who came to my first grade class and read *Cat in the Hat*, the one who made snowflake cookies at Christmas. And then she becomes younger still, now twenty-five, the woman I never knew, the one Daddy fell in love with after she smiled at him on the bus to the north side, the one he surprised with a kiss while they sat on a bench by the river. Then she's younger still, now eighteen, full of the energy only known to the young. She's the woman I never knew, the woman I only imagined, always laughing and cackling on the phone with girlfriends and dancing at bars and parties. And then she's not eighteen, she's twelve, a blossoming, awkward adolescent. The world is wide open for her, no idea she'll meet Daddy, no idea she'll have two children who'll love her more than anything. She's in school learning algebra, gossiping at her locker, sucking milk through a straw from a carton in the corner of a plastic lunch tray. I see every moment of her life that's led to now. Laughing. Tears. Excitement. Sadness. Birthdays. First days of school. Graduations. Her engagement. The wedding. My birth. Jerome. Our apartment. Her wheelchair.

Soon, twenty minutes have passed. A nurse says Momma still has no pulse.

"We have to call it," Dr. Taylor says. She looks at me and Jerome. "I'm so sorry. She's gone."

The staff move back from the bed, gazing at me and Jerome with eyes of sorrow. Jerome falls to his knees, crying. I step forward toward Momma. I can't believe she's dead. I have to make certain for myself.

With the room staring at me in silence, I shake her gently.

No response.

I call her name quietly, "Momma."

No response.

I feel for a pulse, her wrist cool to the touch.

Nothing.

She's gone.

She's left me to be with Daddy among the stars.

31.

Later that afternoon I open the back door to my apartment, the sting of Momma's death still heavy in my thoughts. To my great surprise, Sebastian sits in my kitchen in a chair at the table.

"What are you doing here?" I ask.

"The door was open," he replies.

I'm so used to Momma being home all day watching television, I never thought to lock the door. So much is going to change with her gone.

"You shouldn't have just walked in when no one was home. That's super creepy."

Sebastian shrugs. "It's six o'clock. I know this is the time you usually get home from the hospital."

I consider asking him to leave, but he looks determined to speak to me and I'm in no mood to argue. Hopefully he won't stay long. I close the door behind me and enter the kitchen. It's just as I left it this morning. Dirty dishes teeter in the kitchen sink, the remnants of my breakfast. I spot the cast-iron frying pan on the stove. Momma always loved when I made her eggs in that pan, but I'll never make her eggs again.

I set down my purse and walk to the sink for some water. "This isn't a good time to talk," I say.

"You haven't returned my calls or texts for weeks. What's going on?"

"My mother died this morning." I just blurt it out. I don't know how else to say it. My body clenches as I utter the words. It's the first time I've announced to someone else that she's gone.

"What? What happened?"

Too exhausted to remain standing, I go to the living room and slump into our old recliner, the one I used to sit in when I talked to Momma at night. The space feels so empty without her in her wheelchair in front of the television.

Sebastian follows me, the sofa creaking as he sits down. "So what happened?"

"She got sick," I say.

Before the next word leaves my mouth, I start to cry. Sebastian gets up from the couch to comfort me, but I wave him away. Then I look down. It's easier to talk if I'm not looking someone in the eyes. Slowly, I tell him about Momma's pressure ulcer and the infection that spread to her bloodstream and heart. Then I tell him about the cardiac arrest. Dr. Taylor said Momma had a stroke when a clump of bacteria from her heart broke off and traveled to her brain. She said the stroke was massive, that nothing would have saved Momma's life. I don't believe this. If the staff hadn't been in the break room singing to Dr. Taylor, I'm convinced Momma would be alive.

"So what did you do?" Sebastian says. "Did you go off on Taylor for the delay?"

"I couldn't. After Momma . . . after it was over, I was just empty."

"I'm so sorry," he says.

"She had dozens of notes in her chart. All kinds of people in that hospital were supposed to be looking after her. But she died while everyone was in the break room. They're supposed to leave someone on the floor to monitor alarms, but they didn't. No one was worried enough about Momma to keep watch."

"If it was a massive stroke, it wouldn't have mattered how quickly they responded to the arrest. Probably caused intracranial hemorrhage."

I picture Momma's brain filled with blood, and I shiver. "I don't want to think about how she died."

Sebastian nods. "Are you still on your internal medicine rotation?"

"I haven't been in two days. The school doesn't even know Momma's dead yet. I haven't told them." I slide my phone from my pocket. "Look at the email I got this morning from the dean."

I hand my phone to Sebastian, who begins to read:

Hello Sophia:

I hope your mother is getting better. Please don't worry about the two days of your internal medicine rotation that you have missed. I've spoken with your attending, Dr. Taylor. She completely understands the situation. You can take as much time as you need.

You will, however, have to make up all the days that you miss. Unfortunately, we have lots of student absences, and school policy is that missed activities must be made up. We cannot make exceptions, even for cases of family illness. It's considered a matter of professionalism for all students to complete their required rotations, no matter the outside circumstances. I hope you understand.

Whenever you are ready to come back, please email me. I'll work with Dr. Taylor to arrange make-up dates. Likely, you will either work weekends or overnight shifts until you are caught up. Or you may be required to give up some of your elective time to fulfill your internal medicine requirements.

Sincerely,
SW

"Unreal," Sebastian says, handing the phone back to me. "They're hard-asses about missing time. Always have been."

"I'm not going back for a while. They'll probably make me work nights forever to make up for Momma dying."

Sebastian says nothing, and there's an awkward silence for a minute or so. It bugs me that he came into the apartment without an invitation. I really don't want to see him right now.

"Look, you should go," I say. "My brother went to get some food. He'll be home any minute."

"Why have you been ignoring me?" he asks.

I know this is why Sebastian came to find me, but I thought he wouldn't bring it up after I told him about Momma. I thought he'd leave if I explained what I'm going through.

"Not now," I say. "I can't do this right now."

"I want to know. You've been ghosting me. Why?"

I don't know what to say to him. I don't want to have a break-up argument now.

"Come on," Sebastian says. "Tell me why you're ignoring me." His words feel like a demand, not a request.

"Where did you go to college?" I ask.

Sebastian blinks a few times. "What? Why?"

"Just answer the question. Where did you go to college?"

He sighs. "It was the other derm residents, right? They told you?"

"Why did you say you went to Midtown like me if you didn't? That's messed up."

Sebastian runs his fingers through his hair. "What can I say? I liked you. You're very attractive. I wanted you to like me, too. I wanted us to bond. I wanted you to go into derm like me, so we could spend lots of time together."

"I wouldn't have run away if you said you went to Brown."

"Come on," he pleads. "Guys tell little lies when they meet girls all the time. I wanted us to have things in common."

"Well, anyway, now you know why I haven't wanted to talk to you."

This isn't entirely true. I've also been avoiding Sebastian because the derm residents said he sexually assaulted a medical assistant. They said the dermatology program director had to sit him down to discuss his monstrous behavior. One of them even corroborated the dean's story, that he sexually assaulted a medical student three years ago. But I'm not going to bring any of this up now.

Sebastian rises and paces a few agitated steps around the living room, like my words have touched some deep nerve.

"Look, I miss you," he says. "We're good together. I'm real sorry about your mother. That's awful. But you'll get past this. Then you can get back to gunning. You're going to match in derm. I know it. I mean, it's terrible to think about it this way, but your mom's death probably gets you honors in medicine. No way Taylor's going to give you anything else when she was eating cake during the cardiac arrest."

Suddenly, my head throbs. Sebastian's words feel like rocks against my skull.

"No!" I scream. "No, no, no!" I glare at Sebastian. "I'm not doing this anymore. This gunner thing. I'm out. You want to know why I didn't go off on Taylor for ignoring Momma's alarms? You *really* want to know why? It's because I would have done the same thing in her shoes. If I'd been doing my usual thing on the team? If I'd been following a bunch of patients who I don't know personally? I'd have been eating cake like everyone else. Because the patients aren't the priority. They're just names on my list of chores for the day. It's all about the grade or the promotion or whatever. The patients, people like Momma, they're just pieces on a game board we move around. I'm tired of thinking about people that way. I'm not going to do it anymore."

Sebastian takes this in. He knows only gunning. I'm not sure he'll ever understand how vile I feel over everything I've done in medical school to get ahead.

"Okay, fine. Don't go into derm. It doesn't mean you and I can't be together."

He steps toward me and tries to take my hand, but I pull it away. I can't stand to be touched by him right now. He personifies everything I'm angry about: the hospital, Dr. Taylor, my grades, dermatology, the stupid competition that is medical school. To touch him feels like an embrace of that entire repulsive system.

"I don't want this anymore," I say. "I know how you think. I know how you see the system and the patients and all that. I can't be around a person like you right now."

Sebastian stares at me, his eyes sullen and narrowed. I've hurt him. I didn't mean to, but there's no way to reject his advances without telling him why.

"I gave you so much," he says. "I taught you how to win the game."

"What's that supposed to mean?"

"You can't just cut me out of your life. You owe me."

I stand and head to the back door. I open it and say, "Goodbye, Sebastian."

He hurries toward me, grabs my wrist, and pulls me away from the door. "You can't just get rid of me like this."

I shake his fingers from my arm. "Get out!"

He grabs both of my wrists and pulls me toward him. I shake and twist, but his grip is too strong. I feel his mouth on my neck, his tongue dragging against my skin.

"Stop it," I say, but he keeps kissing me.

Realizing he won't stop unless I hurt him, I thrust my knee into his groin.

"Ow!" he howls, pulling away from me and clutching his balls.

"Get out!"

Sebastian glares at me, breathing through his nose like an angry animal. I see a horrifying fire in his eyes: he's going to hurt me. I turn and run from the kitchen. If I can get to my room, I can shut the door to keep him away. But Sebastian chases me, his footsteps loud against the floor as I flee. I reach the living room, my eyes on my bedroom down the hallway. Sebastian tugs my blouse and pulls, making me stumble onto the rug. I get to my knees and crawl, but I'm too slow. Sebastian grabs me from behind, hauling his weight onto my back, his sickening warmth against my body, his breath on the back of my neck. I try to roll him off, but he's too heavy. With my arms pressed against the floor, I can't reach him to fight.

Then his hands slide down to my waist, slipping underneath me to unbutton my pants. No, no, no. This can't be happening. I feel the movement of his fingers under my pelvis. My mind races for a way out. I won't let this happen. Not here in my living room. Not when Momma has just died.

I squirm, but I can't get free of his weight on top of me. I feel him pulling down my pants. Tears well in my eyes. I look to my left and see Jerome's boots, size twelve shitkickers with mud stuck to the sides. My brother always leaves his crap on the floor, but today that might just save me.

I slide my hand to one of the boots, slipping my fingers between the laces so my grip is tight. Then I flex my arm and thrust it over my head, hitting the side of Sebastian's face. He howls, and his weight shifts to one side. I wiggle from under him, then push him away. I grab the other boot and fling it at his head. He ducks, the boot sailing until it hits the window.

I jump to my feet, my eyes darting left and right. I need a weapon, anything hard and sharp, but I see nothing. Sebastian lurches toward me, his arms out, ready to grab me again.

That's when I turn and sprint to my bedroom.

I fly into the room, slamming the door shut behind me. Sebastian wiggles the handle, but I hold the door closed with all my strength. Then he kicks hard, the door making a loud shudder as his foot lands. He kicks again, and the wood splits, the door nearly severed from the hinges. It won't withstand another blow. I scan my room for a weapon but see only my bed, desk, and scattered clothes. I can't defend myself in here. If he breaks in, I'm trapped.

"Please stop!" I shout, tears streaming down my cheek.

"Let me in!"

"Just leave. Please, just leave."

He jiggles the handle again. He won't stop. I've triggered some primal rage inside him. I close my eyes, knowing the next kick will smash the door in two.

But no kick comes.

I hear a thud outside in the hallway, followed by grunting and movement. Then suddenly all is quiet.

"Soph?" I hear someone say. It's Jerome. Oh, the sound of his sweet voice! I've never been so glad to hear it.

I yank open my door, and my eyes light up at the sight of my brother. He stands over Sebastian in the hallway, the black frying pan from the kitchen in his hand. I throw my arms around Jerome in a giant hug.

"Thank God you're here," I say, still breathing hard.

Sebastian lies unconscious at my feet, a gash in his skull. His chest rises and falls, so I know he's not dead. How could I have trusted this man so much? I remember when I met him as a wide-eyed first-year student. He seemed like a savior after I failed my first exam. But Dean Weaver warned me about him. I should have listened.

"Who is this guy?" Jerome asks. "How'd he get in here?"

"It's a long story," I say. "We should call the police."

"I already did," he replies.

Soon I hear sirens in the distance. They're coming to end the career of Miles Sebastian. He won't finish his dermatology residency. He won't get a job for four hundred thousand dollars a year. I used to want to be like him, but now I want to see him in prison. And I will never follow his advice again.

32.

At six o'clock in the evening a week later, I knock on the door to Mercer's home but get no answer.

It's the day after Momma's funeral, the image of her coffin still aching in my mind. This is the last place I expected to be today. In fact, I went to the hospital this morning to talk about returning to school with Dr. Taylor. But when I was there, something happened that sent me on this journey to Mercer's home. At the hospital, I saw Mercer in the hallway, speaking to her father. A towering man in scrubs with a trimmed gray beard, he seemed furious with his daughter.

"You have to fix this," he said to Mercer.

"You don't think I've tried?"

"Well, try harder. The entire hospital's talking about what you did. It's embarrassing."

"Sorry your daughter's an embarrassment. Must be hard having me in your life."

"Don't act snide with me. Do you know what I've done to get you to this point? I won't let you waste this opportunity I've given you."

After that, Mercer turned and hurried away. She passed me in the hallway but didn't notice me. I saw tears in her eyes.

I can't be certain of what they were discussing, but I'm pretty sure it was the thing with Mrs. Gilbert. Mercer was devastated that Mrs. Gilbert broke her arm because of her progress note. And that's why I've come here today. I have to confess what I've done. I can't bear the guilt any longer.

I study Mercer's home in the wealthy Northwest outskirts of the city, a section far from my rundown apartment. She resides in a cream-colored colonial with a porch swing and nice yard. Charlie gave me her address. He said she lives here alone, the entire building to herself. I wonder if she owns it. Maybe her father bought it so she could live here. Mercer leads a life so different from mine.

I should go since no one is coming to the door, but I'm certain Mercer is home. Her car, a silver Mercedes SUV, is parked along the curb, her white coat and stethoscope strewn across the backseat. I wonder why she isn't answering. Maybe she knows it's me and doesn't want to talk? Maybe she's got music on and can't hear me knocking?

I step down from the porch and walk around the side of the house, my shoes sinking into the grass. In the back, I find a small screened-in porch. I enter and peer through a back window into the kitchen. The space is in a terrible state of disarray, with dirty dishes and food everywhere. It almost looks ransacked.

I knock on the door to the kitchen twice but get no answer. Again, I think of leaving, but it bothers me that her car is out front. She must be home. I jiggle the back door handle and find it unlocked. I know it's wrong to go inside uninvited, but I keep thinking of the tears in Mercer's eyes this morning. More than ever, I want to confess what I've done. I want her to know that I'm the reason her father is so upset with her.

Taking a deep breath, I open the door and enter the kitchen. The smell of rotten food hits me in the face. Flies buzz around the dishes in the sink. Empty frozen dinner trays are stacked on the kitchen island. This is all very odd. Mercer doesn't seem like the type to keep such a messy home.

Creeping through the living room, I find the television on. The evening news blares from the speakers, the anchor talking about a car crash on the interstate. I call Mercer's name but get no response. I walk upstairs and check the bedrooms but find nothing.

I wind my way back to the kitchen to leave through the back door. Maybe Mercer is down the street at a neighbor's house? Maybe someone picked her up so her car is out front? But then I hear the faint, distant sound of music. I think I recognize the song. It's an old Rihanna tune:

When the sun shines, we'll shine together. Told you I'll be here forever.

It emanates from a door in the corner, which I now realize leads to the basement.

I open the door to find a set of rickety wooden steps leading down into darkness. The music rolls up at me from below. I call Mercer's name but again get no reply. I flick on the lights to see a concrete floor at the bottom of the stairs.

Slowly, I descend into the basement. When I reach the bottom, I see boxes and an oil tank. A collection of brooms and mops lies against one wall. An iPhone on the floor plays the Rihanna song.

And then, in the far corner, I see Jennifer Mercer in scrubs, her eyes closed, an extension cord attached to a ceiling beam on one end, the other around her neck. Her feet brush the floor, her legs bent at the knees. She's leaned forward to strangle herself.

My heart plummets.

No, no, no!

I sprint toward Mercer, throwing my shoulder under her chest. I raise her up with my legs, using all my strength to lift her limp body. Then I reach for the cord around her neck. She can't die. I won't let her die. Did I cause this? Did I push her to this point? I wiggle the cord loose and slide it from her neck. Then I slowly lower her heavy body onto the concrete.

Her eyes are closed. Oh, please, no. She can't be dead. The music continues from the iPhone.

Said I'll always be your friend. Took an oath, I'ma stick it out 'til the end.

I rub her chest vigorously, tears in my eyes.

"Mercer!" I shout.

My heart pounds. Why did I change the chart on Mrs. Gilbert? Look what I've done.

"Mercer!" I shout again.

Slowly, she opens her eyes. She gawks at me, then looks around the basement.

I let out a huge sigh of relief. I've never been so happy to see Jennifer Mercer's face as I am now.

"What . . . what are you doing here?" she asks.

I place a hand over my chest and exhale. "Oh, my God. Thank goodness you're okay."

She rubs her neck where a red mark remains from the extension cord. Then she looks at me and her eyes narrow.

"Why did you pull me down? Damn it, Sophia. I don't want to live anymore. Don't you get that?"

I sit beside her, my back against the concrete wall of the basement. "Is this about the thing with Mrs. Gilbert?

There's something I want to tell you about that."

"You honestly think I'd kill myself because of that? Do you really think I'm that pathetic?"

"Well, what is it, then?"

She turns away from me and begins to cry. "Get out. Just leave. You shouldn't be here."

"I'm not leaving," I say. "Not until I know you're okay."

She looks at me, her eyes swollen with tears. "Oh, well isn't that just great. Sophia Abney wants to be my savior. Didn't you fight me in the anatomy lab once? Aren't we supposed to hate each other?"

I realize I need to tell Mercer why I'm here. And I need to start by telling her all that's occurred in my life leading up to this point.

"My mother died," I say. "She had a cardiac arrest while the hospital staff were in the break room, having cake. No one heard the alarm, and by the time they got there, it was too late. And Sebastian tried to rape me. My brother stopped him. Sebastian's in prison now. I had to give a statement to the cops and everything."

Mercer studies me closely. "Are you serious? Don't mess with me now. It's not funny."

"Totally serious. And as you can imagine, those things have changed my perspective."

Mercer wipes her eyes. "So now you want to be friends?"

"I want to tell you the truth."

Then, slowly, my hands trembling, I explain to her how I altered the medical record of Mrs. Gilbert. It's hard to get out the words. My voice shakes as I speak. I'm giving Mercer information she can use to end my career in medicine. She'll certainly tell the dean, and then I'll be kicked out of school. And I'll owe hundreds of thousands of dollars in scholarship money. But somehow, despite all this, I feel relieved when I finish my story. I've been carrying the guilt for so long.

Mercer says nothing when I finish speaking. She just stares at me, processing my story.

"You have to understand," I say, "I was super pissed after you gave me the wrong address for the dermatology dinner. But still, I shouldn't have done what I did. I'm sorry."

And there it is. I apologized to Mercer. I did what I came here to do. Now she can turn me in to the dean and my medical career will be over.

"It doesn't matter," she says.

"What?"

"What you did. It doesn't matter. I don't care anymore."

"What are you talking about?"

Mercer stands and walks to her iPhone, which is still playing music. She taps it off, the room falling silent, then walks back, sliding down to the floor to sit beside me.

"I told my father I was quitting med school today," she says. "He said if I did that, he'd take away my car, my trust fund, everything."

"Wait. What? Why would you quit school?"

"Because it's fucking awful. You can't tell me you're happy. From the first day of first year, I've been looking over my shoulder, making sure I was working harder than everyone else. It's miserable trying to stay ahead of a class full of geniuses. Everyone's always talking about how hard they work. *I just studied this. I just studied that.* God, I can't stand it. I can't stand having to be perfect. I can't stand the grind to stay ahead. Not just you and our class, but everyone. It's all the people at all the schools. I have to beat them all. It's like a full-on sprint that never ends.

"And it's made me into a person I can't stand. I came to med school to help people, you know. I actually thought I could learn how to make people feel better. But gunning for the top . . . it turns you into a demon. The constant focus on grades and status is . . . evil. I don't care about anything else anymore. It's consumed me. And it will never end. In residency, I'll have to compete to be Chief Resident. Then there'll be competition for fellowships, jobs. It will never fucking end.

"And no one else has a neurosurgeon father like I do. He's never stopped hounding me. *How much are you studying? What grade did you get on the exam? Are you publishing papers?* I'm not in school for me. I'm in school for him. He wanted this for me. He's always wanted me to become a doctor. I never really had a choice."

My God. Look at the two of us. We've been ruined by our drive for dermatology, turned into heartless vessels who only know the things that make us stand out when we apply to residency. I had no idea she felt like this. I thought Mercer had it easy and I was the one working my ass off to get ahead.

"But you went to Harvard," I say. "I figured med school was easy for you."

Mercer laughs. "Harvard? You seriously think that place got me ready for medical school? The only good thing about Harvard is the name. My teachers were shit. They're more interested in writing books or giving speeches than teaching students. I learned mostly from TAs, not professors. Even the TAs didn't give a shit. They wanted to get back to the lab to become Harvard professors themselves. I had to learn everything on my own. You got a much better education at community college. I'm certain of it."

I can hardly believe what I'm hearing. I presumed I was the underprepared student since I went to Midtown. But Mercer thought the same thing about herself because she went to Harvard. I wonder if everyone in our class thinks they're deficient in some way, and that all the others are better off.

"It's not just the work that's making me want to quit," Mercer continues. "The school treats us like babies. Mandatory TBLs, mandatory wellness, professionalism violations, PISS surveys for my rotations. I had more freedom in elementary school. They monitor everything I do. It's like I'm in prison."

Mercer is saying things I've thought myself many times. But I always presumed she *liked* the setup of medical school. I thought her father was guiding her through.

"You want to know why I study in the anatomy lab?" Mercer says. "My father sometimes comes looking for me in the library and the study rooms. I have to study among the dead to hide from him. I'm so sick of all of it."

"So quit, then," I say. "But don't kill yourself. There are lots of ways to make a life besides medicine."

"I'm just so fucking depressed," Mercer says, her eyes glossy with tears. "I'm on a shit-ton of pills. My father's psychiatrist friend prescribes them. They're not doing a thing. Med school depression is impervious to all forms of psychiatric intervention. Did you see my house upstairs? It's a wreck. I've been a zombie for weeks."

For the first time since I met her, I actually like Mercer. She's much more likable when she's real. It's too bad medical students act like they have their shit together. We might all be better friends if we let our guard down more. We might even be happier people.

I glance at the deep red mark left on her neck from the extension cord. "So, like, what do you want to do now?" I say to her. "I feel like someone should, I don't know, check your blood pressure or something. Do you want to go to the ER?"

"That would only make me more depressed." She pauses for a second. "I'm actually feeling better because of our talk. I feel stupid that I tried to kill myself."

"I won't tell anyone. It can be our secret."

Mercer nods, her eyes looking at me softly. We're bonding in a way I never imagined possible.

"But what's next, then?" I say. "How can I help you? I don't want you to feel like you want to die ever again."

Mercer laughs. "I'm a UWorld question. *Twenty-five-year-old female is brought in after a suicide attempt. Which of the following is the best next step?*"

"My answer would be electroconvulsive therapy. But I'd probably be wrong."

"Yeah, and then UWorld would tell you that ninety-five percent of students got the question right and only three percent picked ECT, like you."

"UWorld should be examined as a cause of mental illness. Maybe it's not a surprise you're depressed. Maybe that's the point of medical education."

Mercer smiles, and it's the happiest thing I've seen in a long time.

"There's one thing you can do to help me," she says.

"What's that?"

"Stay here with me tonight. I don't want to be alone. We can order food and watch movies."

To my surprise, this request warms my heart. There's nothing I'd rather do right now than hang out with her. I guess I had to drive Mercer to suicide for us to become friends.

"Of course," I reply. "But I need you to answer one question for me first."

"Okay?"

"You couldn't think of anything better than Rihanna to play when you were about to die?"

Mercer starts laughing loudly, and I do, too. She leans her head on my shoulder, cracking up, deep belly laughs rolling from her body. We laugh like two dear friends who've had too much wine. And for the first time since Momma died, I think maybe the world isn't such a dark place.

33.

The day has finally come. I have to go back to school.

A week has passed since I found Mercer unconscious in her basement. Now I sit in Dean Weaver's office, my body planted before her imposing desk, the dean gazing at me with her hands clasped.

Clang, clang, clang.

The sound of a jackhammer rattles from outside the office window, where construction workers in orange vests have gathered in the parking lot.

"Sorry about the noise," the dean says. "They're starting construction on the new skin center. Have you heard? We're expanding the dermatology division over the next five years."

This should excite me because it means more work for skin doctors, but it doesn't. I've lost my passion for dermatology. I don't know if I ever really had any in the first place. I just loved the money.

"You said you wanted to talk to me before I went back to my rotations?" I say.

Weaver gazes at me with sympathetic eyes. "Everyone is so, so sorry about all you've been through with your mother and Miles Sebastian. It's just awful. I can't recall a student going through so much tragedy all at once."

The jackhammer fires up again outside the window.

Clang, clang, clang.

"Thank you," I say. "But if it's all the same to you, I'd just like to get back to my internal medicine rotation."

"Of course," Weaver says. "But first I want to tell you something. Sophia, I want you to know that you're one of the best students we've ever had at State Medical School. Apart from your first exam, your grades in the first two years are outstanding. Top of your class. It's amazing you performed so well while also working in Dr. Murrow's lab and organizing a shoe drive for the homeless. I've met very few students capable of achieving so much. Plus, your evaluations so far in third year are fantastic. Dr. Canning says you're one of the best students he's ever seen. He loved having you on the surgical service. He asks me about you all the time. Dr. Taylor loved you on your internal medicine rotation, too. She told me about a patient you cared for on hospice. Said you were one of the most empathic medical students she's ever known."

I can't believe the words coming from Weaver's mouth. Nearly everything I've achieved has been through lying or breaking the rules. In my first two years, I skipped lectures and labs and conferences unless they were mandatory. I used an Anki deck created by Russian spies to crush my exams. I've published papers through Dr. Murrow's lab, but his post-doc did nearly all the work. My "shoe drive" for the homeless was a pathetic gag to pad my resume. And on my surgery and internal medicine rotations, I've gamed the system to impress the attendings. For God's sake, I considered suffocating an old woman to get honors! I'm not the kind of person who deserves praise from the dean.

Clang, clang, clang.

The sounds outside the window somehow seem to grow louder.

"It's hard to come back after what you've been through," Weaver continues. "But I want you to know that your future is exceptionally bright. We give an award at graduation called the Excellence Award. Maybe you've heard of it? It recognizes one student for outstanding potential as a future physician. You're going to win this award. You're miles ahead of everyone else in your class. Just keep going. Keep doing the amazing things you do. Medicine needs more people like you, Sophia."

The words pound my head like thunder. Medicine does *not* need more people like me. I'm a hustler who pretends to care to advance my own standing. There's something very wrong with a system that rewards me over others.

"Didn't Sebastian win the Excellence Award?" I ask.

Weaver's lips turn downward in a frown. "Unfortunately, he did. I was opposed, but the committee selected him. In your case, however, we won't be making a mistake."

Little does she know, I'm Sebastian's protégé. They *are* making the same mistake again. But I say nothing about this because I don't want to talk about Sebastian anymore.

"And I don't know if you've heard," the dean says, "but Jennifer Mercer has dropped out of school. She was very shaken up by the error she made in her patient's chart. Her father thinks she's going through a deep depressive episode."

Over the past week, Mercer and I went shopping and ate lunch and got pedicures, all of it put on her father's credit card. Mercer is *not* depressed. At least not anymore. Medical school was keeping her down, pressing her mind into dark depths of misery. Since she made the decision to quit, she's happier than she's been for a long time.

I keep thinking about what Mercer said to me in her

basement: *And it will never end. In residency, I'll have to compete to be Chief Resident. Then there'll be competition for fellowships, jobs. It will never fucking end.* Once you become a gunner, you can't stop seeing medicine as a competition from top to bottom.

I wish I could quit like Mercer, but I'm trapped. To leave school would violate the terms of my dreaded Albert Mitchell Scholarship. The award that once filled me with excitement and pride has now become my shackle. It holds me to this life in medicine, whether I want it or not. I never realized once you accept money to pay for medical school, there's no easy way to turn back.

"You and Jennifer were the only two people in your class pursuing dermatology," Weaver goes on. "Since she's dropped out, it should be an easier match for you."

Clang, clang, clang.

God, will that infernal noise ever stop? With each word from Weaver's mouth, it seems to grow louder, the sound making my head seize with tension.

"I think you'll be the top candidate for the dermatology residency here next year," Weaver says. "You're practically guaranteed a spot."

It occurs to me I'm getting everything I ever wanted from medical school. I'm the favorite of my teachers and the dean. The dermatology program loves me. There's little standing in the way of me and $437,000 a year. And yet I feel disgusted with myself.

Clang, clang, clang.

The noise is so loud, my head feels like it'll explode.

"So," Dean Weaver says. "What do you say, Sophia? Are you ready to get back?"

Suddenly, the jackhammer stops. The room falls quiet, and the tension in my head fades.

That's when I realize I can't do this anymore.

"No," I say. "I'm not ready to come back."

A puzzled expression falls over Weaver's face. "What do you mean?"

I rise from my chair and stand before Weaver's desk, my eyes down, my mind preparing for what I'm about to say. Am I really going to do this? If I speak my thoughts aloud, there's no turning back. But I can't act like a fraud any longer.

"I changed the chart on Mercer's patient," I say.

The dean blinks a few times. "What?"

"I wanted Mercer to get a bad evaluation," I explain. "So, I used her badge to enter the EMR under her name. Then I changed her progress note. I'm the one who caused the entire mess with her patient."

Dean Weaver stares at me with a stunned expression. Saying aloud what I've done brings a feeling of nastiness to my bones. I'm a horrible person who's done horrible things. And I'm tired of pretending I'm something else.

"That's not all I did," I say.

Slowly, I tell Weaver every shitty gunner thing I've done since starting medical school. I tell her about using pirated materials to ace my exams. I explain how I sabotaged Mercer's experiments in the lab. I admit to starting a fire to get out of the mandatory yoga session in first year. I tell her how I lied to my attendings about what specialty I was going into. I even tell her how I considered putting a pillow over a patient's face so she'd die faster. By the time I finish, I have tears in my eyes. The vile nature of my behavior has fully seized me. I see my true self, and it overwhelms me.

The dean listens with her jaw hung open in surprise.

"Everything I did was my own choice," I say, tears

rolling down my cheek. "I take full responsibility. But this system promotes gunners like me. It's not about the patients. It's about winning. You've made medicine into a competition! And the stakes are huge. If we win, we get our choice of specialty and training program. We get a career worth millions of dollars. If we lose, we take the leftovers, the specialties others don't want. Do you realize how insane that is when we're supposed to be helping people? We're not even tested on whether the patients feel better; we're tested on naming their disease or ordering the right blood test or impressing an attending. You've made human suffering into a game. Our goal is the grade. Our goal is to please the attending. That's seriously messed up."

The Dean looks at me with a grave expression. "This is shocking. I . . . I can't believe you did all those things. I've spent my career trying to get this student body to act professionally. Your behavior is a slap in the face."

"Act professionally? Are you serious? The faculty aren't professional so how can you expect anything different from students like me? My God, Murrow ogled me every time I went to his lab. Dr. Canning asked me out on a date and *he's married.* And Dr. Taylor never sees patients but you just promoted her. It's ridiculous to hold students accountable for professionalism when you don't do the same thing for our teachers."

Weaver keeps her eyes fixed on me. "I can't believe what I'm hearing from you. I don't know what to say. You were a shoo-in for the Excellence Award."

"Just like Sebastian was, right?"

Weaver gives me a look but makes no reply.

"You know who should win the Excellence Award?" I say. "Charlie. He always follows the rules. He is one hundred percent about his patients. All he cares about is helping people. But he's hardly on your radar, is he? He barely gets by because he comes to lectures, reads the textbooks, and doesn't use pirated resources. He does *everything* you tell him to do, and because of that, he's invisible. The attendings hardly notice him because he's quiet and does his job without trying to kiss ass. No one even sees him. You see only people like me. How can any of us become compassionate when it's like this? We see the Charlies of the world getting nowhere, while the Sebastians match in dermatology and win the Excellence Award. That's the system you've built."

I stop speaking and catch my breath. I'm hyperventilating as if I've run a race, but I'm only standing before Dean Weaver's desk. Yet despite my breathing, I don't feel tired or exhausted. I've been lying to the dean and my attendings for so long. Speaking the truth feels cathartic.

Weaver leans forward, her chair creaking as it rocks. "You need to tell Jennifer Mercer that you altered the chart on her patient. She needs to know that."

"I already have," I reply. "She doesn't care anymore. She wants out, just like me."

"You'll have to go before the academic advancement committee for this. And they'll probably recommend expulsion. You know what that means for your scholarship, don't you?"

"I'll deal with the money. It's better than playing this game anymore."

Weaver scratches her chin. "Is this because you lost your mother?" she says. "Is that why you're behaving this way? Are you trying to burn down your life?"

Momma. I do want out of medicine because she's gone. But I'm not trying to burn anything down. I'm trying to save myself.

And that's when an idea hits me.

Suddenly, I see another way to approach this. Maybe, just maybe, I can get out of medicine without becoming buried in debt. Maybe Momma can still save me, even though she's gone.

"I'm going to make you an offer," I say. "I have a way for both of us to get out of this."

Weaver narrows her gaze at me. "You're in no position to make offers."

"You can send me before the AAC, and I'll tell them everything I told you today. I'll admit what I've done. They'll recommend expulsion, and I won't fight it."

"You'll admit what you've done? You won't fight us? That's your offer?"

"In return, I want the school to pay back my scholarship money."

Weaver's eyes widen. "What? We can't do that. We would never do that."

I don't know why I didn't think of this before. It's the obvious way out.

"If you don't pay back my money," I say, "I'll sue the hospital over my mother's death."

Weaver sits bolt upright in her chair, her eyes wide with surprise. I can't believe what I'm doing. The dean is a powerful woman, and I'm threatening her. But it's the only way for me to leave this school without getting crushed by debt.

"Your mother died of a stroke," Weaver says. "It's very sad. I wish something could have been done."

"My mother died while the staff were singing Jolly Good Fellow. You talked to Dr. Taylor, didn't you? She must have told you what happened."

Weaver says nothing. She knows I'm right.

"I don't belong in this school after what I've done," I say. "You need to kick me out. You *should* kick me out.

But the hospital screwed up. My brother talked to a lawyer about my mother's death. We could sue for *millions*. I can testify that the hospital staff was eating cake while she died. Do you really want all that to get out? I'll let it go if you just wipe out my scholarship debt. A small price to pay for the life of my mother."

"You falsified records and broke someone's arm," Weaver says. "And now you want me to let that go?"

"You can have the lawyers draw up papers. I'll sign documents swearing I won't sue over my mother. And you can kick me out of school. All I want is my scholarship paid back."

Weaver stares at me, her brow furrowed, her eyes angry. She's mad that I deceived her into believing I was a good student. She's mad that I gamed the system without getting caught. But mostly, I suspect she's mad because she knows I'm right. You can be a superstar in medical school without being a saint. People like Sebastian or me, people who understand the game and play it masterfully, can rise to the top. And people like Charlie, those who don't play the game at all, are forgotten, invisible, and ignored. Weaver wishes this weren't true, but she knows it is.

"Let me make some calls," Weaver says. "I'll let you know what I find."

This is her way of saying she'll agree to my offer. I can see it in her eyes. She wants to kick me out and also protect the hospital from a lawsuit. My arrangement achieves both of those goals.

"But while you're waiting to hear from me," she says, "I want you to get out of this school and never come back. It pains me to say that, because I had such high hopes for you. But I want you to leave for good. I'm going to see to it that you never work inside a medical institution ever again."

She means this to hurt me, but I don't take it that way. I came here expecting to return to my rotations today, to go back to grades and honors and picking a specialty. But I didn't want that. Ever since Momma died, all of medicine has felt meaningless to me. Being asked to leave and never come back is the best thing anyone has said to me in a long, long time.

34.

Five years later, I place the last cardboard box in the back of the moving van outside my apartment. It lands with a thump beside a stack of similar boxes. My T-shirt is soaked with sweat from the August sun beaming down from the blue sky above.

"That's the last one," Jerome says, walking up next to me, beads of sweat on his brow.

I look back at our town house, the rickety building where I lived in the first floor apartment my entire life until now. Sometimes I still can't believe we're finally moving out.

"I'll follow you in my car," I say to Jerome, who nods in reply. He'll drive the truck to our new home, while I follow in my Honda Civic, the car I bought three years ago to replace my old Fiesta. That shitbox of a vehicle was barely running with one hundred and fifty thousand miles on it. But thanks to my new job I had enough money to finally replace it.

"Charlie text you?" Jerome asks.

Charlie. He's now a practicing family medicine doctor in the city. He lives across town near Mercer. He graduated in the middle of the class, and matched into his third choice for residency. This would have crushed me back when I was a gunner, but Charlie didn't mind. He loves his work—he is *so* happy to be an attending physician. I sometimes wonder if this is because he took the opposite path from me, the non-gunner approach. Maybe if I hadn't pushed so hard for the top, I wouldn't have burned out.

But at least we're still close friends. And, of course, he insisted on helping with the move today. He went ahead of me and Jerome. He promised to turn on the central air conditioning to cool the new house before we arrive. What a treat that will be. I've never lived in a home with central air conditioning before.

"Just got a text from him," I reply to Jerome. "He's already at the new house." My brother and Charlie are friends now, too. They play Halo online each night after Charlie finishes charting on his patients.

"He's probably unpacked some of yesterday's boxes for us."

I smile. "Yeah, probably. That would be just like him."

My phone buzzes in my pocket. I slide it out, trying not to drip sweat onto the screen. The caller ID says it's Mercer.

"What's up, lady?" she asks when I answer the call.

Mercer and I have been best friends for the past five years, ever since I pulled her down from the ceiling in her basement. After dropping out of medical school, she found a job as a bartender. As she put it, "It's the furthest thing from medical school I could think of." The bar where she worked went up for sale three years ago. Her father agreed to buy it so that Mercer could run the place—he had finally accepted she was never going to be a doctor. She renamed it the Harvard Hideaway. She even created a special drink with gin, lemon juice, simple syrup, and edible gold dust. It's our favorite. It's called "the Gunner."

"What's up is I'm moving," I say into the phone. "You know that."

"Yeah, well are you all packed?"

"I am. Why?"

"'Cause I'm going to meet you at your new place. I'm bringing dinner."

"You don't have to bring dinner."

"It's from the bar. Wings and sliders. There's enough for everybody. Me, you, Jerome, and Charlie—we're all gonna eat in your new kitchen. I'm not taking no for an answer."

The image of the four of us eating together in my new house makes me smile. I agree to the wings and sliders then tell Mercer I'll meet her in about twenty minutes at the new place. I end the call and look at my brother sitting on the back of the moving truck, gazing at our old apartment.

"Let's go back inside before we leave," Jerome says. "Just want to lay my eyes on the place one last time."

I agree and follow him into the building. I open the flimsy door to our apartment and find my way to the tiny kitchen, now completely barren, not a dish or pan in sight. Memories come rushing back. Of Daddy in this room when he was still alive. Of me making food for Momma. Of Sebastian coming after me.

Jerome walks to the sink and drinks water straight from the faucet. I stroll through the empty living room and into my old bedroom, the hardwood floor bare, the closet empty. I spy something in the corner next to the radiator. When I walk across the room, I see it's a Burger King hat.

I pick it up, studying the brown material and logo. This hat holds tremendous sentimental value. I got it five years ago, just after I was expelled from medical school.

After Momma died, Jerome found a great lawyer, an uncle of his idiot friend Fernando, if you can believe that.

A shark who had won so many malpractice lawsuits that his nickname was "ambulance crusher," he threatened to sue the school for twenty million dollars over Momma's death plus go to the newspapers. He said that my testimony alone, of running to get the staff while they ate cake, would sway any jury. He vowed that he'd generate coverage in the news that would sink the hospital's reputation "into the underworld."

The hospital lawyers quickly agreed to settle for the small price of paying back my scholarship. They even agreed to decline criminal charges against me for falsifying medical records and the many other terrible things I did as a gunner. The trivial price of my scholarship money plus forgiving my gunner crimes was a bargain to them, well worth it to avoid an embarrassing and costly courtroom battle. Momma, it turns out, had saved me. The gunning left me soulless and burned out. When she died, I was broken. But in her death, she gave me a way to escape medicine altogether.

After my expulsion, even though I wasn't burdened with debt, I still needed money. Jerome got me a job at Burger King working the cash register. It paid shit, but it was enough to cover our bills. It was super weird to go from the hospital to Whoppers and fries, but at least I didn't have to worry about grades or honors or class rank.

Six months later, I was promoted to night manager. Two years after that, I was made district manager, overseeing six stores. And a month ago, I became senior product manager with responsibility for over one hundred restaurants in a three-state radius. My new job pays $150,000 a year, which is far from a dermatologist's salary, but it's as much as some doctors make in low-paying fields. And most importantly, it was enough to secure a mortgage for a home in the suburbs. You see, Jerome is the regional supply manager at Burger King, making $110,000. Together, we had enough for a down payment on a two-story colonial with a nice yard and garage. I cried when we signed the papers for the loan. My dreams had finally become a reality.

I never thought a job in fast food would bring me the money I always wanted, but I was wrong. Because here's the thing I've learned: if you're smart enough to succeed in medical school, you're smart enough to succeed in other places, too. There are many ways to make money in this world. I'm so much happier dispensing shakes and diet Cokes than I ever was gunning in medical school.

Sometimes I worry that more people will leave medicine like I did. What if no one wants to become a doctor because of the craziness of training? Someone will have to figure this out. Maybe one day they'll realize the competition is suffocating. I was vying with my classmates for everything: grades, Anki card totals, UWorld percentages, residency spots, and ultimately, money and status. The patients were just noise in the background.

Charlie somehow ignored the competition and stayed focused on helping others. Maybe that's the key. But for lots of students, people like me and Mercer, this is impossible to do. It's in our nature to push ourselves to be the best. I wish med schools would stop encouraging this part of our character. I wish they'd value the Charlies of the world more, and the Sophias, Mercers, and Sebastians a lot less. After all, you don't get into medical school unless you're bright. Why make us compete to prove who's the brightest of the bright? Maybe someday they'll find a way to make this happen.

But none of this is my problem anymore.

I flip the hat onto my head, where it fits snugly over my hair. Then I leave my bedroom for the final time. I find Jerome in the living room, gazing out the window.

"I wish we were taking Momma with us," he says.

"Me, too," I reply. "But she'd be happy with where we are."

"Yeah," Jerome says. "She would."

I take my brother's hand, and we leave the apartment. Outside, Jerome climbs in the moving truck and I get in my Civic. He pulls the truck from the curb, and I follow him down the street. I glance in the rearview mirror to see my old apartment fade away in the distance.

THE GUNNER RULES

1. ANY MINUTE NOT DOING ANKI IS A WASTED MINUTE
2. NEVER LEARN FROM SCHOOL INSTRUCTORS
3. ALL RESEARCH IS WORTHLESS UNLESS IT GETS PUBLISHED
4. FOR COMMUNITY SERVICE, THE SADDER THE POPULATION THE BETTER
5. NOTHING MATTERS ON A ROTATION EXCEPT THE ATTENDING
6. THE ATTENDING'S SPECIALTY IS YOUR SPECIALTY
7. NAIL YOUR PRESENTATIONS
8. KNOW YOUR PATIENTS

ACKNOWLEDGMENTS

Special thanks to all the people who supported me in writing this story. In particular, my wonderful wife, Susan, and my children, Luke and Ella. My fantastic book coach, Savannah Gilbo plus all the folks at the Spun Yarn beta reading company. Also, Karen Boston at the Word Slayers, Anthea Strezze, Kristen Strange, and my fantastic medical student beta readers, Perpetual Taylor, Jeska Guirguis and Rudy Valentini. And, of course, thank you to the many, many students who have shared their experiences with me over the years. Without their stories, I could never have written the Gunner.

Jason Ryan
October 2023

Made in United States
North Haven, CT
02 April 2025

67525857R00181